A CHILLING PERFORMANCE

"You know what really astonishes me?" he said to the mirror. "How easy it is! I mean, if there are no witnesses to murder, and you have no apparent motive, what chance is there of being caught? Why didn't I think of it years ago?"

"Conscience?"

"You're being obtuse."

"No. Let's say—it was a judicial killing. I, self-appointed President of the Equity subcommittee for the Preservation of the Purity of our Art, have decided that Mr. Wilde unfortunately had slipped below par. Under the rules of our union that meant that he had to be acted against with 'extreme prejudice' as they say in the CIA."

"Now look, old chap, your motives were hardly so altruistic. It was a personal murder."

"Yes, I like the sound of that—a personal murder. Put it there!"

He pressed his damp palm against the mirror. He withdrew his hand and stood looking at the imprint, watching his eyes reappear as it dissolved. . . .

"A first novel that combines an excellent murder story with equally excellent satire. . . . Simon Shaw's grasp of the psychological possibilities is as impressive as that of Ruth Rendell. A pleasure to read."
—*The Literary Review* (London)

BANTAM BOOKS BY SIMON SHAW:

MURDER OUT OF TUNE

COMING SOON:
KILLER CINDERELLA
BLOODY INSTRUCTIONS

MURDER OUT OF TUNE

SIMON SHAW

BANTAM BOOKS
NEW YORK • TORONTO • LONDON • SYDNEY • AUCKLAND

MURDER OUT OF TUNE

A Bantam Crime Line Book / published by arrangement with Doubleday

PUBLISHING HISTORY
*Doubleday edition published 1988
Bantam edition / November 1992*

CRIME LINE *and the portrayal of a boxed "cl" are trademarks of Bantam
Books, a division of Bantam Doubleday Dell Publishing Group, Inc.*

*HI-DIDDLE-DEE-DEE—Words by Ned Washington, music by Leigh Harline.
Copyright © 1940 Bourne Co. Copyright Renewed. International Copyright Secured.
All Rights Reserved. Used by Permission.*

*Quotations from Four Quartets, copyright 1943 by T. S. Eliot; renewed 1971 by
Esme Valerie Eliot. Reprinted by permission of Harcourt Brace Jovanovich, Inc.*

*Excerpt from lyrics of "THERE'S NO BUSINESS LIKE SHOW BUSINESS" by
Irving Berlin at page 227: © Copyright 1946 Irving Berlin. © Copyright renewed
1974 Irving Berlin. Reprinted by permission of Irving Berlin Music Corporation.*

ISBN 0-553-29592-6

Published simultaneously in the United States and Canada

*Bantam Books are published by Bantam Books, a division of Bantam Doubleday
Dell Publishing Group, Inc. Its trademark, consisting of the words "Bantam Books"
and the portrayal of a rooster, is Registered in U.S. Patent and Trademark Office
and in other countries. Marca Registrada. Bantam Books, 666 Fifth Avenue, New
York, New York 10103.*

PRINTED IN THE UNITED STATES OF AMERICA

RAD   0 9 8 7 6 5 4 3 2 1

Not Cassio kill'd! then murder's out of tune,
And sweet revenge grows harsh.
OTHELLO, *Act V, Scene II*

MURDER
OUT OF
TUNE

ONE

Eight o'clock, he'd said. It was ten past and there was no sign of her. He always said eight o'clock. He was regular in his habits, a good timekeeper. It was a trick he'd learned years ago in rep. It always annoyed him when people offhandedly characterized actors as being casual in their habits. Lateness was unprofessional. If a rehearsal was scheduled to begin at ten, then it should begin at ten, not at five past, ten past, or whenever people could be bothered to turn up. He had never been late for a rehearsal or an interview in his life. Hannah was the sort of actress who gave the profession a bad name.

He usually sat at the same table. It wasn't reserved especially for him, it just happened that way. It was a moderately decent, moderately popular restaurant. It was never more than a quarter full by eight, and most of the clientele, especially in summer, chose the tables near the windows. Quite often he was the only one sitting at the back, next to the stairs that led down to the cloakrooms. "Ready for a quick get-away through the kitchens, dear," Hannah would say with depressing frequency. Her incapacity for original thought was one of her more charming features.

Tonight he was not alone. Two couples occupied the next table, bright, self-confident, young professional types, too glossy for suburbia, not quite sufficiently in-bred for Sloane Square. Probably Stoke Newington. One of them was talking about Oxford. The other man talked about a big account and discussed making a pitch. They were the sort of people one expected to meet in Covent Garden. Upwardly mobile—or was that last year's colour-supplement jargon? Perhaps he should ask them; they'd be sure to know.

He broke open another bread roll. It was as stale as the first. He'd been coming for twelve years and never yet been served with a fresh one. It was a sort of joke with the waiters. One of them, a spindly little fellow called Ben with hair like a well-used toothbrush, had been there for almost the whole twelve years. For about three years they had acknowledged each other with non-committal nods of the head and faint creasings of the mouth approximating to smiles. Then one day Ben had asked shyly if he might have his autograph. Thereafter he had addressed him as Mr. Fletcher and this had continued for about another three years. It was a thoroughly English relationship. Then one night, when the restaurant was deserted, Ben had sat down with him, and they had shared a half-bottle of white wine and chatted for twenty minutes or so. After that Ben called him Philip. Nowadays he'd shout out "Hi, Phil!" quite loudly whenever he came in, even if he was half in and out of the kitchen or disappearing down the stairs. Every time he winced. He hated being called Phil.

He usually drank white wine. He had a glass now. For that matter, he usually had an avocado for starters, a rare steak for the main course (the menu described it as a "Prime Bar BQ Prairie Slab") and something chocolate for dessert. The food was always adequate, the wine one step up from undrinkable. Albanian Moselle, he had once called it. "One bottle of Albanian!" Ben would call out whenever he saw him. He should have a heart-to-heart with Hannah sometime. They had a lot in common. Of course he'd be lucky to meet up with Hannah any time. Men had died of terminal boredom waiting for her. It was a quarter past eight.

He really didn't want to listen to the conversation at the next table, but he didn't have a lot of choice. Both men had loud voices (they did most of the talking), and in any case the restaurant was quiet. He almost missed the regular pianist. Almost, but not quite. He was the most spectacularly untalented pianist he had ever heard. He had listened for five years to one staple number before realizing that it was supposed to be "Autumn Leaves." For the most part he played Beatles songs. "If I were Paul McCartney I'd sue," Phil had said. Hannah had roared with laughter. "If you were Paul McCartney you wouldn't be sitting in a dump like this with a frowsy old bitch like me, darling," she had said. He had said, "It's not such a dump."

"Jen and me saw the new Bond last night," said one of the loud young men.

"Trust you to be right downmarket, Simon," guffawed the other.

"I suppose you two were at some award-winning Yugoslavian film noir," said Simon wittily.

The female half of the other couple giggled through her nose. "Phil's gone off those since he had to start wearing glasses to read the subtitles," she said, slipping her arm through his.

He would be called Phil, thought Philip.

"Actually we went to the theatre," said Phil.

"Do I detect a smug tone in your voice, you shameless old highbrow?"

"Perhaps they went to the Raymond Revuebar," said Jen mischievously.

"Actually no. My membership's expired. We went to the one just round the corner, you know, near the Aldwych."

"The Aldwych Theatre?"

"No, no, bit nearer. The little one opposite the Strand. What's it called, Carol?"

"What, where we saw the Robert Palmer concert?"

"No, that's the Lyceum. Good concert, eh?"

"Good concert," thought Philip. In the theatre where Mr. Irving scintillated with Miss Terry.

"What'd you see, anyway?"

"That Eugene O'Neill. Al told me to go. He's a theatre freak."

"Recommended?"

"Not on an empty stomach. What'd you think, love?"

"It was a bit long."

"Who was in it?"

"Tessa Sanderson."

"What, the javelin-thrower?"

"Oh no, must have got it wrong. Name like that."

"Who else?"

"Gordon Wilde."

"Oh, I fancy him; don't you, Carol?"

"Mm."

You'll be lucky, thought Philip. The last woman he looked at was his mother. And she died when he was two.

"He was brilliant," said Phil. "Really brilliant. He's already got an award. Apparently it's only still on because of that; it was supposed to finish last week but they've kept it on because of popular acclaim. Actually they're going to Broadway with it, or was it the Edinburgh Festival?"

"Perhaps we should try and see that, Jen. Don't go to the theatre much as a rule, but he's worth seeing."

"He's certainly one of my favourite actors. Must be like the Olivier of his generation."

Philip got up quietly. He saw Ben looking at him quizzically and tapped at his watch with unexaggerated disapproval. "It's twenty past," he said significantly as he passed him on his way to the cloakrooms. No doubt Ben thought he was going for his regular twenty-past-eight crap.

The toilet cubicle had been designed by a crook-backed midget. He edged in sideways and locked it with a hand behind his back. The seat was up and he tossed in the remains of the bread roll, which he had crushed into a Ping-Pong-sized ball. He half expected to see fish come swimming up out of the drains and start nibbling at it. He dropped the seat and sat on it with difficulty. His knuckles and teeth were clenched and his body trembled furiously. He let out a string of obscenities under his breath and, feeling a bit better, muttered to himself for a minute or so.

"Now, boy, get a grip on yourself, calm down . . . deep breaths, that's better; one, two; in, out; remember those breathing exercises. On the diaphragm; now breathe out slowly, m-m-m-m-m-m-m-m-m-m-m-m-m-m . . . that's good, nice resonant sound, feel the teeth humming. Ribs, now; up, down, up down; good lungfuls of crisp lavatory cleaner. Better? Better. No, I'm bloody not better! The Olivier of his generation! Jesus wept. Done for theatre what McGonagall did for poetry. That arse-hole, that toe-rag, that talentless little moron. Bum-sucking toad. How dare they mention him in the same breath as Olivier. Not fit to walk on the same planet. About as much ability as this bog-brush. And as much charm. Nasty little smirking queen. I think I'm going to puke. Vomit. I wish he'd choke on his own vomit. Oh, bother! said Pooh. What's the time? Twenty-five past! I'll murder the bitch. After I've murdered him. Double funeral. Can't sit here all night. Perhaps she's shown up. Perhaps the Pope's become a Moonie."

He got up and pulled the flush. The lock was stiff and he snagged a finger opening it. Bloody typical, he thought. He got through the door by employing a pass-able imitation of Houdini and emerged into the corridor outside with the uncertain step of a prisoner released unexpectedly from solitary confinement. At the top of the stairs he bumped into Ben.

"I've been looking for you everywhere," said Ben, clearly oblivious to the fact that he had seen him go downstairs not five minutes ago. "There was a phone message from Miss Sheridan. She says awfully sorry but she's been delayed at the studio and she won't be able to make it tonight. She'll call you in the morning."

Philip curled his lip. "Have you got ten p? I don't have any change."

Ben fished in his pockets and came up with a sweaty handful of coins. Philip selected one fastidiously and retreated back down the stairs. There was a pay phone in the corner and he dialled Hannah's number. After the statutory three rings he heard the crackle of her answerphone tape. As ever, there was background music; as usual, Rachmaninoff's Second. Hannah only knew two pieces of classical music. One was the Rachmaninoff, which reminded her of *Brief Encounter*. The other was *Swan Lake*, which reminded her of swans on a lake.

"It's Philip," he said, taking his cue from the bleep. "Remember me? Another missed entrance, my dear. What will you do for an encore? I would forgive you were it not for the fact that your absence forced me to listen to the morons at the next table panegyrizing that arse-hole Gordon Wilde. You spell that p-a-n-e-g, et cetera. I'm sure you'll find it in your pocket Chambers. I gather you intend speaking to me in the morning. Sleep well and don't overdo the tranquillizers."

He put the phone down and returned upstairs. Ben gave him a sympathetic look. Philip said, "Be a love and put the Albanian on my tab, will you?"

"It's on the house, Phil," said Ben.

Philip winced. He went to retrieve his coat from the back of the chair and overhead the loathsome four discussing the miners' strike. He gave them a malicious stare and mentally went over the text of a voodoo curse he remembered from a thriller in which he had once appeared. He noted with delight that two of them had ordered Chef's Special, the nearest any restaurant in London got to boiled cat without contravening the Trades Descriptions Act.

"See you next week?" Ben asked on the way out.

"Unless I have to fly out to Hollywood," said Philip. Ben laughed. He always laughed at his jokes. Philip liked him.

Philip wandered down through Covent Garden Market. He'd seen a taxi in Long Acre, but it was a fine night and he fancied a little walk. The market was full of people having a good time and he walked through the thickest part of the crowd, breathing in the good humour. They were mostly very young and he liked being amongst young people. Most of his friends were middle-aged theatricals, like himself, as equally jaded. But he was still slim and fit-looking; he didn't seem too out of place. He took pride in not having gone to seed, in having avoided the alcoholic paunch that disfigured so many of his contemporaries. He stopped and watched a Punch and Judy show. It wasn't very good, but the audience was enjoying it and Philip let himself be carried along by their mood. He laughed as loudly as anyone and a pretty girl with spiky mauve hair smiled at him nicely. He felt ten years younger for that smile.

Philip decided to go down to the Strand and pick up a cab there. You could always find one by the Savoy. He walked down Southampton Street and saw a taxi at the bottom, the last passenger in the act of paying off the driver. Philip gave his address and sat back on the worn but comfortable upholstery. He had always liked cabs. He remembered envying the richer students at drama school who had been able to afford them instead of the bus or the tube. He had decided that he would take them all the time when he became a real actor, and imagined himself sauntering out of the stage door in a floppy hat and cape, imperiously hailing a passing hansom with his silver-topped cane and smiling condescendingly at the forelocking cabby.

"Evening to you, Mr. Fletcher, sir . . ." Or perhaps: "Another triumph, Sir Philip?"

It had never quite happened like that. A few years back he had a small success at the Haymarket and there had been a slight but noticeable change in the behaviour of the cabbies. He had never had the gall to sport the hat and cane, but the tweed cape au Sherlock Holmes had looked suitably theatrical. He remembered one Saturday night, after he had given probably his finest performance. The cabby had been delighted to see him. "I did enjoy you on the telly the other night—you know, the Russian thing. You look different without your glasses."

"That was Anthony Hopkins. Highbury Grove, please."

He was still living in Highbury Grove, in the same modest but comfortable ground-floor flat. He had been there for fourteen years. There was some traffic during the day, but his bedroom gave out onto the back garden (which he shared with the couple upstairs), and it was quiet enough. He was anxious to get home. He wanted to see if there were any messages, and he vaguely recalled thinking over that morning's television page that there was something worth seeing tonight. The cabby drove quickly and dropped him off at a quarter past nine.

He went straight into the living room and was pleased to see the green light on the answerphone. It always depressed him to come home and find the red light still on, it made him feel unwanted. Without bothering to take off his coat, he wound back the tape and listened eagerly.

"Hello, Philip. John here. I had a word with Trethowan's production people. They'd like to see you for the Chekhov tour. Have a look at Dorn, it's a bit old for you, but you could do it. Can you be at the Duchess at a quarter to one tomorrow? Ring me in the morning to confirm, will you."

John Quennell was his agent of two years. He'd been meaning to change him for most of that time. He was annoyed with him. Yes, he knew it was a number-one tour, good dates—Brighton, Bath, Norwich, Birmingham—and odds-on for a West End transfer, but he really didn't want to play Doctor Dorn for six months. Trigorin was his part. He'd done it very successfully in Manchester a few years back. The *Guardian* had called his performance masterful. Why hadn't Quennell got him seen for Trigorin? No doubt it had been promised to some nonentity fresh from a popular television series. He knew the way commercial managements worked. They'd probably have one of those dreadful posters with cartoon bodies and oversized heads stuck on, each with a bubble proclaiming "Star of TV's wacky sitcom *AIDS Clinic Blues*." He wouldn't put it past them. He remembered the story of one famous entrepreneur who, on seeing his production of *Macbeth* for the first time, had turned aghast to his director and demanded, "Where'd you dig this old rubbish up from?" He was tempted to tell Quennell to forget it, but then again, you never knew. Something might come of it, and he'd never met the director before. He could always turn it down anyway.

"Philip, dear, it's Eleanor Thompson, here at the BBC. Just to tell you that the series now looks as though it's going to go ahead, and you should get your agent on to it as soon as possible. Tom de Vere's producing, and you know he likes your work. Fingers crossed. Speak to you soon."

That was the only other message. It was nice of Eleanor to ring, she always remembered him. They went back a long way, and she'd got him quite a lot of work over the years. She'd mentioned the new series often, she seemed very excited by it. It was going to be a big historical epic about the life of Sir Walter Raleigh, the sort of thing the BBC does very well. She said he ought to be up for Raleigh, he looked so good in costume. He was grateful but didn't rate his chances. Quennell, of course, had done nothing about it.

He put the kettle on and sat down to watch the tail end of the news. There was a report of a parliamentary debate in which some left-wingers had heckled the prime minister. He loved those sorts of debates, they were so theatrical. He'd always wanted to appear in a dramatized political biopic but unfortunately he didn't look like anyone famous. He thought that he might have had a good crack at Lloyd George, but he suffered from the disadvantage of not being Welsh. It had been quite a handicap when he'd started his career in the late fifties, not being either Welsh or working class.

On closer inspection tonight's film didn't look so appetizing, so he decided to turn in early. He went to run a bath and while it was filling made himself a cheese sandwich. He sat on the side of the bath, munching and feeling the temperature. He could just see his head in the mirror over the sink. He spent a great deal of time looking at himself in the mirror. He wasn't really a narcissist, just curious.

He put the radio on and sank into the bath. He soaped himself thoroughly, examining his body for signs of wear. There was still no suspicion of a paunch. He looked after himself, drank little, didn't smoke, and kept fairly fit. At least he walked a lot. He was pleased with his general state of preservation. The receding hairline worried him a bit, but his hair fell forward naturally and it didn't look too bad. It was still thick on top. He'd never had matinee-idol looks, but he had a strong jawline and interesting eyes. His photographs never did him justice. But he reckoned he had that invaluable, indefinable actor's asset, presence.

"Yes, I've been lucky in that respect," he said out loud, "in always being able to command attention. My mother remarked upon it when she saw me, aged five, in the school nativity play. I was only playing one of the shepherds, it wasn't a speaking role, but apparently I stood out even then."

"I suppose it was that which recommended you to the Royal Shakespeare Company?" he asked himself. He always played out the interviewer's part in full, sometimes stopping to repeat a question if he hadn't got the inflexion right.

"Yes, I spent two years with the RSC, invaluable training for a young actor. Those three letters, RSC, are a bit of a magical password in the theatre, they open doors for you. I did a lot of rep after that, good work, nice parts, a solid grounding, and though I had to wait a long time for my big break, I kept at it patiently, knowing that it would all come good someday."

"Yes, you had to wait a long time, didn't you. How did your big break come?"

"Oh, quite by chance. Luck's the name of the game in our business. I went up for the part of Doctor Dorn in *The Seagull*. But when I walked into the theatre, the director—a very bright young chap, Tony Elliott—took one look at me and said, 'Why don't you read for Trigorin?' The reading went very well, he persuaded the management to give me the part, and that was that. Six-month tour and six months at the Apollo. The *Evening Standard* award and the film with Dustin Hoffman were the icing on the cake. I owe a lot to Tony, and it was wonderful playing opposite Maggie Smith. Of course she'd always wanted to work with me. It was unusual casting, brave. That's why it worked so well."

"What are your plans now?"

"I'm thinking of going into production myself. Since the demise of Prospect, there hasn't been an established classical touring company. There's a gap; I think it's worth filling. I've had a word with Trevor Nunn and he thinks it's about time I played Othello."

"It must be a bore blacking up night after night."

"Not really. I'm used to it after years of playing character parts in rep. Actually I've a reputation as a make-up specialist. I played Firs in Bristol when I was only twenty-eight. Othello's the sort of challenge which any actor relishes. I'd have a skin transplant if it were necessary."

"Ha-ha-ha. Well, it's been delightful chatting to you, Mr. Fletcher, but I'm afraid that's all we've got time for tonight."

"Thank you, Mr. Parkinson."

He always said "Thank you, Mr. Parkinson," even though he hadn't done any chat shows for ages. He still did his Desert Island discs to Roy Plomley. He supposed he'd have to get used to the idea of being interviewed by Wogan, but he wasn't keen; he couldn't do the accent.

He got out of the bath and did some vocal limbers while drying himself. He usually exercised first and last thing. He was proud of being much more conscientious than any of his friends.

He got into bed and turned on the reading light. He much preferred sleeping alone, it meant that he could read for as long as he liked and talk to himself. He enjoyed his own company. There hadn't been anyone else in his bed for months, no one serious for years. The only woman he'd ever asked to marry him had been Hannah, and she'd laughed. He supposed that he'd be a bachelor for the rest of his life now. He didn't mind that so much, but he missed not having a regular sex life. He'd never been very good at getting women into bed. Women usually liked him, but not in that way. Hannah said he was too placid, too English. He lacked passion, didn't have that dangerous glint in his eye. He could do the glint quite well in front of the mirror, but it never seemed to come off in one-to-one situations. He'd just have to keep on rehearsing till he cracked it.

He read for half an hour before turning out the light. He decided against having a look at *The Seagull*. He practically knew it by heart and he wasn't interested in the part. In any case, Tony Elliott was going to offer him Trigorin. He turned over on his side and closed his eyes. He was asleep by twenty-five to eleven.

TWO

Philip wasn't in the right frame of mind for his audition at the Duchess. He'd arrived early and had too much time to kill. Auditions made him nervous, even for things he didn't want. His nerves had not been soothed by the sight of Gordon Wilde's photograph blown up all over the foyer. There was a sickening quote from the *Observer* underneath, and a "Sold Out" notice by the ticket office. Who would want to spend ten quid to see Gordon Wilde murdering Eugene O'Neill? Lots of people, apparently.

He was told to wait in the Stalls Bar, where he found a young actor he did not know. They eyed each other up warily and when they'd satisfied themselves that they were obviously not up for the same part, shook hands. Philip didn't catch his name. He was up for Treplev and sat rather nervously crumpling up a copy of the *Evening Standard*. Philip didn't want to talk to him. He leaned back against the bar and idly examined the posters on the wall. He liked the Duchess, he'd seen a lot of good productions there. Many of the posters were for Pinter plays.

"Done much Pinter?" asked the young actor.

"A bit," answered Philip reluctantly. *"Caretaker"* in Brighton, *Homecoming* in Swansea."

"I played Ashton at RADA," said the young actor. "Loved doing it. But he's really difficult, isn't he?"

"Not as tough as he's made out, I think," said Philip patiently. "I've a theory about Pinter. People think there's something surreal about the way his characters behave, quite often actors don't treat them as real people. That's a mistake. Pinter's got a wonderful ear. Listen closely and you'll find people who really do talk like that. But directors labour it, for example by trying to invest the pauses with a significance which the text can't support. They treat him with too much reverence. He needs a lighter touch, like Chekhov."

"I'd never thought of it like that," said the young actor. "Why do you say Chekhov?"

Because he wrote *The Seagull*, you blockhead, thought Philip, or didn't they teach you that at RADA? "Directors tend to treat Chekhov too heavily," he said. "A lot of it is very funny. Plays should be done as their authors intended them to be done."

The young man pulled a face. "I don't know if you'll see eye to eye with Tony Elliott then."

"I don't know him. What have you heard?"

"Oh, he's good, really good. I saw this amazing modern-dress production of *The Merchant of Venice* he did at the Warehouse last year. Antonio and Bassanio were really creepy stockbroker types. It got over the capitalist angle brilliantly. Shylock was great. He wore an eye-patch and looked just like Moshe Dayan. Lorenzo dressed up as a Palestinian terrorist for the elopement scene."

"Who was Shylock?"

"Gordon Wilde."

Philip felt like Douglas at the end of *Henry IV (Part 1)*, knocking down one image of the hydra-headed king, only for another to spring up in its place:

> Now, by my sword, I will call all his coats;
> I'll murder all his wardrobe, piece by piece . . .

Perhaps that was it: there was not one Gordon but many; chips off the old clone. Philip politely disengaged himself from the conversation and resumed his perusal of the posters on the wall. He thought of Brighton and Swansea.

The touring schedule had not yet been finalized. Philip considered a list of probable venues unenthusiastically. He thought of grey days in Bradford and Liverpool, nylon sheets in damp-walled bedrooms, a greasy breakfast on a dirty plate. He was getting too old to tour; it wasn't worth the risk of getting bad digs. The thought of Glasgow in winter was enough to prompt psychosomatic chilblains; the thought of Billingham any time of the year, to prompt suicide. Cold dressing rooms and trains, three-quarter empty matinees, slow halves in shoddy saloons . . . what a dreadful way to live. He knew no other. It was the dream itself enchanted him; clutching at the chimera of success.

An ASM came in and called Philip's name. He followed her into the auditorium and through the steps at the side onto the stage, where there were a table and some chairs. Two men were seated behind the table.

One of them was Trethowan's production manager, Bill Childs. He got up and offered his hand.

"Hello, Bill."

"Hello, Philip." They knew each other slightly. Bill said, "Philip, this is Tony Elliott."

"Hi, Philip."

"Hello."

They sat down. Tony was a small man with an unhealthy complexion and watery eyes. He wore glasses. He also wore dirty jeans and a Bruce Springsteen T-shirt with a "No Nukes" badge. He was somewhere in his late twenties.

"You know about the tour, dates and that?" he asked. His voice had a nasal twang.

Philip said he knew about the tour, and that.

"That's great. I won't ask you to read anything, this is like a preliminary chat, just to get to know each other. Right. I'm looking at you for Doctor Dorn. How old are you?"

"Forty-four. I'm a bit young for Dorn. Is Trigorin cast?"

Tony smiled. He had thick lips and he looked idiotic when he smiled. "It's on offer, I'm afraid. Now about Dorn. I can see at once that you've got exactly the right sort of qualities, like a bit elegant, intelligent, you know, gentle, slightly detached. But I have to say the age thing worries me a bit. You know, like he's retired."

"Well, there's no reason why he shouldn't have retired early. And I can age up." Philip wondered why he was saying this. He didn't even want to play Doctor Dorn.

"Right. I take your point and that's fair enough. Let me tell you a bit about how I see the play . . ."

Please don't, thought Philip.

"It's the most incredibly vital piece of writing. I was

really knocked out by it. To tell you the truth, I'd never read it till last week, but it grabbed me by the balls. You know, there's like the most amazing dynamic tension, like catharsis. You've got these people, right, these washed-up highbrows, stagnating in the typical bourgeois country-house situation, and the whole thing's this brilliant indictment of their complete lack of moral and political perspective. It's turn of the century, right. We'll update it a bit and call it 1910. Now look at what's happening all around them. Revolution is everywhere. You've got Lenin in Zurich, right, and what've you got here? Trigorin and Arkadina, right, decadent and without political consciousness. But it's all around them. It's very revealing that Trigorin compares himself to Turgenev. That's how I want Trigorin to be, with a long white beard like Turgenev had. Turgenev is like the embodiment of Russian moral intellectual impotence, you know, writing about country squires and trivial love affairs while the fabric of society crumbles round his ears. That's Turgenev all over."

"Really? I wouldn't have thought you could call the author of *Virgin Soil* politically unaware."

"Er, yeah? Well, I haven't read that one. Anyway, as I was saying, Phil, you've got this decadent couple—somehow I keep flashing on to the Irish situation, there's a parallel somewhere—and they like corrupt the young idealists Nina and Treplev, the spirit of new Russia. I see Treplev as Trotsky. Dorn is a Kerensky figure, well-meaning but sterile. Anyway, the whole crux is that just when the reactionary older generation think they've won and crushed the impulse for change in Nina and Treplev, he gets the last laugh. His suicide, I mean. It's not an act of despair, you see, it's an act of triumph. He's saying I refuse to be a part of the conspiracy. His suicide is a statement of principle, an act of free will.

We're into Dostoyevski territory here, right. Suicide is a revolutionary statement, you see what I mean?"

"Yes, I think I catch your drift."

"We're way behind schedule, Tony," said Bill. "Sorry, Philip, we've got to be out by one; there's a matinee."

"Right, well, great to meet you, Phil." Tony got up and offered his hand. "We'll be in touch, as they say. Who's your agent—oh, aren't you with Harry Foster?"

"No. We, er, split up two years ago. I'm with John Quennell."

"Oh, sorry. Just that I'm with Harry and I thought I saw your name on his client list."

"Must have been a very old list."

"Yeah. Shame, though, he's a good agent."

"So they say. Cheerio, Bill."

"It's all right Philip, I'll come with you. I've got to see in the next chap anyway."

They chattered amicably on their way out through the stalls. Once in the foyer, Bill smiled ruefully at Philip and dropped his voice to a stage whisper. "Sorry about that," he said. "He does go on a bit."

"What made Trethowan use him?" asked Philip.

"Oh, you know what Trethowan's like about 'young blood.' You're right, though, he's not quite the man I'd have chosen for our sort of production, I don't think he's grasped the demands of the commercial theatre. Still, I gather he's okay once the bullshit dries up. I was chatting to Gordon Wilde, who did a show for him last year. Apparently he just rabbits on and no one pays him any attention. The actors just get on with it."

"Have you seen Gordon in this?"

"Yes. He's quite good actually. Same old Gordon, the ten-minute pauses and the drawling monotone delivery. But he puts bums on seats. The critics love him.

Of course it's terrible really, but Trethowan's making a mint. God knows what they'll make of Gordon doing Eugene O'Neill on Broadway!"

"They'll love him. They go weak at the knees at the sight of an English actor with a 'classical' reputation, however undeserved."

"Don't let it get you down, old chap. Nice to see you, Philip. I'll put in a word for you; I'd say you've got a decent chance. 'Bye."

" 'Bye."

Out in the foyer there was a small group of pensioners queueing for returns. Philip often wondered what it would be like knowing you were famous, having people stare at you the whole time. None of the pensioners paid him any attention. He stopped just inside the door to pull up his collar and put on his gloves. He could see that it was blustery outside and it promised to be a cold afternoon. It was early September, the weather was very changeable. Philip disapproved on principle of anyone who couldn't make up his mind and he disliked the uncertain weather intensely. It made him cross. He stood outside the theatre with his hands thrust into his pockets and his eyes fixed on the road. Although he could have got a taxi at once simply by wandering fifty yards into the Aldwych, he refused to budge; he would wait until one turned up Catherine Place. There was no logic in his attitude. But the weather had made him feel put out and he reacted with mindless obstinacy. It was a common mood with him. Hannah said that it was the unattractive side of his character coming out, he could be really small-minded and petulant. Thinking of Hannah made him even more cross. She hadn't rung him that morning. It was just rudeness, there was no excuse for it. He couldn't think why he bothered with her.

A taxi was pulling up. He saw the passenger reaching forward and handing over a note, the taxi would stop about five yards from him. He caught the cabby's eye and opened the door. With a muttered "thank you" the passenger got out.

"Why, hello, Philip!"

He was already half in. He turned back in surprise, not recognizing the voice. He felt rather foolish, one foot in the back and one out, twisting himself awkwardly. When he saw who it was, his lip twitched.

"Hello, Gordon."

Gordon Wilde laughed. He seemed pleased to see Philip, he said as much. He giggled with delight. God, you've got ugly teeth, thought Philip. In fact, you're an ugly bastard all round. He said, "You're looking very well, Gordon." Actually Philip thought he looked dreadful, but then he always had. Gordon had prominent bones, his facial skin was crumpled up and his eyes looked sunken. He was famous for his gaunt, haggard look, and there was no denying it was effective in certain parts. Dracula, for instance.

"Haven't seen you for ages, old thing!" declared Gordon, slapping him on the back. "Where was it?"

"Acton, I think." Acton was a safe bet. Everyone had met everybody else at some stage in the BBC rehearsal block. "How's the show going?" asked Philip, wishing at once that he hadn't.

"Oh, you know." Gordon shrugged with what he intended to pass for modesty. "To tell you the truth, I'm not looking forward to taking it on. New York's such a bore in September."

"Isn't it just."

"Still, it'll only be six weeks. Limited season. I've had a lot of offers and I don't want to miss anything. You've played Trigorin, haven't you? Tony Elliott insists it's just perfect for me. I'm flattered, but there's a series in the offing and talk of a film. Lovely to run into you. Drop by sometime. I'll fix you tickets. And make sure you come round and see me afterwards. Matinee—must dash!"

Philip watched him stride confidently round to the stage door as the cab pulled away. He got only half-way before the first autograph hunter intercepted him. He wondered how many times Gordon had been asked to scrawl his illegible signature. It wasn't even his real name. He remembered young Gordon Wilberforce, spotty and anorexic, mooning about drama school complaining of his name. "It lacks something, I'm not sure what, Gordon Wilberforce," he used to say. "I just don't think it's very dynamic." Only Hannah had dared say what everyone thought. "It suits you down to the ground, dear." Gordon had never liked women. He loathed Hannah above all her sex. "I think I'll call myself Gordon Wilde, after Oscar," he announced one day. "What's wrong with Oscar Wilberforce?" Hannah had asked. Philip now regretted not having contributed to that conversation of twenty-five years ago. He sat back in the taxi thinking of appropriate stage names. How about the double-barreled effect, as in Gordon Shit-Features? Or just a one-word name, in the French fashion, like—Shitface.

The cab dropped him at twenty past one. He paid up hurriedly and rushed into the drive. He didn't like being out at lunch-time, he loved listening to the radio. He hoped it would be Robin Day on the *World at One,* he'd just catch the end of him. He'd make himself a light snack and then settle down to listen to the *Archers.* He didn't want to miss anything: a friend had tipped him off that a well-known character (he wouldn't say which one) was about to get the chop. He hoped it wasn't Walter Gabriel or any of the Grundys.

His thoughts far away in Ambridge, he didn't notice

the human heap piled up in his porch. As he mounted the step, the heap moved and he started. Bright-red lips pouted a kiss at him, cat-green eyes flickered wickedly.

"Hello, darling."

"Hello, Hannah," he said warily.

THREE

"Oh, darling, you're so funny!"

Hannah roared with laughter. Actually she didn't so much roar as gargle. She was the only person Philip had ever met who really did laugh like a drain: her guffaws rippled as if through some curious effluent simmering in her windpipe.

"I don't think it's that funny," said Philip.

"Oh, but it is, darling, to think of you being jealous of silly little Gordon . . ."

"No, it's not jealousy," said Philip, trying to sound reasonable. "I am genuinely amazed that the likes of Gordon Wilde bask in popular acclaim while demonstrably talented actors languish in obscurity. The time is out of joint—"

"Oh, it must be such a strain, Philip dear, being saddled with the only truly perceptive critical brain in London."

Philip bit his lip. There was no point in getting into a slanging-match with Hannah, he was too polite ever to plunge into the verbal hilt, a constraint that in no way affected her. The force of her sarcasm was blood-curdling. Even after twenty-five years she still had the capacity to wound him to the quick with a word, and she knew it. She reclined on the sofa and smiled at him luxuriously. She had kicked off her silver sandals and lay with her feet tucked up under a cushion. She was wearing a long black evening dress. Her black bag and mink stole were slung carelessly over the back of the sofa. She dipped a couple of fingers into the bag and pulled out various objects: a powder compact, a lipstick, a bottle of pills, a cigarette holder and a packet of Dunhill International. Using the same two fingers, she replaced the compact, lipstick, pills, and extricated a cigarette, which she very cleverly fitted into the holder, using the same two overworked fingers and (briefly) a thumb. She inserted the holder between her lips and flickered her eyelids.

Philip understood the signal. She never carried a light on the grounds that it reduced one's opportunities for casual sex. Wearily Philip trudged into the kitchen and returned with a household box of matches and an ashtray. He lit her cigarette.

"How long had you been waiting outside?" he asked her, when he had settled back in his armchair.

"God knows, darling. Simply ages. I was thinking of giving it up, but was frankly too tired to move."

Philip had tried very hard from the first not to ask her why she had fetched up on his doorstep in the middle of the day wearing evening clothes. He had kept a straight face and not so much as batted the proverbial eyelash. Hannah had offered no explanation.

"Why don't you keep the key under the mat any-more?" she demanded almost querulously, exhaling like an overheated steam engine.

Philip flicked his hand in front of his face, parting the wave of smoke. "There was a break-in upstairs. They just smashed the window in with a brick, amazing no one heard. God knows why they didn't come in here, but I don't want to make it any easier for them."

Hannah snorted unbecomingly. "Frankly, dear, I think it makes much more sense to leave the key in plain view. If they're going to break in, they're going to break in anyway. So much less mess to clear up if they don't have to smash a window!"

Philip looked at her carefully. He could think of several things to say, but none of them sounded too bright. He wondered if she'd been reading one of those awful lateral-thinking books. On second thought, he doubted it. He'd never known her to read anything more de-manding than the *Daily Mail*.

"Hannah, you don't have to answer this, but you'll understand why I have to ask. My question comes in two parts: Why are you dressed like that, and why are you here?"

"Pass."

She drawled the word seductively, then gurgled richly with laughter. It still occasionally disconcerted Philip that her voice had a deeper register than his. It had not always been so: he remembered the nervous little girl from Shipley, Yorkshire, gormlessly gaping at the rest of the class on their first day at drama school, cruelly caricatured in the boys' changing room for her flat vowels. Her transformation had been swift and little short of miraculous. Within a few months all traces of little Yorkshire Annie had disappeared. Out of the chrysalis sprouted a gaudy butterfly, London Hannah, cosmopolitan and sophisticated, sexually knowing and sexually known. She always looked either as if she were on her way to a ball or just returning from one. Suddenly all the men who had ignored her, even laughed at her, clustered round. She would choose from them seemingly at random, picking one to accompany her to the theatre one night, another to accompany her to bed the next. She wasn't going to get involved; nobody could ever accuse her of duplicity. She knew what she had, and she knew how to use it: she was going to screw her way right to the top.

She'd managed to screw herself about half-way there and then lost interest. She had some talent and got maximum value from the opportunities she earned in the sack. She was a very creditable Ophelia in 1963 and made quite a name for herself as Rosalind a year later. She was hopelessly miscast as the Duchess of Malfi, but at the time she was being escorted by a fashionable member of the aristocracy and the publicity ensured her a string of movie roles, during the course of which she seemed to lose her clothes about as fast as her credibility. In the mid-seventies she attempted a come-back to the theatre and was laughed off the stage, although in fact she wasn't half bad. She had shrugged her shoulders philosophically and stepped with apparent ease out of the limelight. She didn't work much these days, usually appearing only once or twice a year in B-rated cameo roles. These fleeting appearances were rewarded out of all proportion to their true value, and as a consequence she was able to continue to keep herself in the style to which she had been determined to grow accustomed since drama school.

All things considered, she looked remarkably well.

Bits of her had fleshed out, but her waist was still recognizably a waist and there were no visible folds in her skin. Her black hair was still lustrous and thick, her eyes had never lost their alluring spark. He still fancied her.

In a way it made it worse that she had once fancied him. It would be much easier to put such thoughts from his mind if there were no memories to fuel them. But passionate images stormed his brain each time he thought of her: he'd never had another woman like her; there was a hard-porn projection room working on automatic repeat somewhere in his memory banks. They'd been together for six months in all, a long affair by Hannah's standards. This had happened ten years ago, quite by accident, long after Philip had given up the idea of ever getting anywhere with her. She'd locked herself out of her flat one night and asked to sleep on his floor. The next thing he remembered they were in bed together; neither of them could quite recall how. But it had obviously seemed like a good idea at the time, and a week later it was given the official stamp by an oblique reference in the William Hickey column. Philip had never before felt so important, but he knew all along that it couldn't last, and when he read in Nigel Dempster that she was seeing some teenage blond playboy with a string of racehorses and a name in the city, he accepted the inevitable with tact and grace. Only once had he succumbed to delusion when, early in the affair, he had rashly proposed to her. Her reaction had restored him instantly to common sense. He had never let her know how much she'd hurt him. He bottled things up and was embarrassed at the thought of laundering his emotions publicly. He didn't think she knew that he was still infatuated with her.

Hannah said, "I'm dressed like this for obvious reasons, and I'm here because I wanted to see you and apologize for last night. I just happened to be passing."

"Passing from where to where?"

"From Hampstead to Putney. I went to a fabulous party."

"Highbury does not lie between Hampstead and Putney."

"Really? My geography's so hazy. Frankly, dear, I couldn't face going all the way home in the middle of the day. The flat looks ghastly. It's so much cosier here."

Philip sighed. It was useless expecting her to have forewarned him: she never used the phone, she relished the unexpected entrance. She seemed to have fastened on his home as a likely place to crash out. He felt disinclined to probe her deeper motives. Perhaps there was a corpse back in her flat at Putney. She courted the extraordinary. Why in God's name did she have to come and bugger up his day?

She refused alcohol, drooled at the mention of a coffee. He escaped into the kitchen and breathed in lungfuls of smokeless and perfume-free air. Hannah was a walking pollutant, psychologically as well as physically. He put the coffee things onto a tray and added a plate of biscuits and a bottle of paracetamol, covering the likeliest options.

"You are a sweetie," she said, and added coyly, "putting up with me." He smiled vacantly. She sipped at her coffee. "So Gordon invited you along to see him, eh? Well, he always did have a high opinion of you." Philip began to say something, then thought better of it. He looked sulky. Hannah wagged her finger at him and made a mock grimace. "You know very well that little Gordon used to look up to you at drama school. You can't blame him for being successful."

"No, it's not his fault, you're right. I can't remember

who started it all. I think it was some daft critic in one of the Sundays, claiming to have discovered this young protean genius acting his socks off in some obscure venue. Croydon, I think. That alerted the others. Discovery is the critic's dream, usually of an actor or writer. They're on safer ground with directors because none of the critics have ever quite worked out what it is they do, so any number of mindless dipsomaniacs have been hailed as creative geniuses in the arts pages of august organs. But to do a Harold Hobson and spot a Pinter! Ay, there's the rub . . ."

"Philip, you really are a bore when you're in this mood. You've been getting a lot worse lately."

"Don't lecture me, Hannah, please!"

She looked surprised. Philip's lips were pursed, his whole expression unusually grim and tense. Although he was frequently obstinate and irritable, he rarely lost his temper. But just now he looked very near to blowing his top.

Hannah swung her feet to the floor and dipped them into her sandals. "May I use your bedroom, darling? I'd love a nap."

He leaped to his feet with peculiar alacrity. "Yes, of course." He offered his hand and led her to the bedroom. He drew the curtains for her and, as she stretched herself out on the duvet—it was warm, she declined the offer of a cover—he neatly tucked her shoes under the bed and hung up her stole.

"Always tidying up after me, dear . . ." she murmured sleepily. "You'd make someone a lovely wife."

"Thank you. Have a nice sleep. You can rest for as long as you like."

"That may be a long time. It really was the most exhausting party. I'd have asked you along, but you wouldn't have liked the company . . ."

His hand was on the door handle, he had been about to go out. He stopped and stood still. He had had his suspicions when she mentioned Hampstead, but Hampstead was a big place; they both knew loads of party givers in Hampstead. Nonetheless he felt a little psychic twitch. He asked as casually as possible, "Why, who was there?"

"A lot of nice people. But it was Harry Foster's party . . ."

"Ah."

"I thought you might say something like that."

"Something like 'ah'?"

"Yes, or perhaps 'aaargh!'—like in the comic books."

"You mean you stood me up for Harry Foster?"

"No, I stood you up because I was unavoidably detained at Elstree. Don't sound so jealous, you're not twenty-one anymore." She yawned expansively and apologized unconvincingly. "I'll leave you to it," he said, as he turned out the light and closed the door. Out in the hall he took a deep breath and then three quick strides down to the bathroom. He locked himself in with an exaggerated flick of the wrist and sat down heavily on the bath. He stared angrily at his face in the mirror. He stuck out his tongue at the reflection and, placing his thumbs against his ears, waggled his fingers.

"She's right, you know," he said to himself. "You are getting a lot worse." The face in the mirror stared back at him morosely, a slight sneer creasing the skin above the lip. "Don't look so pleased with yourself," he said. The face arched an eyebrow in surprise; clearly it did not think that it looked pleased with itself. "Oh yes, you do," he said. There was a pause. Nearly a silence. Having done Pinter, he was acutely aware of the distinction. He smiled wryly at himself. "It really is a bit much, though," he muttered, in a tone above a stage whisper. He noticed that his voice was cracking a bit, dropping into his throat. Good projection was a trick, an exercise of a state of mind. "Not only bugged by Gordon Wilde, but now Harry Foster too . . ." That was better, the long vowel sound at the end especially crisp . . . "And Trethowan's hardly my favourite person to begin with. Will the line stretch out to the crack of doom?" He spat the words into the mirror. He was so close the glass frosted. He held his breath and watched the smudge dissolve. He turned away, and back suddenly, catching the sudden look of horror in his eyes. "Is this a dagger that I see before me, the handle towards my hand?"

He was off now. He belted through two of the Macbeth soliloquies, three of the four Hamlets (missing out the obvious one) and chucked in "Now is the winter of our discontent" for good measure. By now he was sweating, his hair felt hot under the low bathroom lamp. He glanced at his watch. It was 2:30. He ought to ring Quennell, tell him how the audition had gone. He ought to, but Quennell inspired so little confidence, he felt loath to talk to him. Damn him!

"And screw you, Harry Foster!"

His savage delivery took him by surprise. That was exactly the tone he'd been wanting for a smiling damned villain! Perhaps he should try and conjure up a picture of Harry Foster every time he wanted to express loathing. That sounded suspiciously Method. No, that wouldn't do at all, it went right against the dispassionate grain, the keynote of his classical training—an actor who emotes strangles his voice. More importantly, Othello might end up strangling Desdemona.

"Let's just leave it at this, Harry: to be honest, I find you rather a pathetic creature; I'm sorry for you. Let's face it, being an agent and suffering from the inability to

spot talent if it comes up and bites you on the bum must
be a serious handicap. One day soon you're going to be
kicking yourself so hard it'll bring tears to your eyes."

He spoke to Harry very softly, with genuine sympathy. Over the last two years he'd practised lots of ways
of meeting him. He'd perfected cutting him dead, and
was rather good at the terse dismissive approach. But on
the whole he thought ironic condescension the most satisfying tone. It implied subtly that superiority of spirit
and intellect which Philip felt so keenly. Mind you, he
thought, nine out of ten delinquents and pop stars
would be intellectually superior to Harry.

"Frankly, Harry, I despise you. Yes, your actions
were beneath contempt. You didn't even have the de-
cency to tell me face-to-face. Not even a phone call. A
letter. And a second-class stamp. All that bullshit: 'Dear
Philip, we are changing direction in the agency and are
having to reduce our list of clients . . . I think you're a
smashing chap (oh yeah?) but feel that your interests
would be better served elsewhere, et cetera, et cetera.'
As I said, Harry, pretty despicable, eh? I'm sure you had
my interests at heart while you were taking your per-
centage all through the good years . . . and I thought
you were my friend. Well, no one makes friends with the
great white shark!"

He smiled with his mouth only. Slowly the facial
muscles relaxed, smoothing the creases, until the face
was blank and expressionless. The eyes glared out of
their sockets: his stare was hard and pitiless, without
feeling or emotion. He'd seen it in countless movies—
the eyes of the gun-slinger, the hit man.

"I'm tired of looking at you, ugly-mug," he said suddenly and turned out the light. He fumbled for the door
handle in the semi-darkness and went out. He felt restless and bored. He hadn't eaten, but he didn't feel hun-

gry. He wouldn't have minded going for a walk, but it was drizzling now and thoroughly unpleasant. The long afternoon stretched out in front of him uninvitingly. It was the sort of day when he just wanted to shut out the whole world altogether.

He fitted a tape onto his reel-to-reel recorder. He preferred the reel-to-reel for serious listening, it meant that one could go on uninterrupted for hours; you didn't have to stop and change sides every twenty minutes or so. You could fit an entire Wagnerian opera onto one tape. He thought about putting on *Lohengrin* but decided that he wasn't quite in a Wagnerian mood. He gave long consideration to his mood: not quite Wagner, so probably . . . Berlioz. He had a fine recording of the "Symphonie Funèbre et Triomphale," the blurb on the back sleeve of which began "The legend of Berlioz as a great noise-maker has been a long time dying . . ." He smiled to himself at the recollection: and what was wrong with being a great noise-maker? He loved it, the drums and the fanfares, the thundering chorus . . . music to wave your arms about to! Only he wasn't quite in an arm-waving mood. What about Frederica von Stade singing *Les Nuits d'Été*? Ideal for hors d'oeuvres. He wound on the tape, put on his headphones and settled comfortably in his armchair, feeling keyed up and energetic. The beautiful opening of "Villanelle," the thrilling energy of the singer's voice, implanted a delighted smile on his face.

"Just how important is music to you, Philip?"

"Oh, very important, Roy. I've never had a formal musical training, something I've always regretted, but I always turn to music for relaxation and stimulation. As an actor I feel that the human voice should be treated in much the same way as an instrument."

"A Stradivarius in your case, Philip?"

"More like a ten-bob mouth organ, I'm afraid, Roy."

"Ha-ha-ha! We'll leave our listeners to decide how best to characterize your marvellous classical diction. And what have you chosen for your next record?"

"Of course one is so limited with only eight, so I think variety's all-important, and here's one to kill two birds with one stone, as they say: I love the music of Brecht and Weill, and I love great jazz. What could be better than Louis Armstrong singing 'Mack the Knife'?"

"An excellent choice. Now what about your one luxury?"

"I'd like an eighteen-year-old nymphomaniac masseuse, please."

"You shall have one. And one book besides the Bible and Shakespeare?"

"You're allowed multi-volume works, aren't you?"

"Yes."

"I'll have *The Joy of Sex*, volumes one and two."

"Philip!"

"Huh?"

The headphones had been ripped off; he leaped out of his chair as if electrically shocked.

"Philip, what are you talking about?"

Hannah was standing there, hands on hips, her feet dug in and a furious expression on her face.

"What the bloody hell's it to you, Hannah?" he spluttered.

"There are places for people like you. They're called loony-bins."

"Hannah, I'm just . . . singing along to the music."

"Bloody peculiar lyrics, dear!"

"Look, what the hell do you think you're doing? This isn't the Spanish—"

"It's the bloody phone, Philip! Been ringing non-stop for the last half-hour, and there am I trying to get some sleep and wondering why the hell don't you answer it, and here you are all along, with your earmuffs on, blabbing away to yourself twelve to the dozen like a complete imbecile. Here is the phone. Somebody is on the other end wanting to talk to you. Bloody speak to her!"

Hannah threw down the headphones and exited with panache. If it had been in the theatre, thought Philip, she would undoubtedly have got a round of applause. Mind you, she slammed the door so hard that the set would have probably fallen down. Philip picked up the phone. He grunted into it.

"Hello, it's Eleanor," said the voice at the other end.

Philip made an effort to sound more cheerful. "Thank you, my dear, for your call yesterday. And sorry to have kept you waiting so long. Lovely to speak to you."

"And you. Look, it's about the Raleigh series. Sorry to keep on, but Tom's seeing people already, and although he liked the idea when I put your name forward last week, there's still been nothing from your agent. Pressure's what's required with Tom. For pity's sake, get Quennell on to it."

"Is Tom seeing Gordon Wilde?"

"He's seen him. Why do you ask?"

"I just seem to see Gordon Wilde everywhere I turn these days. Tom's looking for a name then to play Raleigh?"

"Well, you know what they're like at the BBC . . . still, if anyone has it in him to cast from the gut and not from the c.v., it's Tom, but you won't get anywhere unless you're seen . . ."

"Point taken. I'll get on to Quennell right away."

"Sooner, please. Must dash. I think I hear Tom coming back down the corridor. 'Bye."

Philip put the phone down, lifted it again and dialled his agent's number. It was engaged. He sank back wearily into his chair and stared out of the window. Outside, nothing happened: clearly the natural world did not empathize with his inner state. He said to the outside world, "How all occasions do inform against me . . ."

"Talking to yourself again, dear?" Hannah's voice from the kitchen. He heard her bashing about, shuffling cutlery and dealing crockery. The coffee grinder made its coffee-grinding noise.

"Why don't you go back to sleep?" he called out.

"Bloody waste of time now. Coffee?"

"Yes. Sorry."

He went into the kitchen. Hannah made a terrible cup of coffee, he was just in time to snatch the filter and beans away from her. She had the grill on and was burning thick wedges of bread. The loaf stood on the draining board, squashed and hacked about by Hannah's misuse of the carving knife. It looked as if it had been mutilated by a mad axeman.

She rescued the toast just in time and buttered both slices. She offered him one and smeared her own with marmite and peanut butter. He stared with grim fascination at the disgusting thing as it disappeared bite by bite into her mouth. He looked around at his kitchen, his neat, well-ordered kitchen, its tidy symmetry of pots and appliances hopelessly disturbed by two minutes of Hannah. Had he once seriously thought that he could live with this woman?

"Ever been up for the part of Attila the Hun?" he asked.

"Piss off," she said. She knew very well what he thought of her personal habits. She didn't much like his either. "You're a fastidious old prig," she said, and then, between mouthfuls, "what did Eleanor want?"

"About this Walter Raleigh thing at the BBC. Apparently Quennell's still done nothing about it and of course Gordon bloody Wilde's already got his club-foot in the door . . ."

"I thought he was playing Trigorin?"

"I think he's still open to offers."

"Well, he can't do them both, can he? Why don't you give him a ring? If he's not doing Trigorin, perhaps he can put in a word for you. He's got a lot of influence with Tony Elliott, you know."

"Trethowan wouldn't wear it. He wants a name."

"Perhaps, but not necessarily. Doing a classy Chekhov with a high-profile young director like Tony Elliott is a bit radical for Owen. He's not aiming at his usual penguins-and-pensioners audience—"

"—the theatre of gynaecologists and chartered accountants."

"Pardon?"

"Just a phrase of Jonathan Miller's. Go on."

"Well, if Elliott could be persuaded he wanted you, Owen might not stand in his way."

"I suppose there might be something in that."

"I've got intuition, Philip. And I'm pretty *au fait* with the way Owen works . . ." Her voice had slipped into its lowest gear, the famous sotto-voce seductive drawl. He acknowledged it with a mirthless smile: it always annoyed him when Hannah referred to her past affairs. She had such awful taste in men! The thought of her with old fatty Trethowan still made his stomach turn, even after all these years. Jealousy always made him feel uncomfortable. He got up and began to tidy the kitchen. "Yes, I might give Gordon a ring," he muttered absentmindedly.

"Do!" said Hannah firmly. "You've nothing to lose." She banged down her empty plate and wiped her mouth with the back of her hand. Philip gave her a bit of paper towel. "Thanks," she said. "And thanks for the bed. I think I'd better be getting back to Putney. Would you be a dear and call me a taxi?"

Philip went next door and ordered a minicab. While he was at the phone he tried Quennell's number again. It was still engaged. Hannah drifted in, carting her bag and stole. They sat in silence for a few minutes.

Philip heard the cab draw up outside. Through the window he saw the driver open the gate and make his way up the drive. He saw Hannah to the door. "Do phone Gordon," she said, pecking him on the cheek. He said that he would. He closed the door on her and breathed a sigh of relief to be alone again. He went back into the living room and put on his headphones. He selected another tape.

"Ha!" he laughed out loud. "Ring bloody Gordon Wilde? Grovel to that little creep for work? You must be joking! Ha!"

He turned up the volume and relaxed into his arm-chair. He had better things to think of now than Gordon Wilde. He was about to enter the realm of the Grail and the Swan Knight.

FOUR

The phone woke him. He must have been asleep for some time: the tape had run out and the room was gloomy. He had slumped into an awkward position and his left side was asleep. He dragged himself over to the phone. It was his agent.

"Been trying to get you all afternoon, Philip. How did it go?"

How did what go? thought Philip. "What's the time?" he asked.

"It's gone seven o'clock. Thought I'd give you one last try before going home."

"Thanks. Er . . . the audition went okay, but I'm not right and frankly I don't want to play it anyway."

"Yes, I know. Now look, Tom de Vere wants to see

you at the BBC. Can you be at Threshold House on Monday at eleven?"

"Eleven's fine."

"Excellent. Please do phone afterwards. By the way, there's a cheque in the post for you, from the training film. Good luck on Monday!"

A good thing there's some money on the way, thought Philip, as he wandered into the kitchen. And a good thing he phoned when he did. Philip sat down and turned on the radio. He was in time to hear the beginning of the *Archers*. While he listened to the day's events in Ambridge, he went through a few bills. He had a very orderly system: the blue, non-urgent bills were stuck up on a cork-board to the left of the cooker; the red, urgent bills occupied a similar board but on the other side. One could tell at a glance the prospective drain on resources. Funds had been a bit low recently; the training film would take care of the next month's rent and at least the gas and the TV and video rental. He wasn't in financial straits as yet, but over the last couple of years work had been too sporadic for comfort. Only recently had he begun to explore the periphery of his profession, the expanding video industry, voice-overs, even commercials (which he had always considered beneath him), and he regretted not having done so earlier: there was a great deal of money involved, one could easily get in a day what one could earn in a week on the West End stage or on television. He had earned £500 for two days' work doing the training film, in which he had appeared as a bank manager advising trainees on their career structures. It had been terribly easy, money for old rope. But is it art? he asked himself. Who gives a shit?

Of course a certain amount of pride-swallowing was required. His first commercials casting had appalled him. He had gone to a studio in Soho, where he had found a dozen or so actors in his age range clustered around a coffee machine. Later he discovered that they represented only one batch and that the producers would be seeing people all day. He found the impersonal nature of his treatment humiliating. When at last he was called in (late), the director didn't even bother to introduce himself. Philip was given a soiled Xerox of the script and told to deliver his only line into a camera. The director kept his eyes on the monitor. Philip spoke the line once trippingly and on the tongue and was told that that would be all. As he walked out of the door, an assistant bawled, "Next!" and the queue of hopefuls shuffled along. His agent had kept telling him not to take it so personally. They were just looking for the right face; his acting ability simply didn't enter into it. Nonetheless he couldn't help feeling like a failed entrant in a cattle-show. It took a dozen such casting sessions for him to get used to the process and a dozen more (and three years) for him to get his first commercial. But when the repeat fees started coming in, lost dignity was somewhat salved.

He felt more comfortable doing the voice-over work. Unfortunately there were a great many specialist actors in the field and his opportunities were limited. One or two small video companies employed him on a near-regular basis. Generally they required him to supply commentaries to short films hyping a particular company or its products. A job never took more than an hour and was always well paid. Those actors who did it full-time earned a fortune, although few of them were publicly known. It was a world entirely removed from the popular conception of an actor. Occasionally Philip felt guilty at the thought of making more in a couple of hours than a hard-working rep actor made in a week, but the work was never frequent enough for guilt to exert a profound influence. A more common feeling was that engendered by the absurdity of most of the scripts that came his way. Putting one's all into a description of some dully obscure industrial process demanded rigid concentration. He had had particular difficulty with a series of programmes concerned with the artificial insemination of heifers. It was hard to keep a straight face while trying to match one's voice to images of a farmhand stuffing his fist up a cow's back passage. This was not a line of work for which his drama-school training had prepared him.

He felt stale and uncomfortable after his sleep. He was also hungry. He decided to have a quick bath and order a take-away. There was rather a good Chinese round the corner. He didn't eat many take-aways as a rule, in fact, he was a good cook, but this evening he couldn't be bothered. He still felt restless and bored. He ran his bath.

He ordered the meal by phone and walked round to collect. It was cool by the time he got back. He reheated it in the oven and watched a natural-history programme on the television. It was about the breeding habits of lizards. One of the lizards looked just like Tony Elliott. Philip poured himself a whisky.

At the beginning of the nine-o'clock news he poured another whisky, and another at the end. They were good measures, generous doubles. As a rule Philip drank little whisky. In fact, he rarely touched any spirits, and the three-quarter full bottle of Haig on the sideboard was at least two months old. He drank it neat, and he drank it quickly. Picking up the bottle again at a quarter to ten, he noticed that the level was significantly lower. He felt light-headed, but not drunk. He knocked back another glass.

A film had begun on the TV, but it looked tacky and

he couldn't be bothered to follow the plot. He turned it off and put on a record. His inclination, if not his mood, was towards the intimate and mellow. He listened to Ella Fitzgerald.

When the record was over he turned the telly back on and watched the *News at Ten* on ITV. It was similar to the news at nine on BBC. He wondered why he bothered to watch it. It was something he did often. Sometimes he'd pass a whole day religiously switching in to hourly news bulletins, every hour on the hour, despite there being no noticeable difference in the contents. If he was staying up and the other channels were off the air, he'd tune in to the World Service and hear some more of the same. He would also listen again to programmes like *Brain of Britain,* which he'd heard earlier in the week on Radio 4. Of course he knew all the answers the second time round, so he could pretend that he was a genius. He usually listened twice to each episode of the *Archers,* and would hear the whole lot again in the Omnibus edition on Sunday. He liked being on familiar territory. He liked God to keep the universe well ordered.

After the fifth whisky he decided to stop. His head was swimming and he felt a little sick. He turned off the television, put on the other side of the Ella Fitzgerald, and read the *Times.* The leader column burbled incoherently about the Common Market, and Bernard Levin was ranting about left-wingers and the erosion of what little was left of the Great in Britain. A large part of the correspondence page was devoted to the fag-end of months of letters devoted to a subject of such mindblowing banality that Philip forgot it the moment he turned the page. He flicked through the obituaries and the sports pages and settled at last for a leisurely perusal of the "Entertainments" column.

He didn't want to see any films. There were some interesting-looking fringe shows, but the West End seemed pretty stale. *42nd Street, Cats* and *Evita* were probably all booked in for the next millennium. Surprisingly, *Daisy Pulls It Off* was still going, its audiences no doubt swollen by bemused foreigners out for a good time in Soho. And Gordon Wilde was doing Eugene O'Neill at the Duchess.

Philip threw down the paper and poured another whisky. The level was down to a third. He had drunk half a bottle. He felt like a cigarette. He hadn't had a cigarette in ten years.

It was gone half past ten. A Western had started on ITV. The newscasters would be in the bar by now, or getting into their taxis. People everywhere would be coming out of cinemas and theatres and going into bars or taxis. Except at the Duchess. Gordon would be in full flow.

Philip looked at his watch. He was aware that he was drunk, he knew that he had to make the effort to concentrate on the hands going round. He made a simple calculation laboriously: it couldn't last less than three hours, the interval couldn't be less than fifteen minutes, it was unlikely to go up late—they'd be out no earlier than 11:15. It was twenty to now.

"I can just imagine him, beaming all over his stupid face, taking his curtain call to an adoring public. It's Thursday; will the theatre be full? I expect so. Gordon puts bums on seats. Toilet seats, maybe, but seats all the same."

Philip got up, feeling queasy. He went into the bathroom and splashed water into his face. He was thirsty, he drank down a few cupped handfuls. He put his hands firmly against the sink, feeling the cold enamel on his palms. He raised his head and confronted himself in the mirror. He felt steady and in control. He glanced purposefully into his eyes.

"This is on the level, not just man to man, but something more fundamental than that—actor to actor. You're right about Trigorin, it's not your part. It won't do your career any good at all getting stuck into another long run. Your instinct's right, you need a film or a telly. I've always respected you, Gordon—"

"Not as much as I've respected you, Philip. You know, there's no justice in our profession. When we were at drama school I used to say that you were bound to make it to the top, while I thought I'd never even get my first job! It's a travesty, Philip, don't think I don't know it—"

"It's not your fault, Gordon—"

"No, no, listen Philip, hear me out: I feel that I ought to make it up to you in some way, even out the score, for my conscience's sake. You're a fine actor, Philip; I'd like to put something your way."

"You don't have to put yourself out for me!"

"But it's no skin off my nose, old friend, is it? I mean, I've made it—however unjustly—and I'm not without influence. It wouldn't hurt me to put a word in the right ear for you. You deserve it!"

"Yes, you're right, I do deserve it . . ."

Philip walked out of the bathroom and into the living room. He stood uncertainly in the doorway, watching the television in the corner. Two gun-slingers were preparing for a shoot-out in a saloon bar. One was overacting madly; presumably he was the star. The other actor stood impassively, waiting for his cue to draw. It came, and after a flash and puff of smoke he fell forward noiselessly, clutching his stomach. The ham actor holstered his pistol and called to the barkeep for a whisky. He looked down scornfully at the body of the good actor.

"There just ain't no doggone justice . . ." muttered Philip. He walked over and turned off the telly. He faced the silent room.

"This town ain't big enough for the two of us, Gordon Wilde!"

He looked at his watch. It was a quarter to eleven.

He picked up the phone and dialled from the pad. After a few rings a voice asked if it could help him.

"Yes, I'd like to order a taxi. I'm in N5. How long will it take?"

He was told that it would take about ten minutes. He gave his address. He said that he would be going into the West End.

FIVE

Traffic was heavy in the centre of town. Philip's cab got stuck in a jam down Bow Street. Seeing that it was nearly quarter past, he paid his fare and started walking. It was a cold, drizzly night; people were running everywhere with turned-up collars and umbrellas. Rather stupidly Philip had forgotten his own umbrella. He pulled on his gloves and walked briskly towards the Aldwych.

As he turned into Catherine Place he saw that the pavement ahead was crowded. The show was clearly over. Philip listened out for comments. They were generally favourable: the evening had been too long, but Gordon Wilde was magnificent. Philip turned down the side of the theatre.

He stopped. Gordon was standing outside the stage door, ringed by autograph hunters. He chatted away easily and scribbled his name with well-practised fluency. He kept turning to a young man at his side. The young man whispered in Gordon's ear and Gordon laughed. Gordon took the young man's arm and began to steer him through the crowd. The fans parted good-naturedly.

Philip watched the two of them come towards him. Gordon was talking earnestly and they seemed engrossed with each other. The young man was about twenty-five, with dyed blond hair and a pale complexion. He was thin and slightly delicate-looking. Gordon ran a hand through his hair playfully.

Philip stepped aside. He was just in time. From the shadows he watched as the two of them drew abreast and then turned into the brightly lit main street. They passed within a few feet of Philip, but paid him no attention. As they went by, Philip heard a snatch of their intimate conversation. The young man's voice was light and tremulous.

". . . actually I'm feeling a bit queasy, Gordon."

"Then we'll have an early night, dear . . ."

They linked arms as they passed through the rapidly thinning crowd. A few people looked at Gordon, but away from the stage door (where it's open season), a studious politeness characterized the English theatre-going public, and the star was not molested. Philip watched the two backs—Gordon's conspicuous in an off-white gaberdine—disappear up towards Covent Garden.

Philip felt cheated. As so often when he was being irrational, he was quite aware of it, but that didn't mean he intended doing anything about it. He mumbled ill-temperedly to himself: there was something distasteful, to say the least, in the sight of Gordon Wilde running off with his little blond catamite. By God, he must have gone like an express train to get out of costume and into mufti that quickly! It wasn't that Philip had been late (when was he ever?). No, he'd timed it perfectly, choosing just the right moment to knock on the star dressing-room door and find Gordon draped in his silk kimono sipping a well-earned G&T. One glib introductory line like '. . . did enjoy the show tonight, Gordon!' and he'd be away. Instead of which he had had a wasted journey!

He watched the two backs walking up the road. He could still see them, just. They had crossed the road and were passing the Drury Lane Theatre.

The cold and his irritation had sobered him up. He remembered suddenly that Gordon lived in Covent Garden.

He set off after them. He crossed the road at a run and settled into a brisk walking pace, head and weight forward, hands in pockets. It was late, the pubs and theatres were closed, everywhere except in the clubs the night-life was dying. As Philip turned right past the Drury Lane Theatre, the only people he saw ahead of him were Gordon and his companion. They turned left up Drury Lane. Philip hurried after.

He couldn't see them. He stood on the corner, gazing blankly up the street. A car went past, but the pavements were deserted this side of Long Acre. They couldn't have got that far already . . . where were they?

He heard them before he saw them. They were standing in a doorway on the other side of the street. Philip saw the pale outline of Gordon's gaberdine. He couldn't hear what they were saying, but there was an angry note in Gordon's voice.

A taxi turned into Drury Lane, catching the two of them for a moment in its headlamps. Philip saw Gordon jab a finger accusingly at his friend. The young man looked upset. Gordon turned away sharply and began walking up Drury Lane. The young man rushed after and laid a hand on his sleeve. Gordon brushed him off, but when he persisted, stopped and exchanged a few words with him. A couple passed them, having to unlink their arms in order to get by on the pavement. Philip saw the look of surprise on the woman's face as she overheard something Gordon said.

Philip hung back on the corner. The woman glanced back over her shoulder and said something to her companion in what she no doubt presumed was a whisper. Philip heard Gordon's name.

Gordon was walking again. The young man followed, but at a distance, his eyes on the ground. Every step he took expressed sulky reluctance. They walked on, over the junction of Great Queen Street. Philip followed.

They walked past Macklin Street and took the first right. Philip was less than thirty yards behind. They hadn't seen him. Philip stood on the corner and watched them walking away. He didn't know the name of the street. He looked for a name. It was Stukely Street. Stukely Street was narrow, dark and quiet. He saw the gaberdine turn into an alley.

He got to the alley just in time to see the two men step through a heavy black door. Light from inside splashed onto the pavement. The nacreous oblong was steadily contracting as the door closed. As Philip approached he heard the creaking of the springs. Only the tiniest sliver of light remained.

Philip put his hand against the door. It was heavy, burglar-proof, the sort that swings back and locks itself automatically, and sometimes needs a good shoulder to open. But there is a moment between the door shutting and the lock clicking in. And at that moment Philip held it a fraction off the latch.

There was an intercom by the door with four buttons, the three lower ones marked with the names of companies. The top space was unnamed, Gordon's flat. It seemed that he was the only resident. Philip heard his footsteps vaguely on the stone stairway above.

A door slammed upstairs and the landing lights went off. Philip pushed his way through the heavy door and let it slip back into place gently. He climbed the stairs.

It was dark. A single corridor led off from each landing. Feeling curious, he walked down one and tried the locked doors. There was no sign of life. He continued climbing.

Suddenly he heard Gordon's voice. Philip was just past the third landing, there was only one floor to go. He froze in the act of taking another step. A door opened on the next landing and the light went on.

"You're a tramp, Kit, a slovenly little whore!"

"Gordon, stop being beastly . . ."

"Oh, piss off, you mincing little tart!"

The door was slammed. Philip heard Kit sobbing and Gordon's voice, muffled, shouting after him, "And don't bother coming back!"

Delicately, on the balls of his feet, Philip retraced his steps down to the next landing. He heard Kit coming after and darted down the corridor. He dived into an alcove at the end, in front of another locked door.

Kit shuffled past, sniffling loudly. Philip heard him go all the way down and listened for the click of the front door shutting. The lights, automatically timed, went off again.

Philip emerged from his hiding place and walked back up the last flight. His heart was beating furiously, his throat was dry. He longed for another drink, he didn't know if he had the courage to bluff it out with Gordon. He stood on the top landing, hesitating. It was not too late to turn back.

He pressed the doorbell.

"What the hell do you want now?" Gordon's voice was distant. He was nowhere near the door.

"Er . . . Gordon, is that you?" Philip called out loudly. He heard faint footsteps pattering towards him. "Who is it?" demanded Gordon. "It's me," said Philip, not very helpfully.

The door opened a few inches, Gordon's face appeared above the level of the chain. His eyes widened. "Philip?" he asked, perhaps not quite sure; it was very dark on the landing.

"Yes. Hello, Gordon. Mind if I come in?"

Gordon gaped blankly. He looked as if he was trying to think of something to say. He couldn't. He closed the door and, after a moment's grappling with the chain, opened it fully.

"Come on in," he said and then, over his shoulder as he turned away, "How did you get in downstairs?"

"I was about to use the intercom but then I passed some chap coming out. He seemed in quite a hurry." Gordon muttered something under his breath. "Pardon?" asked Philip. "Nothing," said Gordon. "Nice flat," said Philip. He meant it.

They were standing in the living room. The kitchen lay through one door, the hallway by which they'd entered through the other. Philip presumed that the bedroom was on the other side of the hall. It was a charming, surprisingly spacious penthouse flat, quiet and ideally situated. There was a lot of glass in the windows, the room had a light, open feel to it. It was tastefully decorated, in pale colours. The tone was modern, but solid, comfortable. There was a Hockney on one wall and an expensive-looking metal sculpture in one corner. Gordon went to an art-deco drinks cabinet. "Whisky?" he asked, pouring one for himself, which he knocked back in one without waiting for Philip's answer.

"No, thanks," said Philip. "Do you have anything soft?"

Gordon poured him an orange squash, which he filled with water from a glass decanter. He brought it over.

"Thank you, Gordon. I expect you're wondering why I'm here."

"It had crossed my mind. Sit down." Gordon sat in a big leather armchair, glass and bottle in hand. Philip settled himself opposite, on the edge of a big white sofa. "I came to see the show tonight," he said. "You told me to drop by afterwards . . ."

"Huh? Did I?" Gordon still looked surprised. He had another drink.

"Yes, I missed you at the stage door, but I remembered where you lived, so . . . here I am!"

Gordon looked at his drink. He said, "Actually this isn't the most convenient of times, you know . . ."

Philip felt embarrassed. He sat back and looked down. Between them stood a low table, white-legged and glass-topped. Some magazines lay in a neat pile on one side. On the other stood a champagne bottle, unopened, with two empty glasses. There was an ice bucket on the floor.

"Sorry," said Philip. "Er . . . it seems I interrupted a celebration."

Gordon gave a hollow laugh. "I don't think that bottle will be opened for some time. Well, seeing as you're here, Philip—what do you want?"

It was Philip's turn to look surprised. When he said nothing, Gordon smiled. "Cat got your tongue, Philip?"

"No," he said unconvincingly.

Gordon chuckled and filled his glass. "Come off it, Philip. We've hardly seen each other in the last five years. Twenty-five years, come to that. I meet you in the street and casually say 'Drop by sometime,' and here you are on my doorstep at half past eleven the next night! Well, that seems a little odd to me. Sorry if I'm being naive, but I can only think that you want something."

Suddenly Philip understood at least a part of the secret of Gordon's success. In a business where people spend their lives equivocating, where cotton wool and padding, half-promises and quarter-truths are the staples of discussion and negotiation, the man who cuts across all that, the man who knows exactly what he wants—and gives the impression that he's going to get it—has a head start. How many times had Philip sat politely through auditions and interviews, skirting gingerly the ground he wished to occupy? And how many times had Gordon Wilde marched straight up and taken it?

"You're right," said Philip, thinking, there's only one way to play this game. "There is something I want. No doubt I'm being impudent, but . . ." He stopped. What did he think he was doing? People who got places didn't prattle on apologizing for themselves. Look at Gordon. "I wanted to ask you if you'd accepted Trigorin."

"No, I turned it down. It's buggered up Trethowan a bit, but the BBC are doing a series about Walter Raleigh and I want to play the part."

"Ah." Philip raised his glass of orange squash. His hand was trembling. "Have you been offered it yet?"

"No, but I'm working on it. In any case I'd rather do nothing than another long run. I need a break. Why are you asking me all this?"

"A mercenary motive—"

"That goes without saying!"

Philip checked himself again. He was sweating, he felt uncomfortable. "Perhaps I shouldn't have come," he muttered.

"Indubitably," said Gordon. "But now you're here you might as well get it out."

Philip bit his lip. He cursed his own stupidity: he had been thankful to see Kit running out, he'd thought it a golden opportunity to catch Gordon alone. God, I must be stupid, he thought; why didn't it occur to me that Gordon might not be in the best of moods?

Philip spoke quietly. "I've a favour to ask. You know Tony Elliott well. If you're not playing Trigorin, could you put in a word for me?"

There was a silence. Gordon stared at him. Philip didn't know how to interpret his expression. He shifted uneasily and put down his glass of orange squash next to the champagne bottle.

"You can take your gloves off, if you like . . ." said Gordon with casual mockery. Philip was still wearing his coat and gloves; he made no effort to remove them. Gordon asked, "Why do you want me to intercede on your behalf? Haven't you got an agent to do that sort of thing for you?" Before Philip had a chance to reply, Gordon made a curious guffawing noise and slapped his thigh. "Oh no, how silly of me; I'd forgotten Harry Foster kicked you out . . ."

Philip reddened. He was ashamed and angry. "I'm with John Quennell," he said.

"Well, we all have our cross to bear, dear . . ." drawled Gordon archly. He poured himself another drink. Philip remembered that the more he drank, the more camp he got. Gordon said, "Why on earth should you expect me to talk to Tony about you?"

"For old times' sake."

Gordon laughed. "Don't add hypocrisy to your other vices, dear. I know that you can't stand me."

"Gordon, I—"

"For Christ's sake, leave it out, ducky! Every time I meet you I watch you practically turn green with envy, and to be quite frank, I rather enjoy it. I know that you didn't give me a chance in hell when we left drama school. I can't tell you how satisfying it is to have proved you wrong!"

Gordon drank down his whisky. Philip said carefully, "I may have been wrong about you in the past, Gordon, but I have the greatest respect for you."

"Oh, for God's sake, Philip!" Gordon was on his feet, expansively waving his whisky bottle in front of him. "I know bloody well that you just think I'm a jumped-up little pansy occupying your rightful place at the summit of the acting tree. And now you think you see a way of using me, just because I'm the little fairy who happens to be perched on the top. Well I've got news for you, buster. Even if I did think you were the best thing since eye-liner number five, even if I did think you were perfection itself for gloomy old Trigorin, I wouldn't dream of compromising myself one fraction of a millimetre on your behalf, old thing, and do you know why? Because you're nobody. Absolutely nobody. No name, no clout; as far as I remember, not much talent either. Tony wouldn't have you. And Trethowan wants someone to fill his theatre. What do you think the punters would say if they saw your name on the poster, dear? 'Philip bloody who?' they'd say. You're as anonymous as a traffic warden, ducky!"

Ducky! Gordon spat out the word malevolently. There was spittle on his chin. The whisky bottle hung limply at his side, he was tottering on his feet.

"You're drunk," said Philip.

"Not half as drunk as I'm going to get. Why don't you piss off now?" Gordon held up the whisky bottle and glared at it. He shook it, as if unwilling to believe it was genuine. He unscrewed the top.

Philip stood up.

Gordon looked down, to right and left. He couldn't see what he was looking for. He dropped the whisky top and muttered incoherently to himself. He crouched down and began patting the floor suspiciously.

Philip clasped the neck of the champagne bottle.

Gordon turned round and felt with his hand round the side of the chair. He gave a little grunt of joy as he found his whisky tumbler, which had fallen onto the carpet. He straightened up, filling his glass.

Philip hit him over the head with the champagne bottle.

Gordon fell noiselessly. There were champagne and broken glass everywhere. Philip's trousers and shoes were wet. He stepped back, dropped the neck of the bottle and watched Gordon. The whisky bottle had landed facing him, the top a few inches from his chin. The golden brown liquid was trickling out, staining the expensive carpet. In a moment Gordon's face would be wet. He didn't move.

Philip knelt down. He took off his glove and felt for a pulse under Gordon's ear. There was nothing. He lifted an eyelid and saw the pupil staring blankly ahead. He had no idea if that meant anything. He put his finger between Gordon's lips, feeling for a breath. There was none.

He found it very hard to believe that he had killed him with one blow to the head.

He sat down on the sofa and picked up his orange squash. There was a little left, he drank it. He frowned at Gordon's body. He didn't know what to do. Should he call an ambulance? If Gordon really was dead, then he'd have to go to prison. If Gordon wasn't dead, he'd probably do him for GBH. In which case he'd still have to go to prison. Either way his career was in ruins. Why had he hit Gordon? He hadn't meant to. He'd just sort of unconsciously picked up the bottle and . . . and hit him. Because he was being so unpleasant. A spur-of-the-moment thing . . . my Lord. Would a jury understand?

No, a jury wouldn't understand.

He put down the orange squash carefully. He had picked it up with his left hand, his gloved hand. He realized that he had kept his gloves on the whole time, he'd left no prints. No one had seen him come in. He'd avoided Kit on the staircase. And there was no sign of a forced entry. An idea began to take shape in his mind.

He remembered the couple Gordon and Kit had passed in Drury Lane. The woman had recognized Gordon. She had overheard the row.

Philip remembered Kit running down the stairs in tears. He had made a lot of noise. Perhaps somebody outside would have seen him, would remember him . . .

Gordon groaned.

Philip stiffened. He hardly breathed. A minute passed.

Gordon groaned again. This time it was unmistakable. An eyelid flickered. His arm twitched.

Philip got up smoothly. He walked over to the corner where he had seen the expensive-looking sculpture. It was bronze, a twisted, near-human shape about eighteen inches high. He picked it up. It was very heavy. He rested it on his shoulder as he walked over to Gordon.

Gordon lay spread-eagled, his head at a slightly odd

angle, a long white expanse of neck showing between his collar and hairline.

With all his strength Philip aimed at the bare neck. His arms shuddered as the bronze sculpture thudded into flesh. He dropped it, and crouched down to examine its impact.

There was blood now. Blood under the ear, blood where the skin had torn above the broken neck. Philip stepped back quickly, inspecting his hands for blood. He could see none. There wasn't much anyway. He was fairly sure that none could have got onto his clothes.

Philip looked around the room. He wasn't looking for anything in particular, just checking. He felt down the sides of the sofa, in case anything had fallen out of his pockets. He made sure he still had his wallet, his keys, his monogrammed handkerchief.

He carried his empty orange-squash glass into the kitchen and washed it up. For all he knew, Kit didn't drink orange squash.

He looked at his watch. It was five to twelve. Gordon Wilde had been dead for ten minutes.

No one saw Philip as he left Gordon's flat. Stukely Street was deserted. He threaded his way out into Kingsway, passing no one on foot, only a few cars. Kingsway was busier. He hailed a taxi and gave an address just the wrong side of Highbury Corner. From there he walked home.

He was in bed by half past twelve.

SIX

That weekend Philip went down to Maidenhead to stay
with his Aunt Marjorie. He had only rung up the day
before, and she was delighted at his unexpected visit.
"How lovely!" she exclaimed over the phone. "I was
beginning to think you'd forgotten all about me." Philip
laughed. "But not about your home-made cakes!" he
said. Her cooking was superb. She lived in a picturesque
old miller's cottage, in a little lane about a mile back
from the A 4, midway between Maidenhead and
Taplow. In fact, although the address was officially near
Maidenhead, it was from Taplow Station that she collected him.

Philip put his suitcase into the back of the old Ford
Estate and climbed into the passenger seat. She was

looking very well, he thought. Most of his other relatives had died off. She was a sprightly sixty-five.

"Pleasant journey, dear?" she asked, wrestling the car into first gear. It always amazed him that the old banger still went.

"Yes, thank you," he said, putting down on the floor the pile of newspapers he had bought in Paddington. She glanced at them briefly as she turned out of the station.

"Didn't you know that actor fellow who got done in?" she asked.

Philip peered down at the folded copy of the *Daily Mirror*, which lay on top of the pile. A photograph showed the top of Gordon's head, below the caption "Actor Slain in Gay Murder."

"Yes, slightly," answered Philip.

Marjorie quizzed Philip about the murder on the drive home. "You seem to be quite an expert," she said, impressed by his grasp of the details. Philip indicated the papers. "I read them all on the train," he said. "As a rule I don't buy the tabloids, but I have to admit that the headlines have a lurid fascination for me." Philip summarized what he knew: "The police are treating it as a homosexual killing. Apparently Gordon and his boyfriend had a row that night. Gordon had certainly been drinking heavily; they estimated he must have had four times the legal limit! Anyway, the police think that Gordon may have got rough and the boy hit him in self-defence. Alternatively, if the *Sun* is to be believed, Gordon told him that he had AIDS and the boy panicked. They haven't found the boy yet."

"Oh, I just heard on the news that they had. He's been taken in for questioning."

"Then I'm sure the truth will be out before long."

Gordon's murder featured heavily in all the TV

news reports that day, and his photograph made the front pages of even the quality Sundays. The next morning Marjorie brought up the *Observer* and *The Sunday Times* for Philip to read in bed, and he carefully scrutinized every column inch concerning the case, after first checking how Hampshire stood in the bowling and batting averages. It was hard to change the habits of a lifetime.

Marjorie cooked him a delicious lunch—her gooseberry crumble was divine. He went into the village beforehand and bought her a bottle of sherry and a bunch of flowers. "What a kind boy you are," she said. In the afternoon he took the dog for a walk in Burnham Beeches. Marjorie said she had things to be getting on with, and would he mind going alone? Actually he was rather pleased to be alone. The Beeches were full, but he knew them well and took the least-travelled paths. He had spent a lot of his boyhood in the Beeches, and in Black Park near Iver Heath. Black Park was by Pinewood Studios, it was often used for location work. He told people that seeing the film sets had inspired him. It was a lie, but a convenient one: he was asked often (all actors are) when he had decided to go on the stage, but the truth was that he didn't know. It had just happened. It sounded pretentious to talk about one's destiny. It was easier to refer to the film sets in the park.

He'd spent most of his teen-age summers with Aunt Marjorie. After his mother died he didn't really think of his father's house in Chiswick as home. He'd never been close to his father; his new stepmother hardly concealed her disinterest. It was to everyone's advantage that he should spend his summers in the country. He was glad he'd come back. He'd been feeling guilty about neglecting Marjorie, he hadn't seen her since the Easter before. He was touched by the warmth of her welcome. She gave him tea and chocolate cake when he got back. It was wonderfully cosy sitting by the real log fire. He'd be sorry to leave. She said that he'd be welcome to stay for a few more days, but he explained that he had an important interview the next morning. He promised to come back soon. She wished him luck and waved him goodbye as he boarded the quarter-past-seven train.

Just as he was walking through his front door in Highbury, the phone began to ring. He walked into the living room, turning on all the lights, and, after a moment's hesitation, picked up the receiver.

It was Hannah.

"I've been trying to get you all weekend," she jabbered excitedly. "Why didn't you leave your answerphone on? Have you heard about Gordon?"

"Of course I've heard about Gordon," he answered coolly. "The only people in the British Isles who haven't heard by now are a few hermit sheep-shaggers in the Orkneys."

"Don't be flippant, it's serious."

"Believe me, Hannah, I know just how serious it is . . ." In answer to her questions he explained his movements over the weekend. But he didn't make any sorrowful noises. "Of course it's a pity he died," he told Hannah. "It's a pity anybody dies, but I can't pretend that I'm all cut up about it. It gives us pause, that's all . . ."

"Anyone would think you were glad!"

"Of course I'm not glad. But I'm not going to lose any sleep over someone I hardly knew. You must see that that's an honest attitude. What's it to you, anyway?"

Philip's matter-of-factness took her by surprise. He knew that she didn't give a damn about Gordon. Not many people did really, at least not among those who knew him. But it was too good a subject to pass up; even down the phone he could feel her straining at the leash, she wanted desperately to strike a melodramatic posture. Perhaps he should let her. It would be easier. Only not tonight. How about dinner tomorrow, he said. She assented enthusiastically. Eight o'clock, he said. He had a feeling that for once she might even be on time.

He went into the kitchen and put on the kettle. Thoughtfully he watched it boil. It was true what he'd told her: three nights had passed since the murder and he'd never slept better in his life. He wouldn't have been surprised if he'd woken up sweating furiously, dreaming of Gordon bloodied like Banquo, advancing towards him . . . that was apt: sleep—that had been what Macbeth had lost, "Sleep that knits up the ravell'd sleave of care." He'd never played Macbeth, and always wanted to. He had done "If it were done when 'tis done" as an audition piece for drama school and he'd had a special fondness for the play ever since. It was a difficult part, there were sudden jumps in Macbeth's character, almost as if intervening scenes had been lost. It was hard to grasp those moments at which he changed from being the loyal, honest servant of the king into the power-mad psychopath, bloodthirsty and ambitious for absolute power. Perhaps those sort of extreme changes were impossible to delineate in people. Perhaps they just happened.

He made a cup of cocoa and took it into his bedroom. It was nearly midnight, he had an important interview tomorrow, he should be getting some sleep. It was no use thinking about Gordon now. It was too late for that. He hadn't meant to kill him, not at first, anyway, but it had been Gordon's fault: people who where that unpleasant really should not be surprised if they were hit over the head with champagne bottles. Perhaps it wasn't very sporting to break their necks afterwards, but they shouldn't have started it in the first place.

Philip finished his cocoa and turned out the light. He was asleep in a few minutes.

He arrived early for his interview at Shepherd's Bush. Prior to interviews he was usually nervous, but this morning he felt curiously unworried. It wasn't that he didn't want the part—he did, as much as any he'd ever been up for; it would make his career. But his mind was already engaged. Engaged only, not occupied: the matter of Gordon's death, of which he read in *The Times* while waiting to be called, stimulated his brain in much the same way as the paper's chess problem, or crossword. There was nothing actually to be solved, rather a kind of reverse process, whereby he was reading the solutions and trying to deduce the clues, to see if anyone could possibly piece together the truth about Thursday night. He checked the reported details of the story (as he had done on the previous two days) and correlated them mentally. It seemed that circumstantial evidence had been found to implicate Kit (they didn't say what it was), and so far no one had mentioned the possible involvement of a third party. On the other hand, Kit had not been charged, he was still "being questioned." But the implication was that he would be charged shortly. Apparently he was an actor, and Gordon had picked him up in the backstage bar of the National Theatre a few months back. Philip had always considered the backstage bar at the National seedy.

Tom de Vere's interviews were running fifteen minutes behind. Eleanor came down herself to apologize, and she escorted him up in the lift to the second floor.

"Curious, your asking about Gordon on Thursday morning," she said, as they walked along the corridor.

Philip frowned. He couldn't remember saying anything about Gordon. He looked at her blankly.

"You asked if Tom had seen him," said Eleanor. "You must remember. It was the day he died."

Philip thought about what she'd said. He thought that he'd better sound amazed. "What an extraordinary coincidence," he said with great emphasis. Eleanor nodded sagely and led him into Tom's office. She closed the door and left them alone.

"Nice to see you," said Tom, extending his hand and offering Philip a seat. He seemed pleased to see him, but that was a trick all good producers knew. And Tom was a good producer: he had as fine a track record as anyone in television drama. "How have you been keeping, and what have you been up to?" Tom's tone was relaxed, avuncular without being patronizing.

Philip filled him in on the last year and a half, that being the length of time since they'd seen each other. It didn't take him long: a couple of rep productions, a few bits on telly. He tried to spin out the voice-over and video angles, making it sound as if he had been consciously devoting his time to them, at the expense of what he called his legitimate career. He pulled a rueful face and joked about the seductive force of money.

"Fair enough," said Tom. "I know there's a fortune to be made in that line. If I were an actor, I'd think it worthwhile investing some time and effort in it."

"Yes, but it's not what I came into the business for. Certainly it's technically demanding and there's satisfaction to be derived from doing it well, but it doesn't compare with real acting. I've had a bit of a break, and the rest has done me good, but now I feel like getting my teeth into something."

"Well, get your teeth into this," said Tom, and handed over a thick stapled script on pale-blue paper.

Scripts usually came in different colours, to differentiate between episodes. Pale blue (or lilac), pink, lemon—all the colours of lavatory paper. Tom asked him to look through a couple of pages. "This is near the end of the last episode, the last of six. Each of them deals with some significant aspect of Raleigh's life, perhaps a major event like the expedition to Cádiz, episode four, or, as in the case of episode one, general scenes of a courtier's life in the reign of Good Queen Bess. The last episode deals with El Dorado and ends with his death. This is the big scene on the eve of his execution, the 'has my life all been worth it?' scene. He's an old man, sitting in the Tower, his completed *History of the World* in front of him, telling his life story to his gaoler's little son. This is the principal narrative device, by the way: the whole thing's cast in the form of a flashback, so that you have the effect of inevitability, what with his death casting its shadow from the first scene. Anyway, that's enough of my voice. Let's hear a bit of yours!"

Philip read the long monologue. It was a good bit of writing, Philip was impressed. He said as much when he had finished. Tom concurred. "I'm also impressed by your reading. Would you look at this bit . . ."

Philip was there for half an hour in all. He read four passages, carefully selected from very different parts of Raleigh's life. A lot of concentration was required on Philip's part, he had to treat the exercise as if he were going for the perfect take with no rehearsal. Tom seemed satisfied. It was so difficult to tell—producers and directors trot out the same platitudes regardless of what they really think; an actor can get paranoid—most do—trying to interpret subtle nuances. The simple phrase "we'll be in touch" can mean almost anything, very rarely what it appears to mean. Certain accepted stock phrases mean quite simply the opposite of what they say, such as "I'll call you back tomorrow," which means I won't call you back tomorrow (or any other day), and "it's 99 percent certain," which means it's off. "I'll be in touch" is less easy to interpret. For one thing, it implies no time limit. It's quite possible to be phoned back five years later.

As he got up to go, Philip was unable to resist saying "I understand you saw Gordon Wilde for this part?"

Tom looked embarrassed. "It's a strange thing," he said, "but Gordon was speaking to me about it only a few hours before he died."

"You mean you offered it to him?"

"Oh God, no!" The denial was spoken sharply. Philip raised an eyebrow. Again Tom looked embarrassed. He spoke a little uncomfortably. "To tell you the truth, Gordon was being a pain in the arse. I don't want to speak ill of the dead and that, but—he wasn't a friend of yours, was he?"

"No."

"Well, of course it's appalling about his death, and he was an inoffensive sort of chap, but, to be brutally frank, I never really rated him as an actor. Not at all what I was looking for in Raleigh. Though, for God's sake, don't tell anyone I said that!"

Philip assured him that he wouldn't. He left the office with a very high opinion of Tom's judgement.

He went home and rang Quennell to report how well the interview had gone. He was in high spirits. He had barely put down the phone when the doorbell rang.

He went to answer it, half expecting Hannah. Instead he found two men on his doorstep. The younger one was casually dressed and had the shifty-eyed opinionated look of a cabby. The other man, who was about Philip's age, was conventionally dressed in a moderately good suit, and looked as if he might have been an accountant. The accountant did the talking.

"Philip Fletcher?" The smile was well practised, genuinely false. Not so much an accountant as a car salesman. Philip admitted his identity. "I'm Superintendent Turnbull, CID. This is Sergeant Harris. We were wondering if we could have a word with you?" He showed Philip his identity card, flashing it open and shut and returning it to his inside pocket in one deft movement. For all Philip knew, it might have been a bus pass. He smiled affably. "Have the neighbours been complaining about the music again?" he asked, looking puzzled.

"No, sir," answered the Inspector seriously. "We'd like to talk to you about Gordon Wilde."

"Yes, of course. Come in . . ."

Philip took deep, slow breaths as he led the way into the living room. The blood was pounding through his head. He would have liked to have taken a drink, but was afraid that his hand would shake. His knees were trembling; he sat down as quickly as possible in the armchair. He crossed his legs casually and concentrated on looking the Superintendent in the eye. He knew from experience that surprisingly little of his nervousness would show—actors know that stage fright rarely looks as bad as it feels, and a clever actor can always conceal his nerves.

It's a script, thought Philip. He knew the words, he'd watched the scene in countless films, even been in some himself: two episodes of *Z Cars,* and one of *Softly, Softly.* It always started with the policeman showing his badge, in this case a policeman cast against type, not the " 'ello, 'ello, 'ello" stereotype. The script-writer was probably very proud of Turnbull: he'd perhaps written him as a light-opera lover, or a connoisseur of Impressionist painting.

This was an early scene, but which one was it? Was it innocent questioning, a red herring, or was the Inspector trying to trap a suspect? Was it really going to be "Where were you on the night of . . ." and "Anything you say may be taken down . . ."?

Philip thought it was time to deliver his own first line.

"In what way can I be of assistance, Superintendent?"

"It's just a routine inquiry, sir—" (Philip couldn't have written it better himself) "—we're checking up on all Mr. Wilde's acquaintances, to see if they can throw any light on the case. Could I ask when was the last time you saw Mr. Wilde?"

"By an odd coincidence, on the very day of his murder, around lunchtime."

"And where was this?"

"Outside the Duchess Theatre. I'd just been for an audition. But it was the briefest of meetings, and the first time I'd seen Gordon in ages."

"Are you quite sure that was the last time you saw him, sir?"

"Saw him? Er, depends what you mean by saw him . . ."

"And what do you mean, sir?"

"I mean . . . look, I'm sorry, I'm rather confused. What are you getting at?"

"Christopher McCullers says that he saw you outside the Duchess on the night of the murder, in fact no more than an hour before the murder."

"I'm sorry, you've got me there. I don't know the gentleman—"

"Kit McCullers. Mr. Wilde's companion. He says

that he saw you outside the stage door after the performance. Did he, sir?"

"Er . . . ?"

"Pardon?"

"Yes, excuse me. Frog in the throat." Philip got up
and walked purposefully to the sideboard. He poured
out a half-glass of Perrier water and took a sip. "Could I
offer you gentlemen anything?"

"No, thank you."

The Superintendent paused. He was gazing at Philip
with an intent, inscrutable expression. He parted his lips
slightly, about to speak, and Philip interrupted
smoothly: "Yes, I did see Gordon, it must have been
about quarter past eleven . . ." This is it, thought
Philip, Oscar-winning performance or bust . . . "To
tell you the truth, I'm rather embarrassed to admit it.
When I met Gordon that lunch-time he suggested I
come round and see him after the show one night. I
don't know if he meant it literally but I had personal
reasons for wanting to see him. Anyway, when I got to
the stage door, and saw that he was . . . occupied already, I thought better of it, so I went home. I didn't
want to intrude, I didn't speak to Gordon. In fact, I
didn't even think that he'd seen me. As for Kit McCullers, I'm afraid I wouldn't know him from Adam."

"He says that you taught him at drama school, sir."

"Good God!" Something sounded in the under-
growth of Philip's memory: the Inspector had trodden
on a twig. Philip got up and went to the bookshelves by
the fireplace. He took down a photograph album and
leafed through it quickly. He knew what he was looking
for. He held it open on a double page, one side displaying a faded theatre programme, the other a photograph
of a smiling group of youngsters. "I've only done one
drama-school production. Here it is, the Beaux' Strata-

gem at Central. I remember: he played Archer, rather well . . . but his name wasn't Kit McCullers."

"A stage name, sir. His real name is Chris Christianson, but apparently he thought people might confuse him with Kris Kristofferson. Be that as it may, I was interested to hear that he had seen you. It makes you one of the last people to have seen Mr. Wilde alive."

Suddenly Philip felt an almost overwhelming desire to confess. The sensation was physical, he felt it in his stomach. Curiously it wasn't the first time he had experienced such a sensation; he remembered an occasion years ago when he had witnessed a motor accident and the police had asked him to go down to the station and make a statement. The sergeant he had spoken to had been very much like Superintendent Turnbull, in manner, at least. There was something about that warm, sympathetic attitude that inspired confidence. It drew you in, acted almost like a verbal anaesthetic. It made Philip feel that if he came clean he would suddenly feel enervated, lighter than air, and it would in any case be worth it for the look of approval guaranteed to light up the avuncular policeman's face. It was the same species of urge one sometimes had to shout out a rude word in a crowded place, and Philip knew that it had to be resisted forcefully. After all, he had wanted to confess all those years ago, when he hadn't even done anything.

Yes, I was the last person to see Gordon alive, thought Philip. That's because it was me who killed him.

Philip bit his lip. He said, "Yes, I suppose it must. I'm sorry but it hadn't occurred to me, or I'd have come forward."

The Superintendent was still staring at him rather hard. During the ensuing pause Philip rose to refill his glass. His actions were a study in casualness.

"Are you sure I can't offer you gentlemen anything?" he inquired pleasantly.

The Superintendent shook his head. "Would you mind telling me, sir, the nature of the personal business you referred to with Mr. Wilde?"

"Yes. Of course." Philip settled down again and assumed a rueful expression. "I wanted to ask him a favour, that's all. It may seem rather odd that I should confess to embarrassment over such a simple request, but the fact is that in the theatrical world it's unusual for one actor to intercede on another's behalf and I wanted to be discreet. I was going to ask him to suggest me for a part. But as I say, as soon as I saw that I'd be intruding I thought better of it."

"Can you remember the time?"

"Yes. The show had just finished. It was quarter past eleven."

"Could you give me your impression of Mr. Wilde's and Mr. McCuller's behaviour when they came out of the stage door? I know you only caught a glimpse of them but it would be very helpful if you could remember."

This is important, thought Philip. He leaned back in his armchair, rested his chin on his hands and appeared contemplative. He had to think quickly, the Superintendent was certainly keeping him on his toes. "It's funny you should ask that, but I do have a vivid recollection of Gordon that night. Perhaps because it was only for a moment, it's fixed in my mind, like a fast exposure on a camera. He looked upset, and the tone of his voice—I just heard him as he passed—was angry. I didn't hear what he said, but I remember I was surprised. Surprised to see him angry, because listening to the audience's comments, it had been a particularly good show."

"Thank you, sir, that is very helpful and confirms

other eyewitness reports. I wonder if you could come down to the station sometime tomorrow and make a statement. You may be needed as a witness."

"Certainly, Superintendent."

"I'll send a car to pick you up. We'll call you in the morning."

Only when the two policemen had gone did Philip realize that his shirt was drenched with sweat. He pulled off his jacket and tie and walked into the bathroom, unbuttoning his shirt. He ran the hot water and flannelled himself down. Once he'd started it seemed silly to stop, so he stripped off altogether and had a thorough wash. Feeling much better, he wrapped a towel about his midriff and sat on the edge of the bath. He was unable to resist a smirk.

"Going all right, old boy," he said to the mirror. "What do you think?"

"I think that was a pretty smooth performance, all in all. Great shame it's not on video for posterity. Got out of that jammy moment with exemplary skill. Remember that Stanislavski improvisation exercise? The old master would have been proud of you!"

"You know what—what really astonishes me? How easy it is! I mean, if there are no witnesses to a murder, and you have no apparent motive, what chance is there of being caught? It's so straightforward. Why didn't I think of it years ago?"

"Conscience?"

"The play's the thing . . ."

"You're being obtuse."

"No. Let's say—it was a judicial killing. I, self-appointed President of the Equity subcommittee for the Preservation of the Purity of Our Art, was merely engaged upon the important business of maintaining standards. And there's a great deal more work to be done,

I'm here to tell you! Mr. Wilde unfortunately had slipped below par. Under the rules of our union that meant that he had to be acted against with 'extreme prejudice,' as they say in the CIA."

"Now look, old chap, your motives were hardly so altruistic. It was a personal murder."

"Yes, I like the sound of that—a personal murder. Still, it will have beneficial if unlooked-for repercussions . . ."

"Now that's honest."

"Put it there!"

He pressed his damp palm hard against the mirror. He withdrew his hand and stood looking at the imprint, watching his eyes reappear as it dissolved. He was fond of that trick.

"Good evening, Philip, nice to have you on the show. You don't mind if I call you Philip?"

"Not at all, Terry. In fact I'm delighted!"

"Begorrah, you're just saying that!"

"No, I always said I'd do anything to get on your show."

"Short of committing murder?"

"Oh no—I've done that all right!"

Ha-ha-ha!

The bathroom walls shook with the sound of canned laughter.

SEVEN

Eight o'clock, he'd said. She's said seven. The unprecedented alteration of a long-established routine disquieted him, as if in itself such tampering with the ordered structure of the universe could bode only ill. He was at his usual table by half past six and, once Ben had got over his surprise, supplied with a Balkanized Bordeaux.

He had not meant to be so early, but the end of the day had found him in town at a loose end. Earlier he had decided that he must write some letters and stir up his sluggish career. Of course, that was what his agent should have been doing, but the gap between expectation and reality was assuming canyon-like proportions, and it might well be, he acknowledged to himself with an attempt at fairness, that the time had come to set his own house in order. He'd written therefore to some of the better reps and to a couple of television casting directors in Manchester whom he had never met. He hadn't written such letters in years. That had been the occupation of his youth, slipping a c.v. and photo into a plain brown envelope and dispatching it to the far-flung provinces. Dropping the neatly addressed pile into a letter-box made him feel gauche. Was he taking a step backwards or wrestling manfully with his fate? Sisyphus or Hercules? At last he had convinced himself that he was making a positive effort. Looking through *Contacts* (the actors' handbook) he was amazed to find how few of the rep directors' names meant anything to him. Keeping in touch was half the battle in this game. Surely one or two of these new names must at least know of him by reputation. But they weren't going to employ him unless he put himself under their noses.

He examined his stock of photographs. They were five years old, and although there was nothing particularly wrong with them, familiarity, as ever, was beginning to breed at the least discontent. He sorted through his contact sheets and found an enlargement that he had never used before but which he now found he liked better than all the others. It showed him slightly in profile from his right side (his best side) with an appealing, slightly ironical look in his eye. The expression seemed much more human than that in his current entry in *Spotlight* (the actors' directory). Why had he never used it before? Five years old . . . that was the last batch under Harry Foster's regime. Photographs, of course, had always been one of Harry's self-proclaimed "strong points." Perhaps that was an essential insight into the medium itself—the fact that photography should attract so many bullshit artists. Harry was never happier than when poring over a contact sheet with an eyeglass, or

holding a transparency up to the light and pontificating
on effects of shade and light and the relativities of perspective. That these things were important Philip had
no doubt. But it was equally certain that Harry didn't
know the difference between a negative and an affirma-
tive. Harry had hardly been unique in this, nor in the
vehemence with which he clung to his malformed opin-
ions. It was a common phenomenon that people in the
casting end of the business automatically assumed that
they were experts in the subject. Time and again in
Philip's experience one casting director had commented
enthusiastically on his picture only for a colleague to
suggest at the next interview that he change it forthwith.
If he had collected every comment that had ever been
made to him, he would have been able to fill "Pseuds'
Corner" for a year.

It had been this new photograph (the Ironic Profile)
that had brought him into town in the afternoon and left
him with so much time to spare. There was a photo
reproduction centre behind Charing Cross Station to
which he had been coming for years. He didn't trust the
post, he always went in person, and so, having ordered a
hundred 10-by-8 prints, he found himself footloose at
the Embankment with no more rhyme or purpose than
the vagrants laid out in their cardboard boxes. It was
then that he had had an idea. Marching up purposefully
through Trafalgar Square—as purposefully as the
massed ranks of pigeons and tourists would allow—he
crossed over to the north side and passed through the
portals of the National Portrait Gallery. It was his favourite gallery, he knew every room and corridor, and
without a second thought he at once traced his steps to
the pantheon of sixteenth-century faces, where he low-
ered himself onto a padded bench and stared thought-

fully at the anonymous full-length portrait of Sir Walter Raleigh with his son.

Most actors of Philip's acquaintance were prone to superstition. He respected, or tolerated, its traditional manifestations—the embargo on whistling or mentioning the Scottish play backstage—but he had no time for those actors who refused to discuss or consider any job in the offing, saying only "I'll talk about it if I get it . . ." Philip deplored sloppy research. What was the point of going up for a part and doing nothing about it by way of preparation? Would, say, an industrialist turn up at an interview without an idea of the post for which he was applying? Philip had already dipped into Raleigh's own writings, and if recalled would study him in detail. It might make the disappointment of failure more acute, but how else could he gain an insight into the character?

The man in the portrait was about fifty, near enough Philip's own age. He was tall and had a good figure, the slim waist accentuated by the tapering cut of his doublet. His eyes were small and blue, the trim beard greyish-white. He had a long, thin nose and a high, smooth forehead. His fine features and elegant manner appealed to Philip. Although as a character actor he prided himself on his versatility, he was inclined temperamentally more to the refined than to the vernacular. At the same time he recognized the immense possibilities of a startling combination, remembering John Aubrey's comment that Raleigh "spake broad Devon until his dying day."

His eyes moved along to the next picture, a similarly full-length and anonymous portrait of Sir Francis Drake. The two invited, demanded, comparison. Here were the most famous seafarers of the Elizabethan Age, but at once one knew that of the two, Drake was the more natural sea captain. His whole bearing expressed robustness and vitality. He was shorter, far stouter than Raleigh, with full whiskers and red, puffy cheeks. He stood solidly, with one hand resting on a globe, declaring the physical world his domain. He stared you full in the face. But then so, too, did the sitters in most of the other portraits in the room. There were about twenty-five in all. Philip noticed that Raleigh was only one of two or three whose gaze had looked beyond the artist. Perhaps it was only coincidence, but even his son, young Walter, stared right at you. The comparison with Drake was perhaps simplistic, but it was tempting: the aggressive sea-dog holding the material world in his grasp; and the aesthete, with no less aggression or ruthlessness than the other, but with at least a part of his thoughts fixed beyond, as his eyes also were fixed beyond. In his own time Raleigh had been something of an enigma. His portrayal would require a clever, subtle actor.

"Just up my street really," said Philip softly to himself.

He was still lingering over the delightful vision of himself in wig and doublet adorning the front cover of *Radio Times* (this was an hour later in Covent Garden) when he became aware of Ben, who was standing at the entrance of the restaurant and talking to a taxi driver pointing furiously in his direction. Philip knew that it was a taxi driver because taxi drivers make a particular psychic intrusion into an atmosphere. Also there was a black cab sitting outside. A premonitory numbness crept over him as he watched the taxi driver approach.

"Mr. Fletcher?" It was pointless to deny it; he nodded. "Miss Sheridan's waiting outside. She asked me to come in and fetch you." He didn't doubt it. Who else but Hannah could have persuaded a London cabby to run an errand for her? Moreover, the man had assumed an unmistakable air of self-importance, as in royal lackey. Philip glared at him with sudden suspicion. He remembered Hannah roaring with laughter as she recounted the story of how she had gone out on the town one night without any money and screwed the taxi driver as payment in kind for a fare to Putney. Was it common practice, even the same man? What sordid commercial exchange might he be party to e'en yet?

Instantly bad-tempered, he shuffled off in the cabby's wake. "Albanian on the tab?" called out Ben as he exited. He gave a backward nod as he stepped out into the taxi.

There was another man in the back with Hannah. For one moment he had visions of a taxi drivers' orgy, and then he recognized Tony Elliott.

"Darling, how lovely to see you!" cooed Hannah, and then: "You know Tony, don't you?"

"Phil, hi! How you doing?"

Philip smiled weakly. He was saved an exchange of pleasantries by Hannah's instant launch into overdrive:

"Last-minute change of plan, darling, knew you wouldn't mind. Ran into Tony in Owen's office. Quite a gathering, all discussing poor dear Gordon. We left them to it actually. Owen's awfully worried about what he's going to do with his Sea-Gull now—" (Philip made a mental note of advice.) "—And though perhaps one might think it a bit callous, one sees his point of view. And of course Tony, you poor darling, such an important production for you. Well, Philip's free, aren't you, dear, you'd be willing at a pinch, wouldn't you?"

She actually paused. Squirming with discomfort, both their sets of eyes turned on him (he sat opposite on a flip-down chair), he tried desperately to come up with a quick riposte. Failing that, a slow riposte? But he managed no riposte at all. He slumped in his flip-down chair, skewered on her open question. Her roar of laughter covered his dying fall.

"Poor dear Philip, you're looking so confused! Well, that's hardly surprising. Look, I'm so sorry about to-night to spring this on you, when you're all set for a quiet tête-à-tête à deux (incidentally, I hope you're not hungry; I'm ravenous, but that's too bad!)—suddenly, hey presto! it turns into a ménage à trois (now don't go getting any ideas, boys!), but Owen had these tickets for the theatre and because of this Gordon business he couldn't go, so he offered them to us, and I thought well, waste not want not, and I just knew you'd want to come, Philip, because it's one of those Restoration things which you adore—what's it called, Tony?"

The sudden non-rhetorical question took Tony by surprise. Mastering conversation with Hannah was an acquired art: like an angler one had to sit passively holding a limp line, waiting for the abrupt tug that demanded a response. Tony floundered.

"Er, I'm not sure actually. The one at the Lyttleton, you know."

His "you know" was directed at Philip, an appeal for complicity. Philip was stony-faced. Why are we here with this prat? he thought. Why does she keep booby-trapping my life? Was this really her idea of a casting session or just a coincidental cock-up? For Christ's sake, beam me up, Scotty.

They were crossing Waterloo Bridge. The battleship-like superstructure of the National Theatre loomed on the far side of the Thames. Philip felt his heart sink into the mud below.

The taxi deposited them outside the box office. While Hannah and Tony collected the tickets, Philip drifted into the foyer. He could have done with a drink but the queue at the bar looked forbidding. For that matter he found the whole atmosphere of the place forbidding. As one who had been nurtured on the great National productions at the Old Vic, he still found it hard to accept the functional geometry of the new Culture Emporium. It was representative of so much that was ugly and depressing in the architectural environment: it was a multistorey car-park; a motorway service station with an airport waiting lounge tacked on at the front. A row of supermarket trolleys by the door would not have looked out of place, but then almost nothing would have looked out of place because the place was anything you wanted it to be, with the possible exception of a theatre.

What Philip found most irritating was the air of cultural self-consciousness. Wander out at the interval and you'd find yourself face-to-face with some exhibition; step back carefully or you'll bump into someone playing an oboe; dive into the bookstall for light relief and wade your way through the one-act plays of Bertolt Brecht (or Peter Hall's diaries if you're into the serious stuff). And all the time your ears are ringing with "the performance in the Olivier Theatre will begin in three minutes/ take your seats, please, in the Lyttleton/ tonight's performance in the Cottesloe . . ." Paddington Station crossed with the *Reader's Digest;* timetabled culture for the masses. Of course the intention was all very fine, but the path to hell is paved with good intentions. It was ironical, thought Philip, that the repertory should include *Animal Farm,* when the building itself fulfilled at least four out of five of the criteria catalogued by Orwell in his famous definition of "Pleasure-Spots." Then there was its size, an inevitable product of a multistorey supermarket culture—Economy Pack Special Offer. Olivier was reputed to have said, "There's a theatre in here somewhere named after me but I'm buggered if I can find it." Backstage, it was labyrinthine. And of course entirely unsuited to human life. Up and down the country actors were expected to work in backstage conditions that would have shamed a battery farmer. Dressing and rehearsal rooms were so often windowless, airless, baking in summer and overheated in winter. Some weren't even equipped with sinks (this is for actors, who wear make-up). Architects gave the impression that geometric symmetry was the sum of all their interest. There was one celebrated instance of a theatre in the south of England built with one communal dressing room, the designer apparently having forgotten that there are two sexes. Yet nothing seemed to change. Amoeba-like, they multiplied, mutually indistinguishable entrants for the Prince Charles Carbuncle Award. Prospero usurped; Caliban enthroned.

"So there you are!"

Hannah slipped a fur-sleeved arm through his. "Tony's gone to buy an ice-cream, he's such a dear," she whispered in his ear.

"And how long have you know the little dear?" he asked, smiling falsely in the continuous effort to suppress his anger. If she caught his mood, she chose to ignore it. "About two and a half hours, darling. Poor little thing was looking so lost in Owen's office, I just had to ask him along and, you know, he could be *aw*fully useful . . ."

"To whom?"

She slapped the back of his hand. "Now, now, behave!"

"I thought we were having a quiet meal together. I'm not in the mood to see a play, Hannah, still less to sit next to the little dear while he dribbles his cornetto down his designer jeans. I'm not sure it isn't past his bedtime anyway."

"Philip, you're so ungrateful. I'm trying to help—"

"I'm not a charity!"

"Careful!" Gently she pried his fingers apart and smoothed out the crease on the cover of the book he had been squeezing for emphasis. She replaced it on the rack. "You don't have to sit next to him. Owen had two tickets and we've bought a third. It's ten rows away. I'll sit with you, and he can sit on his own."

"I've got a better idea—you sit with him and I'll sit on my own." He picked up the book again and examined the back cover with furious intent.

"I've got a better idea still," said Hannah, snatching back the book and waving it under his nose. "I'll go and sit with him and you stick this up your arse!"

"So that's where you two've got to! Come along, we've only got two minutes. What you reading, Phil?"

"Grotowski. And don't call me Phil."

"Eh?"

"Ouch! That hurt, Hannah!"

But she'd gone, and so had Tony, dragged out backwards by the arm, a spinning whirl of toothy grin and chocolate sundae. Philip put down the battered copy of *Towards a Poor Theatre*. Doesn't look like we've arrived yet, he thought savagely to himself.

He caught up with them at the programme desk. Hannah glanced at him contemptuously, then looked away. "I didn't think you were coming," she muttered darkly. "Might as well now I'm here," he muttered back, also looking pointedly away.

"Now how shall we do this?" asked Tony. "There's two tickets together and this one's on its own . . ."

"Give it to me!" said Philip. Tony looked surprised at seeing it snatched so vigorously from his grasp. "See you at the interval!" he called out to Philip's back. "Not if I'm fast," said Philip under his breath. "Arse-hole!" said Hannah crisply.

Philip sank gratefully into his seat. At least the seats in the Lyttleton were comfortable and his was on the end of the row, almost by the exit. It was important to leave his options open. He tried to think of any mitigating circumstances to soothe the oppressions of the evening. None came to him. Of the National auditoria the Lyttleton was the one he liked least. Supposedly a proscenium stage, it gave the impression of a two-dimensional box. It had obviously been designed for use as a cinema and by some mysterious oversight was being used for the performance of live plays. Friends working at the National referred to it as Screen Centre 2. Still, it could have been worse. It could have been the Barbican.

Philip opened his programme. "God, not him!" he stuttered out loud, his eyes halfway down the cast list. "Bloody typical, couldn't act his way out of a paper bag . . ." He became aware that the woman on his left was staring at him. He clamped his lips shut firmly and sank deeper into his chair. Fortunately the woman's attention was distracted by an altercation in the next row. An elderly gentleman in a tweed jacket was declaring to no one in particular that he was going to complain in no uncertain terms to the management. Apparently he had bought a ticket for tonight's performance under the impression that he was coming to see something else. Philip sympathized. The National's programming system defied understanding. Filling in one of their booking forms was like doing a Jumbo Crossword.

The lights dimmed. The tweedy gentleman resumed his seat ostentatiously while the rest of the audience settled down. Conversation dropped. To offset it, the crunching of sweet papers was redoubled. Two entire rows near the front were consumed by bronchial fits.

An usherette remonstrated with a Japanese tourist waving a flash-camera. The curtain rose and light filled the stage.

Philip watched in silence as the first act unfolded. He crossed his legs and assumed a pose of detachment. Mentally he began to tick off his list of criticisms for the interval autopsy. It lacked pace and a sense of style. The set was too elaborate. The leading actor was twenty years too old for the part. The character actors were school of Michael Green. He'd have done it differently. Why hadn't he been asked? Not just for *this*, but ever. In all these years there'd never been so much as a whisper of an approach from the National. Surely Peter Hall remembered him from Stratford? Apparently quite a few of the directors thought well of him, several people had told him that. Then why wasn't he here? When he was renowned for his classical roles. To hell with it! Was he as good as he thought he was? Would he have made any difference if he'd been out there, now, in waistcoat and periwig?

He wasn't feeling too well. It was close in the theatre, people were waving their programmes as fans. He was perspiring freely, it was an effort to concentrate. The audience were laughing loudly. He felt himself caught up in it. The scene was flowing, he knew what was coming next, he'd played two of the parts in rep, but he was laughing himself, despite his familiarity. This was good stuff, there were good actors out there. He'd even forgotten his dislike of the auditorium. It didn't matter. With a good play and a good cast, any space could be a theatre. And this was a good cast all right. Better actors than he perhaps. Probably why they were there and he wasn't. Confidence was draining out of him. He felt weak with insecurity. Worse, he felt sick. His head ached, there was a lump in his throat. The clammy air hummed with laughter, noise. He needed fresh air, quiet. I want to be alone, he thought. Like Queen Christina. The lights were dimming, there was a scene change . . . Now, for God's sake, out! out! out!

He got out as the lights came on again. The doors swung back behind him, muffling the renewal of laughter. He leaned against them for a moment, catching his breath. He walked unsteadily through the foyer, then out by the plate-glass exit doors.

It was cold outside. It had rained earlier in the evening, the feel of dampness was still in the air. He pulled up his collar and muffled his chin in his scarf. Almost unconsciously he climbed concrete steps and found his way onto the terrace. He could hear the traffic on Waterloo Bridge to his left. It was quite dark on the opposite bank. There was the strip of streetlights along the Embankment and, above, a splash of yellow by the underground station, but there were great lumps of shadow too, round the Temple and behind Fleet Street, while back towards the bridge, amongst the Victorian office buildings and the warren of hotel rooms, only occasional lights flickered, like pinpricks in a backcloth. All the life of London lay beyond that dim façade. A stone's throw farther and you'd find the first of the restaurants and bars, the cinemas and theatres, the traffic piling up in the Strand, Trafalgar Square, Haymarket, Piccadilly, Soho, Shaftesbury Avenue. It was as bright as day in Leicester Square. Even in the shadows it was nowhere near as black as night.

"And this too," said Philip suddenly, "has been one of the dark places of the earth."

He looked round quickly, embarrassed at the loudness of his voice. But there was no one there. He was quite alone with the rain and the darkness, and his thoughts. His breathing was steady now, his pulse regular. He felt calm and self-contained, and slightly ashamed that he had allowed his doubts to unnerve him. He was in control. He could hear it manfully.

He stared hard across the river, and no less hard into his memory. He reconstructed methodically another dreary night in London Town. It was like a test, a mental litmus test: he walked again through the dark streets and saw the two of them bickering on the pavement. Step by step up Macklin Street and the little street whose name he hadn't known. Stukely Street. His mind fixed on the picture of that name. The door crushing the light by inches. Bare concrete steps and corridors. The boy running away. He stood at the door again. He had been apprehensive then. There was no compunction in his reliving it. Gordon stood before him. He heard his dry, unpleasant voice. God, how he hated him! Each word, each look intensified it and spurred his dull revenge. The memory flowed, smooth as the river. He heard the crack of glass. His fist tightened at the second blow. He saw the blood. And walked away, and neatly shelved the memory. It would not rise again unbidden.

"They were men enough to face the darkness."

He liked the sound of his own voice, he liked to talk his thoughts through. "And what will I say to Hannah when she says 'And where did you get to?' Oh, I just popped out for a moment, dear, to have a literary thought or two and mull over the heart of darkness. It's in all of us, you know. But no Kurtz me. No horror, horror, horror. No tongue nor heart cannot conceive nor name thee. No, that's Shakespeare, Tony—you know, that funny-looking Elizabethan chap whose plays you murder from time to time. Oh, just a friendly word of warning, old thing, while we're on the subject of murder—you might very well be next! In fact, I could quite easily bash you over the head and heave you into the bosom of old Father Thames there below. Right now. So, *cave*! I wonder how they're getting on in there. Must be nearly the interval. Better act like I had a headache. Better be careful. Don't want to antagonize Hannah any more. Probably thought she was doing me a favour bringing Tony along. Quite sweet, really. Didn't realize she'd be setting him up for the big sleep. Then she wouldn't, would she? Dr. Jekyll and Mr. Fletcher. Bloody cold out here. Could do with a coffee. Or a brandy. Good-night, sweet Thames. Full fathom five thy father lies. Sweet Thames, good-night."

EIGHT

If there was one thing Philip hated above all hate-worthy things—and there were many on his list—it was playing Trivial Pursuit at parties. It was not so much the game which he disliked; on the contrary, he had a knack for storing up useless information and always gave a good account of himself in quizzes. He was so good at *Mastermind* that he had more than once toyed with the idea of entering, but professional considerations dissuaded him: the British public has never taken to their bosoms intellectual actors, and however doubtful the label, there was no disputing the fact that the man on the Clapham Omnibus regarded *Mastermind* as an intellectual activity. Even within the theatre many directors looked on thinking actors with suspicion, which was hardly surprising: the post-fifties revolution in the British theatre had clearly staked out mental creativity as lying within the provenance of the "director." Only the "director" could give off a true air of authenticity while —leaning back in his leather jacket and pulling on an untipped Gauloise—he expounded to the *Guardian* Arts Page on the critique of post-structuralist alienation with reference to Toad of Toad Hall.

Philip looked up from the Trivial Pursuit board. On the sofa opposite, crushed in by a number of female forms, sat Tony Elliott in his leather jacket, puffing on an untipped Gauloise. Though he was only a few feet away, Philip could hardly hear him. It was very noisy.

Someone had just asked a question about the mating habits of hamsters. Tony Elliott had said something terribly funny and everyone roared with laughter.

Philip smiled politely. What made Trivial Pursuit, or "Triv," as it was called, so awful, was the people who played it. He had known almost from the instant of stepping through the door that it was destined to be one of those evenings when, during some lull completely indistinguishable from the other lulls that had peppered the proceedings since their inception, the hostess's voice would be heard baying in the tones of an invitation to tennis through the french windows, "Anyone for Triv?" and the delighted howl of response would put one in mind of a pack of blood-crazed beagles. It was pathetic, thought Philip, that nonetheless he had allowed himself to be caught up in it. He had been forced to surrender to the inevitable.

It was all Hannah's fault. Disasters of this sort were usually Hannah's fault, but, lemming-like, he would always disregard the lessons of history and dive open-eyed into the next farrago.

Even by her own standards, Hannah's behaviour had been infuriating. Having wasted most of the evening at the theatre, Philip had at least hoped that they might spend the rest of it together. But not for the first time he found that their plans were mutually incompatible. A quiet dinner for two might have been the original idea, but it was ancient history now. In any case, quiet dinners and Hannah had never gone well together. And now the witching hour was nigh; Hannah's dawn.

"But darling, Owen's throwing a party tonight and one simply couldn't miss it. Do come, I'm sure he won't mind. You're coming, aren't you, Tony dear?"

Of course he wouldn't miss it for the world, said the little dear. He was clinging to Hannah's arm like a kid out on a treat. Philip wanted to tell them both to stuff it, but as always, Hannah's mere presence was enough to weaken his resolve and make him lose the name of action. He didn't want to go with her, but he didn't want to leave her. He shuffled along miserably in her wake.

In the cab on the way to Hampstead, Philip had sat opposite the two of them on his flip-down chair and listened to their chatter. It was excruciating. Hannah was dropping names shamelessly. Tony was dropping bricks. He prattled on absurdly, tagging together a collection of key phrases—theatre of cruelty, empty space, alienation, social realism and political consciousness, et cetera—with a baffling series of non sequiturs. From something he said Philip deduced that he had been at Cambridge, which was absolutely bloody typical. Philip sat in the darkened cab watching the glinting glasses that marked the obnoxious presence, imagining that he held in his tightly clasped fists a loaded revolver which he was emptying chamber by chamber into the howling, stuttering body. When he tired of this he dreamt of machetes, garottes, and poisoned cups. By the time they got to Hampstead he was licking the stamp on a letter bomb.

Already he was regretting his decision to come. By the time they got through the front door he was in the grip of nausea. He didn't much like parties at the best of times.

Dinner parties were all right—good food and wine, conversation and peppermints, a civilized and sedentary experience. But "party" parties, were full and semi-strangers crowded into demographically dense rooms clutching at glasses, circulating under the demanding eyes of a vulture-eyed hostess, breathing in man- and woman-made pollution while trying desperately hard to hear and be heard above the din of forced conversation or even (Heaven forbid) loud music—no, those sorts of gatherings were inimical to Philip's taste. They were, of course, essential to Hannah's way of life.

She responded to the foul and stagnant midnight air like an asphyxiated diver breaking the surface. She bloomed like an orchid under a sun-ray lamp. She had burst into the den of gossip like a bitch in heat, and like a magnetic limpet mine waiting to explode had fastened herself onto all of importance who passed her by—directors, producers, star actors—all the big ships ploughing their increasingly sodden way through the sea of darting minnows.

Hannah, torpedo-headed, evoking, then bursting, mixed metaphors like balloons . . .

Philip hadn't seen her for hours. She had managed to be out of the room when the Trivial Pursuit board materialized like the Tardis on the Habitat glass table. Fanny Trethowan, arms imperiously folded like the games mistress she might so easily have been mistaken for, had made it clear with a look and a word that exeats were not to be issued. As for an inter-house tournament, four teams were picked and leaders nominated to exhort their charges to play up and play fair. Once again

the appointment of prefect passed Philip by. He prepared to suffer detention in the ranks.

"What was the Rolling Stones' first hit single?"
asked Tony Elliott.

"Bobby Charlton!" shouted out an actor called Pete
who wasn't quite as drunk as he pretended to be. Some
people giggled politely. Pete had said at the outset that
"the answer to any sports question is bound to be Bobby
Charlton," while someone called Jim had said that the
answer to any Entertainments question was always The
Beatles. Now whenever one of those categories came
up, and sometimes when they didn't, Pete would shout
"Bobby Charlton!"

"The Beatles," said Jim.

After the laughter had subsided, Philip observed to
Tony Elliott in a voice loud and clear enough to cut
through the hubbub, "Surely that is not an Arts and
Literature question?"

Tony blinked like an owl and stared down at the
board. Sure enough, Philip's team's tray was poised over
the brown-wedge symbol, not the pink. A wail of disapproval went up from Philip's team.

"Play fair, Elliott, play fair!"

Tony looked embarrassed. "Just testing," he said
with a cringe. He looked closely at the card before asking, "Who wrote *Treasure Island*?"

"Bobby Charlton!"

Members of the other teams groaned. "These questions are too easy!" declared a florid-faced playwright.
Philip's team bent their heads together in consultation.

After discounting from the list of possible authors
Bobby Charlton, Jackie Charlton, Long John Silver,
Robert Newton, Someone at Walt Disney, The Beatles
and Jules Verne, the team came to the conclusion that

the book was the work of George Stephenson, the celebrated railway engineer.

Philip, along with two or three other members of his
team, had long ago resigned from the collaborative process and accepted a temporary state of brain death.
While listening with half an ear to the inane delibera-
tions of his team-mates he became suddenly aware that
Fanny Trethowan had left the room. No doubt she had
gone off to press gang malingerers and malcontents, a
faction to which Philip was determined to aspire . . .

He got up quickly, muttering to his team monitor
that he simply *must* find the loo and squeezed himself
out of the Triv arena. "Back soon," he lied transpar-
ently, but no one was paying him any attention; they had
moved on already to a question of History.

"What was the name of Aristotle Onassis' yacht?"

Aware as never before of the inadequacy of his own
historical perspective, Philip slipped unobtrusively out
of the room.

He found himself in the hallway. Hannah's laugh
gurgled from the other end. He walked towards her.

She was surrounded by men. Philip recognized
Owen Trethowan next to her, his sagging jowls dis-
tended by a sinister smile as he hung on the poisoned
nectar dropping from Hannah's lips. There was no
doubt as to the centre of attention; the queen of gossip
held her court.

"—but darling, it just isn't his own; you can always
tell because they take it from the nether regions and just
glue it on top all short and curly as before. And you
know he has that simply dreadful habit of running his
fingers through his hair! One simply daren't shake
hands with him for fear of ending up with a fistful of
pubic dandruff—

"—of course they're silicon, dear, but they're sagging already. She should have had zips put under her tits, for easy refills—

"—I know for a fact that he hasn't been able to get it up for six months. He's seen three London specialists and made two trips to Switzerland. But frankly, dears, from what I've heard, it hardly justifies the effort—

"—yes, I suppose she has worn well. But then, so has the Eiffel Tower . . ."

Philip inserted himself into the group. He found himself standing between a writer whose name he had forgotten and an actor with a vaguely familiar face. He glanced at the fourth man, standing between Hannah and the actor. At the same moment the man looked over at him. Both sets of eyes met and widened in uncontrolled surprise.

Harry Foster muttered a hello.

It was impossible to make a more expansive greeting. Hannah was in full flow.

"—the poor dear, darling, fancy having your brains bashed out by a priceless modern sculpture. How dreadfully ironic that finally he should come so close to a work of art!"

Not even Hannah's brilliant insouciance could quite gloss over the tastelessness of her last remark. The actor blanched. Owen Trethowan leaned over and said, changing tack in a hearty manner, "Didn't you once represent Gordon, Harry?"

Harry Foster shrugged his shoulders. "I tried to get him on my books several times, but I'm afraid I missed out."

"He must have heard about you, Harry," said Philip.

The corners of Harry's mouth twitched. He had a smooth, rather featureless face and rarely expressed himself with anything more than tics or twitches, often unnoticeable to the untrained eye. Some said that it had been the undoing of him as an actor. For a time in the early sixties it had looked as if he might become something in films, but once he turned thirty the work dried up and, sharp enough to assess his own limitations, he became an agent. He had become very successful but those who knew him well often complained of insensitivity; coldness, even. He was not considered malicious, rather the truth about the inexpressive face was that he had very little to express. Philip had not been alone in thinking him a boring man, but there was nothing professionally disadvantageous in that. Indeed, for an agent it was probably an asset.

"You're looking well, Philip," said Harry.

"And yourself."

"I keep in shape."

He was just the sort of man to keep in shape, thought Philip. A creature of habit and routine. Philip remembered the rowing machine and the exercise bicycle in the corner of Harry's office. They had not been there for show. Philip pictured him sweating it out on the apparatus. He probably gave dictation while bicycling around, he was not the sort of man to waste time, which, as he never tired of saying, meant money. It looked as though the exercise had done him good: the dark hair was very thin indeed these days, and shot with unbecoming grey, but the face was smooth and (artificially) tanned and the figure looked trim.

"Healthy body, healthy mind, eh?" said Philip for no particular reason, but impelled by the organic self-propelled drift of an aimless and unwanted conversation.

"It's healthy bodies and dirty minds I'm interested in, dear," drawled Hannah, breaking into a fit of gurgling laughter like a demented fountain.

Harry seemed relieved by her interruption. He even permitted himself one of his rare apologies for a smile, then said quickly, pointing to someone who was just leaving, "Excuse me, but I have to go and say goodbye to Sir Peter . . ." Owen Trethowan, alerted to the dignitary's imminent departure, also excused himself; he had seen his wife already at the door.

The little group was splitting up. The actor and the writer had struck up a conversation of their own. As Harry brushed past him Philip leaned over and whispered quite distinctly in his ear, "Shit."

Harry did not pause, but as he passed by, Philip saw with satisfaction a savage twitch disfigure his offside cheek.

Philip felt an arm slipped through his. Hannah stared up at him with big dewy eyes. "Will you ever forgive him, darling?" she murmured. Philip felt embarrassed, he hated anyone's pity, but he hated more the sense of injustice that consumed him still. "I have an elephant's memory," he said. "Well, I think you should untie the knot in this particular corner," she said firmly. "It isn't doing you any good, what's done is done, it's in the past . . ." Mechanically Philip began to quote from the *Four Quartets*.

"Well, if you're going to go all literary on me, Philip, the least you can do is get me another drink." She shoved her empty glass into his hand. "Whisky sour, one cube of ice, the usual, I'm sure you know. I'm off to powder my nose. Unless I'm waylaid by some brutal hunk of machismo, I'll see you back here in five minutes."

As she sauntered off, Philip heard Fanny Trethowan's shrill hectoring voice demanding the instant surrender of all Triv escapees. He ran off in the other direction.

A small drinks table had been laid out in the conservatory. Philip poured Hannah's whisky, then went and stood behind a clump of tomato plants. He was just in time to witness through the leaves Fanny Trethowan make her imperious sweep towards the back of the house. He chuckled to himself as she went out again. He had a good look at the tomato plants. Though nothing of a horticulturist, he felt sure that they were particularly weedy specimens. He had a quick look round, taking in the dimensions of the conservatory and trying to work out its position in relation to the sun. It was of course in exactly the wrong position to get any sun at all, which was absolutely typical of a pair of old poseurs like the Trethowans. He could just imagine the conversation over breakfast, the earnest consideration of new "features" to enhance the prestige and value of their property viz. HIM: What say we build a functional carport and convert the garage to a sauna and Jacuzzi? HER: I do think it's time we Axminstered the lawn. HIM: But the chimney flue needs repapering! HER: Sod the chimney flue, the Frogton-Smoggetts have got a *conservatory*. HIM: Then we'll get one too, but with stained-glass windows . . .

Philip heard the conservatory door click shut. Transfixed by fear of Fanny, he held his breath while with his fingers he made a peep-hole in the leaves. Scanty they may have been but the light was dim.

Owen Trethowan was rummaging through a large box of chocolates. He picked a couple out fastidiously and stuffed them in. Rather reluctantly he held out the box.

"Want one?"

Harry Foster shook his head. He took his glass to the drinks table and poured himself a fruit juice. Owen looked relieved, like the dormitory fat boy saved from having to share his tuck.

"Good-o!" said Owen cheerily. "More for me!" He

pulled out a piece of corrugated paper and dived into the bottom layer. He leered at Harry. "Fanny's a proper spoil-sport, she won't let me near chockies, but I'm just *mad* about coffee creams! She seems to think they'll spoil my figure or something."

Harry shared his self-deprecating laugh. Owen's enormous belly wobbled like a jelly.

Go ahead, thought Philip, when you look that disgusting to start with, why not go the whole hog.

"Sorry about the other half, by the way," continued Owen. "She's obsessed with that bloody game. Must be something to do with the time of month. She's got absolutely no shame. Only the other week we were at some first-night party and she tried to get me to invite John Gielgud back for a game."

"God! How embarrassing!"

Trethowan then did a very bad imitation of John Gielgud inquiring after the name of the capital of Mongolia. Harry Foster laughed politely.

As so often at social gatherings, Philip—snug as a bug in a tomato plant—was growing tired of the sound of polite laughter.

"Hannah seems to have got the right idea," continued Trethowan in conspiratorial mood. "She just laughed like a klaxon when Fanny asked her."

"She always laughs like a klaxon," snickered Harry.

"Dear darling Hannah, she does go on a bit sometimes but then she does have her points, eh?" Both men chuckled knowingly. "One thing I will say for her, she's loyal to her friends."

"Oh yes—which in particular?"

"Philip Fletcher, for one."

Carefully Harry picked out the slice of lemon from his empty glass. He twisted it and popped it into his mouth and, sucking noisily, said, "Tell me more . . ."

"Oh, she keeps on at me about what a good actor he is and how he deserves a break. And I do have this problem, what with old Gordorina shuffling off his mortal sheath so unexpectedly, you take my point? I've tried Hopkins, Jacobi, McKellen, but at this notice it's frankly impossible."

"Surely you can't risk Fletcher, Owen. He couldn't fill a telephone kiosk."

"I think I'm going to have to risk someone, Harry. And it'll have to be an experienced actor of Fletcher's age and type. Bill Childs says he did rather a fine Trigorin in Manchester a few years back, he showed me the reviews."

"Well, if you're going to go on provincial critics—"

"Now let's be fair, you can't call Irving Wardle provincial. No, the only thing that's wrong with Fletcher as far as I can see is that he's a nonentity. We're having a go at a few telly names, but if the right fish doesn't bite, then I suspect we could very well be looking at the likes of Philip Fletcher. And there is another point: I'm not too keen on a telly name. It's all right for getting bums on seats in Harrogate, but the West End's more demanding. I'm left with Tony Elliott, you see . . ."

"What's wrong with Tony Elliott?"

"He's an imbecile. Gordon wanted him because he wouldn't get in the way and he's popular with the critics. But the problem is that if I let Elliott loose on an inexperienced and insecure telly star, it'll take more than a few nutty reviewers to save us. That's my problem in a nutshell."

Harry took out his piece of sucked-dry lemon. He examined it for a moment with unlikely curiosity, then dropped it back into his glass. He stared at the glass while saying softly, "Can I take it that our conversation is strictly confidential, Owen?"

Trethowan looked surprised. "Of course. Isn't it always?"

"Yes, you're right, you're about the most trustful confidant I know, which is just as well; it wouldn't do me any good if it came out that I had told you this."

"Told me what?"

"About Philip Fletcher. A friendly word of warning —don't touch him with a barge-pole. The man's a natural piss-artist."

"Philip Fletcher? I don't think I've ever even seen him drunk!"

"No, there were too many embarrassing scenes in the past; some vestige of professionalism makes him control it in public. But believe me, when he's working, his dressing room smells like a distillery. He's so pissed half the time he can't even remember what play he's in. Why do you think he hardly works these days?"

"Are you sure about this?"

"I'm afraid I haven't told you the half of it. Believe me, I hate doing this, it really cuts me up—that man I counted among my dearest friends for years, he was one of my first clients. But in the end I couldn't take any more; I knew that although it wasn't common knowledge yet, it soon would be, and my reputation would be dragged down with his. I had to kick him out. It was the hardest decision of my life, I hardly slept for weeks afterwards. And I feel in a way responsible. But there are limits, and when he started messing about with drugs, I just had to call it a day."

"Drugs!"

"It's too awful, I know. God knows how he's never been busted, his arm looks like a pincushion. I bet Bill Childs didn't tell you he missed an entrance in Manchester because he was snorting cocaine in the bog."

"Jesus—"

"—and that's the gospel truth!"

"Why on earth didn't Hannah tell me?"

"Don't even think of mentioning it to her, Owen. Promise me that. I've seen it happen dozens of times. His close friends just somehow black it out, they don't, won't talk about it; it doesn't exist as far as they're concerned. It's a common medical phenomenon. I mentioned it to her once and she flew right off the handle. Refused even to talk to me for months afterwards. And you wouldn't want that, would you?"

"How extraordinary!"

"In these cases the psychological effect on friends is almost as bad as on the victims. That's why I had to ditch him. There's nothing you can do. I'm sorry, but I had to warn you. Remember, I probably know him better than anyone . . ."

"We'll talk about this later; here comes my wife—"

"Darling, would you fetch up some red from the cellar, we're almost out . . ."

"Coming, darling!"

"I'll give you a hand, Owen."

"Oh, thanks, Harry."

Exeunt all.

They closed the door after them. Once more it was quiet in the conservatory. The party sounds came from somewhere far off, from another part of the action, someone else's scene, a different play altogether.

But in the conservatory no one had bothered to change the scenery. Philip stepped out from behind the arras.

He caught his reflection in the glass and stopped to straighten his tie. In the past five minutes he had passed through a series of violent emotions, the more intense because inwardly suppressed, and he felt both physically drained and wound up at the same time. The effort of self-control had been immense. He decided to go for a walk and clear his head. He found the key to the outer conservatory door and went out into the garden.

It was cold but he did not feel it. It was wet, too, but that he barely registered. He probably wouldn't have noticed if it had been ten below freezing.

Half-aloud he went over the text of his soliloquy: ". . . O double-damned smiling villain . . . O villain, most heathenish and most gross, O Spartan dog! More fell than anguish, hunger or the sea . . . you are not worth the dust which the rude wind blows in your face . . . O villainy! Ho! let the door be bolted: Treachery! seek it out . . . from this time forth my thoughts be bloody or be nothing worth . . . Is this, is this a dagger I see before me, the handle towards my hand . . ."

He had walked once all round the garden and come to the side of the house. He saw a light up ahead and heard voices raised in conversation. He recognized the voices at once and, feeling gravel crunch under his feet, stopped and stood deathly still.

The light came from a low door half-way down the alley. Owen Trethowan's head, at shin level, was sticking out of the door and looking up. He said to Harry Foster, "I think I'll just get one more case." "Righto," said Harry, putting the one he held down on top of another. That would make three cases, enough to cater for the serious drinkers. Why, even a piss-artist like Philip Fletcher should be content with that . . . Harry was leaning through the cellar door, looking down. Philip could dimly hear Trethowan scrabbling around among the bottles below. Philip imagined him kneeling in a corner, squinting at some dusty label. It was curious how cellar lights were always so inadequate. Someone could come quite close without you knowing it.

It would be an easy thing, thought Philip, the gravel

path notwithstanding, to creep up behind Harry Foster and push him down the cellar steps. It would be an easy thing to murder Harry Foster. Easier than murdering Gordon Wilde. And much more pleasurable. The idea of the moment had much to recommend it: that morning Philip had gone down to the police station to make his statement, and in the car on the way back afterwards Sergeant Harris had been very chatty. The police had been lucky in the case of Mr. Wilde, he'd said, crimes of passion were so much easier to solve than other murders. And the most difficult sort to solve? Anything done on the spur of the moment, anything without apparent motive . . .

But wait!

What if he fell and injured himself only? Philip could hardly go down and finish him off afterwards, engineer another broken neck with Owen Trethowan looking on. No, it was too risky. Philip didn't know how big the drop was, it might be a few steps only . . . no, for all its attractions, spontaneous murder was no longer a game he could afford to play; once perhaps, but not *twice*!

Gently lifting his feet clear of the gravel path, Philip stepped back onto the lawn. He watched Owen's head reappear at the cellar door and saw Harry bend down to pick up the proffered case. He had not been observed.

Really, he thought, I'm getting the hang of this.

He walked back to the conservatory door with stealthy pace, with Tarquin's ravishing stride.

"Anyone seen Hannah?" he inquired breezily as he stepped back into the party.

NINE

Premeditated murder was certainly a different kettle of fish. It involved doubt and the appreciation of risk. Philip couldn't afford to foul up; the effect on his career would have been disastrous. But of one thing he was sure, resolution must follow quickly on resolve:

> If it were done when 'tis done, then 'twere well
> It were done quickly.

He had already screwed his courage to the sticking-place.

Deciding to murder Harry Foster was one thing; finding the means, another. He began to cast about with a view to constructing schemes of Machiavellian subtlety. The problems presented themselves to him like clues to a fiendish puzzle. One by one the false solutions were discarded. The mental work was slow but absorbing. He passed a whole week in contemplation of the subject, and then another.

His phone hardly rang in those two weeks, he felt all but cut off from the world. Quennell called once, Eleanor once and Hannah twice. None of them had much to say for themselves. For long periods Philip took to leaving the phone off the hook.

The crux of the matter was this: Philip had committed one more-or-less unintentional murder (it was getting more unintentional in comfortable retrospect), and through a combination of circumstance and cunning managed to bring down no suspicion whatsoever upon himself. He was forced to conclude that luck had been the principal factor and that such a situation could not have been engineered. If Harry Foster were to be murdered openly, then another suspect was wanted. Philip had been unable to find a second Kit McCullers.

He had immersed himself in his chosen victim's life over the last fortnight. He would get up early in the morning and watch Harry leave his Hampstead home for work. He would follow him to his Soho office and pick him up again at lunch-time in one of the pubs or bistros which he frequented. Then, in the evening, he would follow him home and sometimes stand for an hour or so in the street, waiting to catch a glimpse of him through the lighted windows. Philip had got to know a great many intimate details about Harry Foster; for instance, that he had a predilection for very young girls. Philip had seen several arrive at his front door of an evening, and depart again the next morning. Usually they had turned up to appointments in Harry's office a few days earlier, all clutching their 10-by-8 folders or envelopes. Once he had seen one of the girls drop her envelope and a pile of photographs spilled out onto the pavement. He had helped her pick them up.

"Oh, are you an actress?" he asked innocently, looking at the monochrome portraits.

"Trying to be!" she had answered with a laugh. She was very pretty, blue-eyed and blonde, slightly plump-cheeked. She was just Harry's type. By now Philip had a very good idea of what constituted Harry's type. He gave her back her photographs and watched her walk away. He wanted to say something, he felt sorry for her. He wanted to say, "For God's sake, don't go to his place tonight, love. You won't mean anything to him, you'll just be the third this week. All that stuff about getting you an Equity card is just bullshit. He'll screw your socks off and won't even remember your name in the morning." Philip wanted to say all this very badly; he had to restrain himself. He was consoled by the thought that Harry's days of heartless philandering were numbered.

At the end of two weeks Philip had drawn up a series of schedules, like a life plan—to which a death plan would soon be appended—documenting in detail Harry Foster's movements. Philip's neat ticks and comments filled the pages with impressive symmetrical patterns: Harry was nothing if not regular in his habits. He never deviated from the daily routine of comings and goings by more than a few minutes, his life was rigidly compartmentalized. Prior to his study of Harry, Philip had considered himself to be a paradigm of orderliness. But by comparison with Harry he was practically an anarchist.

In order to observe his quarry closely, Philip had resurrected some of his most notable performances.

On the day he had picked up the blonde girl's photographs, he had been playing Baron Tusenbach from *Three Sisters*. "A sensitive performance," the Birming-

ham *Post* had called it. It was a rather older baron these
days: the bushy sideburns, lovingly preserved for years,
had to be flecked with a little grey, and finding that he
had overdone it a bit, he found it necessary to add some
iron to his own hair and eyebrows. He put on the little
steel-rimmed spectacles once more with affection. He'd
worn them several times since, but they'd never suited
him quite so well. They seemed to go perfectly with the
character of the gentle, stuttering and somewhat tuber-
cular-looking man with his old-fashioned pressed suit
and silver-topped cane. The cane was more than an ex-
travagant prop: Philip's baron had an integral limp. The
baron usually appeared on Tuesdays and Fridays.

Mondays and Wednesdays saw Philip's modern-
dress Shylock, an "interpretation of rare power," in the
words of the Coventry *Evening Telegraph*. Philip had
been a bit worried the first time he'd re-created the
make-up—he had forgotten just how big that nose really
was! His principal worry was not that it might look too
grotesque but that it might fall off. However, he tried
out for the first time a new brand of putty and found to
his delight that not even five minutes of vigorous head-
shaking could dislodge it. Grey spray and a goatee
beard contributed to the severe and proud look. He
wore dark glasses as in the original production, which
had had a very Mediterranean look. He was confident
that his creation would have compared well with the
recent (probably plagiarized) production starring the
late Gordon Wilde.

Thursdays only was the turn of Captain Ahab, undoubtedly his riskiest performance. But Philip was convinced that it had been his finest achievement—on an
ill-fated tour ten years previously—and he included it
for sentimental reasons. With Ahab the difficulty was
not merely a question of make-up, although he did find

the business of strapping up his ankle behind his buttocks and fitting his knee into the peg-leg irksome. No, he had most trouble with the American accent. Philip was not naturally good at accents, and difficult ones required a lot of work. He could do a passable standard American, but *Moby Dick* was set in a specific time and place and Captain Ahab was the very model of the Yankee sea-dog. At first Philip had sounded more like Captain Birdseye. But he had kept at it, and after hours of drudgery with his cassette recorder had managed to recapture the essence of his famous performance. It was so taxing, however, that he had to restrict himself to one showing a week.

Saturdays and Sundays saw his finest make-up creation. He had used parts of it subsequently, but the whole thing, one and indivisible, would forever be associated with his Firs, a part he had played with enormous conviction (Bristol *Evening News*) while still in his twenties. He regarded doing Firs as his treat after a hard week's slog. It didn't matter that the make-up took two hours to apply, it was a joy from start to finish.

The young girl in the chemist's had not seemed in the least perturbed when he presented for payment an armful of contraceptives—a sign of the times, he supposed. Did it not occur to her that he must be planning to indulge in some fearful orgy of gratification, or did she consider it just wishful thinking? He would have liked to tell her the reason for his purchase; he smirked to himself at the thought of his secret knowledge.

Once at home, he carefully unravelled the sheaths of latex and, cutting off the ends, filled his table with rectangular strips. Then, smoothing his facial skin bit by bit, he applied glue to the pieces and stuck them on. When he took his hand away, the skin fell back into its natural tightness, causing exaggerated wrinkles in the rubber.

His face and throat fully covered, he didn't look a day under eighty. The old semi-bald wig, false eyebrows and lashes, and a few blacked-out teeth completed the picture. His was a modern-day Firs, no old retainer but a washed-up dependant of the welfare state. He automatically got a half on the buses, no one even asked to see his card. He noticed that people edged away when he sat next to them. Only the occasional passing wino favoured him with a friendly eye.

It had been in the guise of Firs that he had approached Harry Foster the first Saturday outside the newsagent's and asked him for the price of a cup of tea. It was not merely a piece of bravado, rather the ultimate test. Harry's ill-tempered refusal had put Philip in very high spirits. He had suffered his tedious day's vigil gladly and it was by no means inappropriate that it should have been that very evening that he hit upon a solution.

At six o'clock Harry had trotted out of his front door in track suit and trainers. This was something Philip had not seen before, a weekends-only routine. Harry took a few ritualistic sniffs of air, neatly sidestepped the waiting piles of dog shit and broke into a jog. Following a little way as fast as his geriatric disguise would allow, Philip was in time to see him round Whitestone Pond, then disappear off down Spaniards Road. Harry lived in a little road between West Heath Road and Heath Street. Unable for obvious reasons to follow him, Philip settled himself on one of the benches by the pond and hoped that he would return that way.

A half hour later Harry emerged from East Heath Road. Coming to the top of the hill, his jog had slowed to barely above a walk, and as he approached, Philip heard his heavy breathing and saw his beetroot face shining with sweat. Clearly Harry found keeping in shape more of an effort than he was prepared to admit. He embarked on a last circuit of the pond before staggering off home.

Philip was still sitting on his bench as Harry came up. He was almost abreast of him when, spurred by a mischievous impulse, Philip rose rheumatically to his feet and whined, extending a mittened paw, "Have pity on an old codger fallen on hard times."

"Piss off, you old git!" gasped Harry, who had to sidestep clumsily in order to avoid him, and in so doing stumbled and all but fell. It was all he could do to keep on his feet; he looked done in.

Philip smiled to himself and sat back on his bench. As Harry lurched across the other side of the pond he shot Philip a black scowl. Gleefully Philip stuck two fingers up at him.

It was while heading home on the bus an hour later that the idea came to him. It was audacious, astonishing, outrageous even. He dismissed it reluctantly for those reasons. But that night it kept coming back to him. And when he woke the next morning it was to find it lodged indelibly in his mind.

He had to get up early to be out of the house before anyone was about. He had gone to sleep in his make-up, but even so it had taken him twenty minutes to set it straight again and reapply the finishing touches. Then he had gone out, his costume hidden under a long coat, a floppy brimmed hat on his head, his features muffled under a scarf, his eyes lost behind opaque shades. It was the work of a few moments when no one was looking to find a quiet corner and divest himself of his outer disguise. Stuffing the gear into a plastic bag—a tramp's necessary prop in any case—he boarded the bus as Firs.

He sat in the back seat opposite the conductor dribbling and muttering himself into character.

"Where you going, granddad?" asked the healthy-looking young conductor with unfeigned disgust.

"Hampstead Heath, to see the cherry trees . . ."

It didn't take a mind-reader to tell that the conductor thought he was completely cracked. Philip, unable to resist giggling maniacally to himself, did nothing to discourage the idea.

It had been a long but fruitful day. Sustained by intense internal excitement, the strain of acting out the part had not been onerous. By the early evening (when Harry made his track-suited appearance on the dot of six), Philip had made a thorough mental map of his area of operations and put the finishing touches to his scheme. It had lost none of its original audacity, for boldness was to be the key.

This time he kept out of Harry's sight. He watched him from a distance and saw that his run followed the same pattern as yesterday and took about as much time. Running round the pool once on the way out and once on the way back seemed to be a well-established ritual. It was a cold afternoon and there were not too many people about; but nonetheless, as things stood, the enterprise looked all too risky. At six-thirty, when Harry made his final circuit, it was still light. The need for darkness suggested the subtle final touch to the overall plan.

The next week went by slowly. Every evening Philip went out to the pond in his disguise of the day, to check on the number of passers-by through the evening. It was deserted for only short periods, there seemed to be an unconscionable number of dog-walkers out at any one time, but bad weather radically reduced their number. It looked as if the feasibility of the plan was going to depend more and more on the weather. If necessary, he might have to wait for weeks, and that might place a serious strain on his nerves.

On Friday the long-term weather forecast was good. On Saturday when Philip arrived at the pond, an ice-cream van was parked beside it and doing a brisk trade. From buying a cornet Philip was able to ascertain that the ice-cream man would be there until about seven, and yes, he would be working Sunday. He had been on holiday the week before. Sometimes he stopped by the pool, other times outside Kenwood House. Philip digested the bad news rather better than the soggy cornet. He watched Harry come and go and waited till the van departed at 7:15. He went home feeling depressed.

He was woken the next morning by the sound of rain against the windows. He leaped out of bed, flung back the curtains and scanned the grey black sky with a sense of mounting triumph.

Now it had to last.

He passed the day with the curtains drawn, not daring to look out. He spent almost the whole time with his headphones on, listening to Böhm's famous recordings of the Beethoven symphonies with the Vienna Philharmonic. He listened to some movements twice and sat right through a replay of the whole Ninth. At about four, his patience ran out. Hardly daring to look, he lifted a corner of the curtain with one finger and peeked out.

It was drizzling steadily. The leaves of the eucalyptus tree in the front garden were glistening, the brown earth beneath lumpy with wet. A network of canals and puddles latticed the pavement and road. A car drove past slowly, windscreen wipers lazily waving hello, the full beam of its headlamps catching the falling water droplets like moonbeams. Philip stood at the window for nearly ten minutes. Not a single pedestrian went by.

His hand trembled as he replaced the curtain. Excitement and fear consumed him about equally. He hadn't felt this bad since opening in *Charley's Aunt* in Bournemouth without a dress rehearsal. As a rule Philip liked things to be well prepared and he eschewed improvisation. He took longer than usual to fit his wig and retouch the make-up. This had to look good; it would be a one-off performance.

He muffled himself in his hat and scarf and went out, closing the front door after him with exaggerated care; he knew that the couple upstairs could always hear when it was slammed. He knew they were in, he had heard their occasional footsteps. It was a good sign, usually on a Sunday afternoon they went out for a long walk. This afternoon it was important that everyone stayed in.

He ran on tiptoe down the drive and for the first fifty yards along the road. He stopped at the corner to get his breath back and looked hard about him for half a minute. Nothing moved—no pedestrians, no cars, not even a bird or a cat. The drizzle was intensifying. He decided he would take the tube.

It was only when he got down to the platform that he removed his outer disguise. He shuffled down to the end, darted behind an unoccupied bench and shredded himself of the last vestiges of Philip Fletcher. The platform was practically deserted; no one paid him the slightest attention in either incarnation. It was as Firs that he boarded the train.

He arrived outside Harry's house at half past five. He sheltered under a tree on the opposite side of the street, next to a telephone box. He would have liked to stay in the telephone box—which he had checked was in working order—but unfortunately it did not afford an unobstructed front view of Harry's front door. He hunched himself up as best he could against the bole of the tree, feeling drops of water splash down the back of his neck.

It never occurred to him that the bad weather might deter Harry. Real men weren't frightened by a bit of wet, although, of course, as Philip was forced to acknowledge to himself, Harry was only approximately half human.

At a quarter to six, Harry's bedroom light went on. Although he had been expecting it, Philip's heart jumped. That sudden yellow-white glare against the window was the awaited signal; the routine mechanism had been set in motion.

About five minutes later the first-floor light went off and a light went on in the small bedroom upstairs. Philip saw Harry's head bent forward over a desk. In five more minutes he would go down to the bathroom. Everything was going according to schedule.

A young girl brushed past Philip's tree. Her appearance as from nowhere startled him. Her actions alarmed him. She went into the phone-box.

He looked at his watch. It was four minutes to six. He looked at the sky. It was overcast but by no means dark.

Damn you! he thought, looking at the girl.

She was an anorexic slip of a thing, perhaps anything from fourteen to eighteen. Philip found it so difficult to tell with girls these days. Her hair had been carefully spiked in punk style, but now lay sodden flat like a drenched cornfield. Her dark make-up ringed her eyes and ran in channels down her cheeks. She had the look of a lachrymose vampire.

Philip bit his lip. It was three minutes to six, the bathroom light was on. His only hope was that Harry's schedule might be delayed. Or perhaps the girl might not get the number she wanted. But no, he could see her clearly through the glass, her chin tilted up with the receiver tucked in under, her mouth splitting in a wide grin, then opening and shutting in a feverish imitation of a silent movie.

The bathroom light went off. It was two minutes to six. He would have to improvise.

He shuffled out from under his tree and positioned himself on the far side of the kiosk. The girl did not seem to have noticed him. He reached out a dirty-nailed finger (his characterizations were nothing if not thorough) and scratched lightly on the glass. The girl ignored him. He knocked three times very deliberately. She couldn't pretend that she hadn't heard. She turned with a malevolent look, waving him away with one hand. He leered at her, displaying his crooked teeth.

He went right up to the glass and pressed his nose against it, letting his eyes roll cross-eyed out of focus.

"Piss off!" came the plaintive imperative from the other side of the partition.

He withdrew a fraction, still leering, and registered her look of panic. At least he had her attention.

He flashed open his raincoat, revealing his unbuttoned fly and dangling member.

"You fucking old pervert!"

Philip had never in his life seen anyone move so fast. Superman himself could hardly have exited the telephone box with more panache. She stopped once, turning back when she was just under the tree, screaming insults and imprecations.

"Why don't you shut up and wrap your laughing gear round this, darling?" wheezed Philip.

For a moment she looked as if she were about to be violently sick, then she turned on her heels and bolted down the road.

Despite the occasion Philip could not resist chuckling to himself; his interpretation of Firs was certainly one of the more unusual of recent years. He wondered if Anton would have approved.

And then he saw Harry's front door swing open and a moment later Harry himself appeared on the porch.

Philip dived into the phone box, slammed in ten pence and pumped out the numbers. He should have ten seconds or so, the minimum time that Harry took to flex his muscles and psyche himself up before closing the door and setting off.

There was an interminable pause between the dialling and the first ringing tone. Clicks, whirrs and more clicks reverberated in Philip's ear, as if the machinery were digesting its lunch. Then it rang three times and Philip's heart sank . . .

". . . Hello, Harry Foster speaking. I'm sorry you've got the answerphone."

Oh, bother! said Pooh.

". . . but I'm unable to speak to you at the moment . . ."

Oh, sod it, Eeyore!

"—Hello?"

Philip started.

"Hello, are you still there?"

Philip swallowed, took a last deep breath and sighed sibilantly, "Harry Foster please . . ."

"Speaking. Sounds like I got to you just in time, I was going out."

"Well, that's a relief. This is Theodora Babbett from Irving Salzenheim's office in New York . . ." Philip's falsetto squeaked a bit but hopefully it sounded like transatlantic interference.

"Oh, hi, Theodora!" said Harry in the tone of someone greeting a long-lost friend. Philip was momentarily surprised. As far as he knew, there was nobody in the biz with the ridiculous name of Theodora Babbett, but then with Americans you never could tell.

"Oh, hi, Harry. Long time no see," simpered Theodora flirtatiously.

"Ages, isn't it?"

"Wow, yeah!" breathed Theodora (curiouser and curiouser, thought Philip). "Look, I'm sorry to bother you during your leisure time" (pronounced *leejur* with a soft *j*) "but we got a flap on. We're filming the pilot episode of *Cabin Crew* from tomorrow, an everyday story of ordinary folk on the world's airways. The first episode features a psychopathic junkie ex-Nam veteran pilot getting his own back on the flame-haired stewardess who jilted him by hijacking a mercy flight to Africa. A week's filming in London and Egypt and studio in Hollywood, guaranteed minimum seven days. But our chief guest star has just booked out with scarlet whooping fever and we need a replacement fast. Got anyone forty to forty-five, Scotland Yard Inspector type, American green card?"

"Mmm. Andrew Tufnell's available. Hang on, I'll have to check my diary. What dates did you say?"

"Fourteenth to the sixth. You get your diary, I'll take a peek in *Spotlight* . . ."

While Harry was gone, Philip put in a couple more coins. It wouldn't do to have a tone cut in during a transatlantic call.

"Are you there, Theodora?"

"Where else would I be, honey?"

"Ha-ha! Those dates are fine. Found Andrew?"

"Uh-huh. Looks dishy. What's he done?"

Harry recited a comprehensive if unexciting list of credits. Philip heard him out patiently, then said, "Know anything about a guy called Philip Fletcher?"

There was a pause Pinter would have been proud of.

"By an extraordinary coincidence I was chatting to him at a party only the other week, so I happen to know he's unavailable. Besides, he's not in Tufnell's league."

"Whatever you say, Harry" (you cretin). "I'll just check with Mr. Salzenheim and call you right back. Don't go away now!"

"I'll stay by the phone."

" 'Bye, honey!"

Philip replaced the receiver. He looked at his watch. It was nearly ten past. He waited. It was safe to wait in the kiosk now, Harry would be as good as his word. He'd be foolish not to, Theodora had been talking big bucks. Philip pictured him sitting there with the dollar signs flashing up in front of his pale narrow eyes.

It was perceptibly gloomier by half past six. Philip snatched up the phone and dialled Harry's number.

"That Foster?"

"Harry Foster speak——"

"Irving Salzenheim here" (a very aggressive Jewish Ahab). "Why didn't you tell me Tufnell was a faggot?"

"I beg your pardon, Mr. Salz——"

"A faggot, you ass-hole, a pansy, nancy-boy, ass-bandit, whatever you call them in Limey queerspeak——"

"Mr. Salzenheim, I'm scandalized, but even if it were true, what difference——"

"What difference? The ass-hole asks what difference! Jesus H Mohammed, you been living in a time-warp? There's a hot love scene between our chief air stewardess and this detective inspector guy, and actresses won't work with goddamn *queers*! We've got Bettina McMalinowski on contract from Columbia; if I tell her she's gotta smooch with a faggot she'll go apeshit——"

"This is ridiculous, Mr.——"

"Ridiculous, huh? Don't you know you can catch AIDS from breathing down the telephone?"

"That's nonsense!"

"Aw, for Chrissake, Foster, don't ever dream of pulling a fast one on me again!"

"But Mr. Salz——"

Philip slammed down the receiver. He felt exhausted, unfortunately the most enjoyable performances were always the most tiring. Philip got out of the kiosk and resumed his position under the tree. It was twenty-five to seven.

Five minutes later Harry reappeared on his front door. For a few moments he peered at the unremitting rain, then he pulled up a grey pointed hood and set off at a slouching pace into the wind and the wet, looking for all the world like an Olympic pixie.

Philip followed at a safe distance. By the time he got to the pond, Harry was out of sight. Now Philip had to wait patiently, hoping that having thrown Harry's routine out of sync would make no difference. Looking at the foulness of the weather, Philip knew he'd never again get a chance as good as this. He sat down on his chosen bench and uncoiled his ball of piano wire.

A half-hour passed. It was all but dark now and only half of the streetlamps seemed to be working. Out of the shadows of the heath loomed a grey running figure.

A stream of cars flowed up from Heath Street, four in a row, then two more fifty yards behind. Harry stood trotting on the spot, a hand held up to protect his eyes from the glare of headlamps, watching for a gap in the traffic. At last he lurched across, heading for the pond and his farewell circuit.

A blue Jaguar cruised slowly out of Lower Terrace. It swung lazily round the far side of the pond, almost keeping pace with the jogging man. From where he sat,

Philip could hear Harry's agonized breathing over the purr of the engine.

Harry rounded the apex of the triangular pool, he was running down the back straight. The Jaguar accelerated suddenly and disappeared down North End Way. It was dark, it was deserted. Harry was ten yards away.

There was no sound above the pounding of feet and the gasping for breath. Harry was five yards away.

Philip got up and staggered towards him, arms outstretched.

"Spare a bob for an old soldier, guv!"

In the quarter light, Philip saw a spasm of fury jerk across the already contorted face. Harry swerved away, missing Philip by a fraction, cutting in on the narrow strip of concrete between the bench and the water's edge. Philip tensed.

Suddenly Harry seemed to kick his heels three feet in the air. His whole body hung horizontally for a moment and then he fell flat on his face.

Philip sprang towards him. He could still hear the piano wire humming as he laid a hand on Harry's shoulder.

"You all right, guv?"

He didn't sound all right. He was wheezing like a bellows and his arms hung limply under him. Philip found his grip, one hand on his collar, the other round his waist.

"C'mon, mate, geddup!"

Half-dazed, Harry made a token effort. Philip felt him push up weakly from his knees. Philip leaned in close and whispered in his ear,

"Say goodbye, you bastard . . ."

He jerked him up, then down, stabbing his knee into the pit of Harry's stomach. He heard the whoosh of air, the retching groan. He dragged him two feet across the concrete.

He plunged Harry's head into the pond.

The water was freezing, the cold shock almost forced him to let go. The back of Harry's head broke the surface.

Even as he forced him down again, Philip marvelled at the strength still left in him. Though he was completely knackered, the upwards pressure was enormous, the hands that snatched at Philip's arms closed like vices. Philip gritted his teeth and pushed down. The legs twitched, the buttocks rose and fell in sexual parody. And then there were no more bubbles breaking the surface and the body was still. Philip sat on Harry's back, sweating and breathing heavily. It had taken about twenty seconds in all to drown Harry. He was mildly surprised. He'd have thought it would take longer. He looked around.

It was still dark, it was still deserted.

He took out his Swiss army penknife and cut through the two ends of piano wire, one tied to the bench, the other to a rusty iron link on the lip of the pond. The evidence tucked away in his pocket, he grabbed Harry round the waist and pushed him a little farther into the water. He left him half in and half out, the legs splayed on the bank, the head and torso submerged.

Philip got up and ran to the top of Heath Street.

A car came up the hill towards him. He remembered himself just in time, slewed to a shuffling walk and bent himself double with decrepitude. He stopped as the car disappeared. He waited half a minute, dreading the sound of brakes screeching and doors slamming. But there were none of those sounds.

A man was walking his dog up the pavement towards

him, one hand on the leash, the other holding up an umbrella. Philip carried on down. The Alsatian growled at him suspiciously and the man glanced at him with faint distaste. As they walked up towards the pond, Philip pushed on down the hill as fast as he could go.

He passed a pub where he had frequently stopped to drink. God, he was parched, what wouldn't he have given for a pint and chaser! He stood for a moment savouring the idea. And then he thought of the Alsatian sniffing at his ex-agent's corpse. He carried on.

He got into the station, found the stub of his return ticket and stood waiting for the lift. The others in the queue edged away automatically. The lift came whirring up and big black hands threw open the steel doors.

"Tickets, please!" boomed the lift man, a massive grey-haired West Indian who wore a permanent shark's tooth grin and a battered LT cap slanted at an impossible angle.

The queue shuffled forward. Behind him, on the other side of the ticket barrier, Philip heard boisterous young voices. He glanced over his shoulder.

Two boys and a girl were at the ticket office, jostling each other playfully and looking aggressively at passers-by. Besides the fact that one of the boys was tall and the other one short, there was nothing to distinguish between them: their quiffed black heads of hair and leather jackets were identical, they wore the same eye make-up and duplicate jewellery. For that matter, the girl looked almost exactly the same, the only difference being that she was fair. She glanced over and saw Philip looking at her.

"It's him! It's that dirty old bastard!"

Everyone in the station turned round. Philip looked about innocently, hoping to deflect public attention, but whichever way he glanced all eyes were fixed on him. It wasn't surprising really—there was no other candidate for the title "dirty old bastard."

"Let's fix the old git."

"Right!"

The two punk avengers came bounding towards him. Philip felt his knees shake.

"Stand clear of the doors, please!"

Casually the powerful black hand flipped shut the heavy grille. A flick of the switch and the machinery reluctantly stuttered back into life.

" 'Ere! Open up, Sambo!"

Two angry faces pressed up against the grille. Blithely the lift man turned away and opened up his *News of the World*.

"He flashed his cock at me!" came the furious girlish voice as three pairs of black-shot feet disappeared upwards out of sight. The lift man dropped his paper and grinned hugely at Philip.

"She should be so lucky!"

Passengers entering the lift from the northern line a few minutes later were surprised to see the attendant and a particularly revolting old tramp convulsed in hysterical laughter and clutching at each other for support.

TEN

For the third time in a minute Philip sneezed into his chocolate dessert.

"How disgusting . . ." drawled Hannah, spitting out a gobful of whipped cream over the tablecloth.

"I'm sorry, I've run out of tissues . . ." Philip wiped his nose with his napkin. Hannah rummaged in her bag. "You just can't have been taking care of yourself properly," she said, tossing over a packet of handy-andies. "You should try some of these . . ." She emptied the bag onto the table and picked out a dozen or so assorted pill bottles. "Christ, Hannah," he said, "do you want to turn me into a drug addict?" She snorted contemptuously. "Vitamins, darling, vitamins, never did anyone the slightest harm . . . and it's rude to read at table!"

She slapped his wrist mock-seriously. He recoiled with mock pain but did not relinquish the much-folded *Standard* plucked from the detritus on the table. He scanned its pages quickly.

"Page three column two," she said, casually sweeping up a handful of drugs and stimulants.

He opened the paper at page 3. He had been disappointed that morning to find that the story hadn't made any of the front pages. Of course the circumstances of Gordon's and Harry's deaths were quite different, but nonetheless the previous evening's events had been so extraordinary that they ought really to have merited more than passing attention. Instead, under the headline "Theatrical Agent in Bizarre Accident," a mere three paragraphs reported the case.

"*Telegraph* had more this morning," said Hannah. He looked at her expectantly and she went on, "There was a photograph of the pond."

"With Harry in it?"

"I didn't see any sign of him. Unless he was hiding under the Coke tin and the paper boat. No, it was just a mood shot. Rather like they used to have on the back page of the *Times,* you know—'Whitestone Pond, early evening, October.' "

"But no foreign body floating in it."

"You know, I've hardly found anyone who's expressed the least sympathy at Harry's demise. He was unpopular even by the standards of his breed. It all goes to reinforce my theory—"

"You must tell me about it sometime—"

"I will!"

The conversation snapped to a halt. Philip sneezed. "Bless me," he said. "Screw you," she said. She lit a cigarette and blew smoke in his face. His nostrils twitched. "Cow!" he said. She stuck out her tongue at him.

They had been getting at each other all evening. All evening since Hannah had made her entrance forty-five minutes late. Of course Philip was used to Hannah being late, but sometimes her complete unwillingness to apologize made his brains boil. He had buried his head in the menu and ignored her.

"Well, what shall we talk about?" she asked, breaking the silence.

"Phlebas the Phoenician," he responded coolly. He knew she hated it when he was being literary.

"Who's he, centre forward for Juventus?"

Philip could only look appalled. He looked pretty appalled anyway, what with the constant effort of screwing up his nose to try and pre-empt the next sneeze. "I got caught out in a shower yesterday," he had said lamely by way of explanation. "Well, you're a bloody idiot," she replied unsympathetically.

"If you'd told me you were ill I wouldn't have come," she said a little later. "Men! Really, get a little sniffle and you start behaving as if you've less than a week to live. Perhaps you have. Perhaps you're next. You can't open the paper these days without finding someone you know who's popped off. Mind you, he deserved what he got. Jogging and all forms of non-sexual physical activity should be banned forthwith by Act of Parliament."

"Couldn't have happened to a nicer chap," said Philip.

"I take it you won't be sending flowers . . ."

They ate their meal in a silence punctuated only by Philip's nasal eruptions and the constant fussing of Ben the waiter. Ben always went over the top when Hannah was around. He had seen her in a couple of semi-pornographic films during his adolescence and she had made a powerful impression on him. Sometimes when he bent down to take an order or serve them she would tousle his hair, or lick his ear, or stroke his bottom. Then his eyes would loll and his tongue would hang out like a frenzied dog's. The poor sod wasn't to know that random titillation was a by-product of Hannah's most pedestrian dealings with the opposite sex. Ben was under the misapprehension that he was being singularly honoured and Philip was reluctant to disabuse him. Of course no form of singularity featured in Hannah's sexual cosmology; she regarded going to bed with someone as just a way of saying hello. Philip had always wondered what was wrong with shaking hands.

He had not meant to be so short with her tonight. In fact, he had turned up at the restaurant full of affectionate feelings towards her. He still felt warmed by the snippet he'd overheard in the conservatory. Of course that was only as it should be, she knew better than anyone his true qualities as an actor and human being, but nonetheless that sort of altruism was rare in the theatre; so called friends would take the first opportunity to snipe at you behind your back. And Philip had to admit to himself that in that respect he had been in his time as guilty as anyone. What a terrible business to be in, he thought, rather taking himself by surprise, as if he'd never thought of it before—what a ghastly business, all those egos fighting it out for their own corner of quicksand! At least Hannah (rather curiously to those who didn't know her) seemed to be above all that; she just didn't appear to care. Of course she bitched and gossiped the whole time, but to her it was just a game, no jealousies consumed her, her psyche seemed indecently secure; whereas Philip felt sometimes as if a convocation of worms were gnawing at his guts. He finished his chocolate pudding rapt in melancholy thought.

He pushed his empty dish to one side and became aware that Hannah was talking to him. Obviously she had taken his attention for granted, and for all he knew, so inward had his thoughts been turned, she might have been talking to him for ages. He stared at her blankly.

"What are you talking about?" he asked suddenly, not meaning to sound rude, but genuinely bemused.

"My theory that Harry's death wasn't an accident . . ."

"You mean he committed suicide? Threw himself over, knocked himself out and then fell in with his last conscious impulse? Sherlock Holmes, eat your heart out!"

"God, you're in a bad mood!"

"I need a drink."

"Make it a parakeet!"

"A what?"

She sat fuming while Ben brought over a brandy. Ben remained hovering over the table, grinning rather stupidly, no doubt waiting for Hannah to goose him. Philip looked at him pointedly. "That's all, thank you," he said crisply. Ben raised an eyebrow and flounced off with undisguised disappointment. Philip took a generous mouthful of brandy. Hannah took out her powder compact and began dabbing at her face.

"That nice policeman was very interested in my theory," she said offhandedly.

"Why do you keep going on about this bloody theory? What policeman?"

"Superintendent Turnbull of Scotland Yard. My theory that Harry Foster was murdered."

Philip spluttered and spouted brandy and saliva over the tablecloth. He clutched at his napkin and covered his face hurriedly. "At-choo," he said weakly. He was aware that he had reddened noticeably. He was racked by a sudden fit of coughing.

"Are you sure you've only got a cold? I think it might be lung cancer."

Philip cleared his throat. When he judged that he had recovered his voice sufficiently he asked, "How did you come to be talking to Superintendent Turnbull?"

"He came to Owen's office this morning," she said matter-of-factly. And what were you doing in Owen's office? he wanted to ask, but checked himself. He just sat staring at her expectantly. With a show of nonchalance she continued, "He came to see Owen because there was a message from Owen on Harry's answerphone. He thought that Owen could help establish the time of death. Then we got chatting and I said it really wouldn't surprise me to find out that someone had pushed him in . . ."

"Who, for instance?"

"Anyone . . . you, for instance!"

Philip became aware of the hairs on the nape of his neck standing up one by one. He felt his ears burning, melting and dripping flesh onto his shoulders. His eyeballs had both popped out and were hanging on stalks down his cheeks. His tongue, like an outsized feather boa, had curled up on itself and was thrusting forcibly down his oesophagus. He didn't feel one hundred percent. Hannah, for reasons best known to herself, had decided to ignore these violent manifestations of physical disintegration and was carrying on as if nothing had happened.

"Well, you or practically anyone. I mean, doesn't it strike you as absurd that someone should just trip over and fall into a conveniently placed pond? It certainly struck the Inspector as suspicious. I know it was wet and slippery, but what if someone had, you know, helped Harry on his way? He wasn't short of enemies. London is full of people—like you—who bore him a grudge, and while, okay, I grant you that's hardly grounds to commit murder, but well, there are people I've often thought I wouldn't rule out doing in, probably you've felt the same, and if ever there was anyone of whom you'd think, 'well, he'd better watch his step or he'll end up getting it in the neck,' that person was our Harry. You know, he wasn't paranoid or anything, but he happened to tell Owen only the day before that he thought someone was following him. He was embarrassed talking about it, he wasn't the sort to bring up something like that, but he told Owen he'd sort of had this feeling that he was being watched, like some sixth-sense thing, but of course Owen just laughed at him and thought no more about it. And then of course there's the business of that old tramp . . ."

Philip's stomach had risen in a gaseous lump and was trying to force its way up through his teeth. Simultaneously his feet had expanded to three times their normal size and were about to combust spontaneously.

". . . you know, that old tramp they're anxious to interview, there was something about it in one of the papers, I don't know which, anyway the chap whose dog found the body said he'd passed this old codger coming down from the pond who must have been there about the time Harry fell in and as it happens one of the things Harry had told Owen was that some smelly old git had taken to hanging round his house at weekends and demanding money. Now is that a coincidence or is it only a coincidence? I think it's pretty weird and the Inspector thinks so too. Jesus, *I'd* have seriously considered murdering Harry if he'd done to me what he'd done to you; I mean I couldn't have blamed you! And

there are loads of people around who Harry shat on.
Come on, I bet if you're honest with yourself you wish
you had done it!"

Philip sat wondering how long it would take her to
notice that he had just turned physically inside out.

"I could do with another drink. I don't know about
you, darling!"

Somehow Philip retained enough control over his
limbs to cock a beckoning finger towards Ben. Hannah
gaily ordered a Cointreau; Philip just about managed to
point at his brandy glass.

"Well, what do you think?" demanded Hannah.

"Y-e-s . . ."

"Yes what?"

Philip cleared his throat. It was difficult to make in-
telligible speech when your teeth were chattering like a
pneumatic drill. He concentrated very hard. "Yes, I wish
I had pushed him in . . ."

Hannah shrieked with laughter. Ben, infected by her
delirium, himself began to giggle and spilt most of the
drinks over the table. Hannah squeezed the top of his
thigh admonishingly. Ben almost collapsed in unbearable ecstasy.

Philip started laughing. He was still laughing long
after the other two had stopped and he knew that he
would be laughing for quite some time. First the lip
started twitching, then both cheeks went at it like vibrat-
ing jelly moulds. The madness crept down through his
neck and set his shoulders in motion, pumping up and
down so vigorously as to give the impression that he was
contemplating flight. A moment later and his belly was
engaged in a desperate rumba. Both feet were already
tap-dancing on a bed of nails. Other parts of his body
had simply shaken themselves free of all sensation.

He became aware that Hannah was looking at him

with an expression of some concern. Seeing her comically pained look via the veil of tears through which all vision was now diffused en route to his brain did nothing to lessen his diaphragmatic anguish. In fact, the more worried she looked, the more he laughed. His ribs were aching horribly. He noticed between bouts of laughter that he had developed hiccups. Ben had noticed too and was gently patting his back. Ben said in his ear, "I think you should try drinking a glass of water upside down." Philip had never heard anything funnier in his life. He knew that he was completely incapable of drinking anything the right way up. Ben actually waved a glass of water under his nose. Philip could only point at it feebly and attempt to wave it away. Ben's failure to understand only made it worse. Philip felt his thighs buckle beneath him and he slipped onto the floor.

Hannah emptied the glass of water over his head. The shock made him sit up. Suddenly he stopped laughing and felt himself turn green.

"Aaargh!" he said.

Some apoplexed semblance of sense and motion had returned. He picked himself up, tottered for a moment, then bolted for the bog.

Five minutes later he lifted his head out of the lavatory bowl. He had always hated being sick. He had known many people who could happily drink themselves to the point of excess, throw up and then think nothing more of it. Roman behaviour. The thought of it disgusted him. He felt humiliated kneeling in the tiny cramped closet, helpless while his insides emptied automatically. At least he was a little calmer now. The physical horror was over, he had only to endure the shame. He rinsed out his mouth and cleaned himself up as best he could with the standard restaurant sliver of green soap that looked exactly like a plastic credit card. He faced himself unsteadily in the mirror.

"Right bloody fool you've made of yourself, haven't you. Like an ingénue succumbing to nerves. It just won't do, won't do . . . what do you think'll happen when Inspector Plod pays another call? Might as well have your confession signed and sealed . . ."

He felt angry with himself. He punched his face in the mirror lightly, but not lightly enough—his knuckles stung. He took three deep breaths, concentrated on appearing calm, and returned upstairs.

Hannah had gone, which both added to his humiliation and made him feel relieved. Ben came up anxiously, unable quite to conceal his embarrassment. Philip became aware that a lot of people in the restaurant were looking at him. He patted Ben's shoulder and whispered an apology. Ben shrugged, he began to say there was no need for—but Philip cut him off. Every moment he stayed made him feel worse. He said he'd better go at once, he wasn't well. Ben would please put the meal on his tab . . .

He found a taxi easily and was home in twenty minutes. He made himself a Bournvita, took two aspirin and went to bed. He stayed in bed for three days.

On the third day the phone rang incessantly. It had rung occasionally on the two previous days and he had just ignored it. It had seemed like too great an effort even to go into the living room and switch on the machine. He only got out of bed to visit the bathroom or kitchen, and that very rarely. He enjoyed the stale warmth of the bed, the darkness of the curtained room. He had lost all sense of time; he only realized later that he had been there three days.

At last he had to pick up the phone. He knew from the persistent ringing that the matter must be urgent and that he would get no peace until he answered it. He stood in the living room in his dressing gown staring out through a crack in the curtains talking to John Quennell. He muttered something incoherent in answer to his agent's anxious questions.

"Are you feeling all right?" Quennell asked.

"Yes, I've had a flu bug or something, but I'm fine . . ."

"Thank God for that! Tom de Vere wants to see you this afternoon, four o'clock, TV Centre. You'd better be there, Philip . . ."

"What's the time now?"

"Quarter to two. You haven't got long!"

"No. Thanks, John."

He put the phone down.

He sat in his armchair and stared blankly at the ceiling for a minute or more. He noticed that there was a record, by now dust-covered, on the turntable. He reached out and turned on the machinery. The Ninth Symphony came on.

He thought about Harry Foster. Specifically he thought about holding his head under the water, about Harry's lungs filling with that water.

He felt uneasy. Was this guilt? He almost hoped it was, he found his own cold-bloodedness slightly unnerving. He remembered reading that Himmler had been kind to animals and good with children. If you'd met Himmler at a drinks party, probably you'd have thought he was a perfectly pleasant, ordinary man. How could someone who liked stroking spaniels' tummies pull the switch in the gas chambers? How could any normal human being batter another's brains out and then calmly hold a man's head under water without flinching? He recalled that Dr. Crippen had been affable and well liked. That set Philip thinking. He had played Iago in York many years ago. It hadn't been a very happy experience, he had spent the whole time arguing with the director. "Not evil enough, not evil enough," the director had kept saying, "you're a villain, not a bloody Sunday-school teacher!" "What do you want me to do then?" Phillip would ask. "Roll my eyes and laugh maniacally?" The director hadn't seen anything wrong in that. He'd given Philip an all-black costume and a diabolic forked beard. He'd also tried to get him to walk with a twisted limp and wondered about giving him a hump. Philip had won those particular arguments, but he'd been very unhappy with the finished product, a compromise Iago, so torn between extremes of character as to be almost characterless. The experience had always rankled with Philip because it had been a waste of one of the greatest Shakespearian parts. Surely it was so much more effective to play against type, to score one's palpable hits by delicate contrapuntal arrangements rather than bangings and crashings of the full symphonic effect. That was in any case Philip's natural style; he had not been nor ever would be an epic actor—nor was Iago an epic part. Othello, on the other hand—now that would stretch him!

The music had stopped. He realized with a start that it was gone half past two and he didn't have long before his interview. He ordered a taxi and dived into the shower.

He just made it to Television Centre on time. Naturally interviews were running late, but Philip was relieved nonetheless to get there on the dot—he was jealous of his reputation for punctuality. Many actors who were habitually out of work grew sloppy about time-keeping. Philip knew that the self-imposition of routine helped maintain a disciplined frame of mind. In view of his three-day lapse it was necessary to reimpose it at once.

Again Eleanor came down personally to escort him up. She looked eager and excited. "They've been playing silly buggers here for weeks," she explained. "Of course there's a financial tie-up with the States and the silliest casting ideas have been floating around. Everyone from Mel Gibson to E.T. Some idiot in New York wasted a whole week by insisting that we get Marlon Brando to do a cameo of Lord Burleigh. Poor Tom was reduced to tears. He offered to resign twice, but the brass kept leaning on him and demanded that he stay, thank God! So it just got to a point where Tom said, 'All right, I'll do it, but only if you get these jokers off my back and give me a free hand.' And amazingly enough, they did. He's got carte blanche, though he knows his will be the first head to roll . . ."

"So what you're saying is he has the go-ahead to cast an unknown?"

"Yes—amazing but true!"

Eleanor left him outside Tom's temporary office. He stood for a moment summoning up his concentration and his courage, then knocked and went in.

There were two men in the room besides Tom. One was the writer from Owen's party, whose name Philip had forgotten. He was introduced as Paddy Elting, the script-writer. On Tom's left was a bald, corpulent red-faced man of about fifty, expensively dressed and wearing moreover a shrewd hard-edged look. He was the type one would go for if casting the mayor or some such sceptical executive in a New York cop show. Tom introduced him respectfully.

"This is Mr. Irving Salzenheim from New York."

"Good God!" Philip was unable to restrain himself. Instantly he was covered in confusion. Mr. Salzenheim looked surprised. "Er, sorry it's just that I was . . ." (I was what, for Christ's sake?) ". . . er I was talking with one of your employees only the other night . . ."

"Really?" His voice was surprisingly light in texture, not a bit like Philip's own impersonation. "Which one?"

"Theodora Babbett." (Oh God, why did I say that!?)

"Rabbit? I don't think I've ever employed anyone called Rabbit."

"I think he said Babbitt," cut in Tom, "as in Sinclair Lewis."

Mr. Salzenheim glared at him suspiciously. "I remember some lion. Don't recall anything about rabbits."

"That was C.S. Lewis," said Paddy Elting.

"I think we may be wandering from the point," said Tom.

"Too right!" declared Mr. Salzenheim emphatically, giving each of them an alarmed steely-eyed look as if to say, "No wonder you ass-holes lost an empire."

Tom said, "Mr. Salzenheim is our co-producer, he's here in an advisory capacity. This is a full-blooded Anglo-American co-production. After all, Raleigh did found Virginia, and, as we all know, was responsible for the introduction of tobacco into the Old World."

"Not to mention potatoes," mentioned Paddy Elting.

"Well, we haven't concentrated overmuch on potatoes," said Tom, "there didn't seem an awful lot to say about potatoes. But Paddy's written a tobacco scene in the third episode."

"Yes, it was rather hard," chuckled Paddy. "I couldn't get that Bob Newhart monologue out of my head, you know, the joke phone call from London: 'I hate to tell you this, Walt, but come fall we're kind of up to our necks in leaves in England!' "

They laughed. Except for Mr. Salzenheim, who frowned. "I wonder if Newhart's available," he muttered. Tom carried on, "I don't know if Eleanor told you, but I've been given a free hand in casting. I'm going to be quite frank with you: I've drawn up a short list of four and you're one of them. All of you are good, widely experienced, and, if I can say so without disrespect, not known, but I don't consider that a disadvantage. On the contrary, I'm anxious to avoid the 'Oh look, it's Mr. Spock without the ears syndrome,' if you know what I mean. Mr. Salzenheim is still a bit dubious, but I rather think that if the public see an actor who's known for a particular role, they'll say, 'Oh look, it's so-and-so in a ruff.' Of course, if you get this, you'll probably be ever after so-and-so *without* a ruff, but let's hope that the project will be good enough to make that worthwhile. Also it does require you to age up and down considerably, so I won't be making it easy for anyone to typecast you. Anyway, the point of all this is not to hear me talking. Let's read something and give Mr. Salzenheim and Paddy a chance to hear you."

Three quarters of an hour later, Philip was sitting in the canteen taking deep draughts of sweet tea. Eleanor had insisted on buying him a packet of biscuits, but he felt too queasy to eat. Being an actor was ruinous to the digestive system. Eleanor looked at him sympathetically. She said, "You were in there longer than the others. I think that's a good sign."

"Who do you think's the main opposition?"

"Difficult to say. Tom liked Paul Hammond. I gather Dick Jones read well but looks a bit boyish."

Philip frowned. He rather liked Paul Hammond too, both as an actor and a man. He didn't relish the idea of having to murder him. Dick Jones, on the other hand, was both a moron and a shit. As Philip recalled, he lived in one of those penthouse shoeboxes in the Barbican Centre; it shouldn't be too difficult to arrange for him to fall off his balcony.

Eleanor said in a near-whisper, "It's a good thing you weren't still with Harry Foster, isn't it?"

"No, it can't have been good for business."

Eleanor stifled a giggle. "Don't, I feel terrible . . . what a bizarre accident!"

"Hannah thinks he was pushed. Possibly by me," he added ironically.

"I don't know why you bother with that woman," snapped Eleanor abruptly. "I don't think that's very funny." Philip looked at her with an air of mild surprise: it was all right to giggle at his crack about death being bad for business, but to suggest that he had had a hand in it was unacceptable. How curious were the limits of humour and good taste! He leaned forward and said in a very low voice, "To tell you the truth, dear, I wish I had done him in . . ."

"What an absurd notion!" she said, still rather offended. "You couldn't harm a fly."

Philip smiled gently. I suppose, he thought, that friends of Jack the Ripper had thought that he couldn't have harmed a fly either. As a matter of fact, Philip couldn't have hurt a fly: he had never enjoyed boyish pursuits such as tearing the wings off insects or asphyxiating them in milk bottles. He had always considered himself a bit squeamish; he didn't even like gory movies. (His playmates at school had mocked him for being girlish—which meant bookish and non-physical.) But life was not like in the pictures. It was much easier to kill a man than ever he would have thought; why, as easy as shedding a bluebottle's wings . . .

That evening Philip passed in quiet contemplation. Staring at his face in the mirror before going to bed, he had an odd sense of looking at something quite obscure, although familiar. It wasn't that the features had in any way changed (that would be absurd); he didn't feel the approach of a Dorian Gray complex or anything like that. But he experienced a feeling of distance. He couldn't explain it. Nor did it much worry him. But he felt faintly curious.

He had been told that no casting decision would be taken before the weekend. He was somewhat surprised, therefore, when John Quennell rang up the next morning to tell him that he had been offered the part of Sir Walter Raleigh.

ELEVEN

On the third day of rehearsals Philip chanced to come across Dick Jones on his way to the canteen. Although they'd never liked each other—they'd once been rivals for the affection of the principal boy (i.e., girl) while playing the bailiff's men in pantomime—Dick seemed affable enough and managed to sound almost sincere in complimenting Philip on his good fortune. But when Philip had got to the cafeteria and was mulling over his script and a cup of ersatz coffee, a sudden thought struck him: he remembered idly contemplating Dick's murder. Now, Tom de Vere had told him that the final selection had been between Dick and himself, so it occurred to him in a blinding flash of paranoia that what he had considered doing to Dick, Dick could very well do to him. If something happened to him, Dick would still be the automatic replacement. Philip wondered if Dick realized that the final selection had been so close. He was quite renowned for his aggressive temper; undeniably he had some violence in him. Perhaps, thought Philip, he ought to take pre-emptive action and murder him anyway. Then again, he might be mistaken, in which case it would be a bit rough on Dick, as well as risky for himself. He'd just have to take care and not lean invitingly out of any four-storey windows, such as the one he found himself staring out of now.

Just as he was about to go back into rehearsal ten minutes later, a page accosted him with the news that there was a gentleman waiting to see him in the rest room down the corridor. Apparently it was important, the director had sent her urgently to find him. Philip muttered his thanks and wandered down to the rest room. He didn't think to inquire after the gentleman's identity, his mind was still occupied with Dick Jones. He had something of a shock then when the man turned out to be Superintendent Turnbull of Scotland Yard.

"I'm sorry to interrupt like this," said the Superintendent. "But it's important." He waved Philip into a chair. He himself remained standing, with his hands clasped behind like a schoolmaster. "I understand you're playing a major role, sir. My congratulations." Philip mumbled a specious thanks. The Superintendent went on cheerfully, "My wife's a great one for the acting, you know. Well, light-operatic stuff's really her line. She's very big in the local society down in Cheam. They're doing *HMS Pinafore* at Christmas. I tell you what, sir, would you mind if I troubled you for your autograph? She'd be tickled pink!" Philip took out his pen. "Her name's Madge, sir," said the Superintendent.

Philip wrote "To Madge with every wish for success in your forthcoming production. Break a leg! Philip

Fletcher." He tore the scrip out of his diary and handed it over. "I can't think that you came all this way just for that," he said.

The Superintendent smiled as he tucked the autograph away in his pocket. "You're quite right, sir. No, it's just that police work sometimes takes a little while. There have been a lot of leads to follow up and we've only just got round to you. I'd like to ask you some questions about your relationship with Mr. Harry Foster."

"If you will. There's not a lot to tell."

"You had a falling out with him, I understand. Is it fair to say that there wasn't any love lost between you?"

"Yes, but—sorry, could you tell me what you want to know? Harry's death was an accident, wasn't it?"

"The inquest returned an open verdict. Of course there's no evidence of foul play, but I find the accident theory unsatisfactory. I understand that Mr. Foster was not a popular man."

"You mean he was pushed?"

"You could say my mind's like the verdict—open."

"Well, I didn't push him, if that's what you mean."

The Superintendent roared with laughter. It had a hollow ring. "Now, now, sir, no one's saying you did, please don't get me wrong. All I'm trying to find out is if you think anyone might have had cause to wish harm to Mr. Foster."

"Quite a lot of people, I'd have thought. But murder's a pretty drastic step."

"I'm afraid that it seems rather more commonplace from a policeman's point of view. Familiarity breeds—not contempt, but a certain amount of necessary indifference. I'm afraid a CID man who buckled at the sight of a corpse wouldn't stay long in the job. Why, only last week I was reading the autopsy report on Mr. Gordon Wilde, and pretty gruesome reading it made too."

Philip was beginning to feel irritated. He faced a hard afternoon's work and all this was upsetting his concentration. At the same time he couldn't help but admire the Superintendent's technique: his delivery of his lines was immaculate, casual but carefully weighted. He knew exactly how to use inflections and pauses, and exactly when to meet his eye. Yet his manner was superficially so pleasant that it was impossible to tell whether he suspected anything or not. All in all, he would have made a worthy addition himself to the ranks of the Cheam light-operatic and dramatic society.

"Why do you mention Gordon?" asked Philip, matching his relaxed tone.

"It's on my mind at the moment. The trial comes up next month. I don't know if you'll be called as a witness."

"It would be very inconvenient just now."

"I'm afraid that the due process of law cannot take account of inconvenience." There was an abrupt note in the Superintendent's voice. He seemed to be aware of it and he overcompensated with a fatuous grin. "However, I don't think I need to detain you any longer now. Would you just tell me if you can think of anyone who might have borne Mr. Foster an especial grudge? Someone rather advanced in years, for instance?"

No, thought Philip, but I can think of a very good actor with a speciality line in old men. "I'm afraid you've stumped me there, Superintendent. You see, our paths have hardly crossed for years. I'm not au fait with Harry's circle."

"Well, if something does occur to you, perhaps you'd ring. You've got my number. Sorry for any trouble. Oh, and thanks very much for the autograph; it'll be much appreciated!"

The Superintendent put on his hat and made for the door. In his pale tan mac he looked a bit like Clouseau. Only without the bungling. It would be a good idea, thought Philip, to lie low for a while. Just as well he'd decided against nobbling Dick Jones.

Two weeks later they began filming. They were running to a strict budget and the schedule was tight. The first episode was due to be shown in the spring, and only three months had been allowed to get six episodes in the can. The work-load was very demanding and soon Philip was feeling permanently exhausted. Every morning he was up at five and rarely got to bed before eleven. Even when shooting finished early he always had lines to learn. Both Tom de Vere and his director Mark Gilbert were very exacting, and there were frequently many takes of the simplest shots. Early on, Philip suffered a crisis of confidence. Tom, who had once been an actor himself, saw him through it. He understood how even the best actors can suddenly lose their grip on themselves and doubt their ability. Only egomaniacs can perform without doubts, and what passes for supposed arrogance in many actors is really no more than insecurity. Tom made Philip sit through the first rushes and convinced him at last that he had nothing to worry about. Philip found this especially torturous, for he hated watching himself act. But the make-up was so skilful that it was as if he were watching someone else. As the script utilized flashback, they shot many of the later scenes first, so from the beginning he was doing his famous old man's act. He had so many condoms on his face that the make-up department referred to him as Sir Walter F—face. He took it in good part, he was pleased that he had a good working relationship with all the crew—no one could have accused him of starry behaviour! Still he was glad when the bulk of the later scenes were finished and he had only to endure each day the sticking on of a little beard and wig. He looked terribly dashing in costume and he found out that one of the make-up girls had a crush on him. On one of his rare days off he invited her out to dinner and ended up spending the night with her. A week later on location in Devon, he had one of Queen Elizabeth's waiting women on the bunk bed in his caravan. The discovery that he could be attractive to young women did more for his confidence than all the rushes in the world. Over a friendly pint one night Tom joked that he should take it easy: he didn't want to see his star shagged out when there were still six weeks to go. Philip told him good-naturedly to mind his own business and spent the night screwing the assistant designer. He sent a naughty sea-side postcard to Hannah full of suggestive ribaldry. Hannah phoned up Tom to ask what on earth had got into Philip.

It didn't really sink in that he was going to be famous until the *Radio Times* people turned up to take some stills and conduct a few interviews. Actually being asked the questions which he had been rehearsing to himself for twenty years took him by surprise. They wanted to know all sorts of trivial details; for instance, which make of car he owned. As he'd never owned a car, he found this a difficult one to answer. They persisted. He said a Golf Convertible, for no reason at all. The next thing they turned up at the hotel with a brand-new white Golf and made him pose at the steering wheel. It seemed that they were going to do a feature on the "Cars of the Stars." Apparently some lucky *Radio Times* reader would have the chance of winning a "Philip Fletcher Golf Convertible." All he or she had to do was answer a few questions and complete in less than ten words the phrase "I would have liked to own a car in the Elizabethan age because . . ." Because what? Because I'm a complete bloody idiot, Philip thought was the likely answer. He was bemused. Tom warned him that this was just the beginning. He was glad to immerse himself again in the insane hothouse atmosphere of filming.

He read in the cameraman's *Mirror* one day that Kit McCullers' trial had been adjourned. Talk of the trial had become all the rage on the set. An Irish alcoholic called Brendan O'Malley who happened to be in possession of an Equity card and was playing Gondomar (Spanish ambassador) had a book on it. He was offering ten to one for an acquittal and there were no takers. Peter Miles (Earl of Essex) had done weekly rep in Ayr with Kit McCullers and asseverated frequently that he was quite harmless, but not even he would put his money where his mouth was. Brendan had more luck with the sentences. Money was about evenly split between life imprisonment and a token five years for manslaughter on the grounds of diminished responsibility. When pressed, Philip offered ten ducats on the latter. Brendan said that he wouldn't take less than his share of the Spanish treasure fleet. Philip said that for a Spanish ambassador his behaviour was pretty outrageous. Vernon Smith (Sir Francis Drake) offered to stake all on the outcome of a game of bowls.

Over Christmas they flew out to Morocco, which was to double for the next fortnight (in unlikely partnership with South Devon) as the New World. Philip enjoyed the climate but didn't like the action scenes; he suffered from seasickness. Peter spent the whole time getting stoned on hash cakes. Brendan went off with a succession of Arab boys and caught a nasty dose. Fortunately he'd finished his part, so his committal to a nursing home didn't interrupt the schedule.

Back in England they spent three days filming the famous scene where Sir Walter lays down his cloak for Queen Bess to walk over. It took so long partly on account of the weather, which was seasonally bad (a risk Tom had lost a lot of sleep over when he'd decided to film in winter—at least it was good for the night shoots!) but also because Mary Denbigh had been cast as Elizabeth. Mary was a celebrated stage actress but had little experience of working with a camera. She was an RSC stalwart and bored everyone rigid with tales of Stratford. It quickly became apparent that she thought all this beneath her. Every time Mark tried to give her direction she froze over with aggrieved grandeur. Peter, who had been with her at Stratford, said that she'd been a pain in the arse there too. Mark wanted to sack her but had no way of making up the lost time. Eventually they got the twenty-second scene in the can. Tom raced through the rest of the script and cut out as much of her as he could.

The final run-in involved location shooting in London, particularly Hampton Court and the Tower. Mary kept interrupting important takes to demand why various of her lines had been cut. Tom confided to Philip that he would like to strangle her. Philip bet him that if he did, no one would ever find out it had been him, she had too many enemies. Tom laughed and said yes, it would be a case of the Harry Foster's. Philip was completely taken aback. "Sorry, I know that was a bit tasteless," said Tom. "I merely meant that there's that Scotland Yard Inspector going on about the possibility of murder and there are so many suspects he doesn't know where to start looking. Ha! I know, Philip; why don't you just come clean and make it easy on yourself!"

Philip creased up his nose as at a bad smell. Tom apologized for his warped sense of humour but carried on laughing.

Later that day Philip was surprised to come across an article in the *Guardian* devoted to Superintendent Turnbull. The tight-lipped smile in the accompanying photograph made Philip feel chill; he could sense the icy hand of coincidence gleefully waving two fingers at him. He raced through the column breathlessly. There was no mention of Harry Foster, nor even of Gordon Wilde. The article referred only to an outstanding record in criminal detection. But Superintendent Turnbull, it transpired, was about to take early retirement. Philip's heart leaped. Apparently he'd been lured into Civvy Street. Not only that, he'd actually written a book! Superintendent Turnbull was clearly an impressive man. His superiors were quoted as lamenting the sad loss to the force of such an outstanding officer. Outstanding indeed for the egregious Plod to string not merely two words but an entire book together! *Memoirs of Knacker* was expected on the bookshelves within the month.

Mightily relieved to discover that the bloodhound was forsaking the trail, Philip repaired to the location canteen for a cup of coffee, only to learn that Harry Foster was the topic of tea-time conversation. King James I (of England, VI of Scotland) was talking about Harry's missing diary to Ben Jonson, Will Shakespeare and assorted members of his court. He was saying that it really wouldn't surprise him if the diary could throw some light on Harry's unfortunate end. He had been on Harry's books and he said he'd seen this diary one day lying on his desk. It was about the size of the *Encyclopaedia Britannica*. He understood that the police had searched the office for it but in his opinion it was much more likely to be found in Hampstead. Apparently it contained such scandalous comments on everyone in the business from A to Z that Harry hadn't felt safe leaving it in the office. The court was in general agreement that it would make pretty juicy reading. Philip excused himself hurriedly and walked out, leaving his coffee unfinished.

They finished shooting one chilly February morning in a mock-up of the Old Palace Yard at Westminster. A crowd of Jacobean extras filled the foreground, ranged behind a line of soldiers. Drums rolled and a camera tracked slowly across the set, recording the last journey of old Sir Walter Raleigh. He came on, feeble but proud, his face carefully made up to the ravages of age and sickness. Sound recordists manoeuvred their microphones, but the background noise in the first part of the scene was to be faint; the images were to be accompanied by Philip's voice reading Raleigh's own poetry. Philip had already recorded the lines:

> Give me my scallop-shell of quiet,
> My staff of faith to walk upon,
> My scrip of joy, immortal diet,
> My bottle of salvation,
> My gown of glory, hope's true gage;
> And thus I'll take my pilgrimage.

Slowly he mounted the steps of the scaffold. He faced the crowd, the lights, the cameras. A boom microphone hovered above his head out of shot. There was silence as he made his farewell speech, asserting his loyalty to the crown, his love of his country and his unshakeable belief in God's mercy and justice. Hardened technicians looked at their feet; the script-girl brushed a tear from her cheek. Sir Walter gave a purse to the executioner and knelt to the block. He stretched out his arms and the axe came down. When the director shouted "Cut!" there was spontaneous applause.

"Got it in one!" declared Mark Gilbert. "It's a wrap!"

"Bloody brill, mate!" said the Earl of Arundel.

Everyone clustered round Philip as he got down from the scaffold. Tom de Vere shook his hand warmly and told him it was the most moving scene he'd witnessed in twenty-five years of television drama. Champagne corks popped.

Philip said to Tom, "I'm having a little party of my own on Sunday. I do hope you and June can come."

A glass was pressed into his hand. Already exhilarated, he felt the bubbly alcohol go straight to his head. He beamed hugely at the people queueing to shake his hand. Stars were dancing before his eyes.

TWELVE

Two girls called Annabel came in to do the catering for Philip's party. Annabel One was a short, plump energetic girl whose speciality was choux pastry. Annabel Two was a willowy blonde renowned for her salmon mousse. Both girls had infectious giggles and preposterous vowels, or should it have been preposterous giggles and infectious vowels? After half an hour's chat in the kitchen Philip found himself sounding just like them. He went into the living room feeling like a fugitive from the *Sloane Ranger Revue*.

The table and sideboard were packed with food and drink. Although the sofa and chairs had been pushed back to the walls, there was very little room for twenty-four people. These last few days Philip had begun to think for the first time that his flat was too cramped; he

felt the need to expand his living space. He could afford
it now, the cheques were rolling in. John Quennell was
already talking about massive buyout fees from commercials and that morning he'd biked round two scripts
from the ITV companies. Sometimes after an actor has
just established himself in the big league there's a lull
before the offers come in, but not in Philip's case.
Quennell had been a revelation. No doubt frightened by
the thought of losing his new star to one of the big
managements, he'd pulled out all stops on Philip's behalf. Yesterday he'd lunched and dined with two of the
most influential film-casting directors; tomorrow he had
an appointment with an American associate of Irving
Salzenheim. Salzenheim himself had been raving about
Philip in Hollywood, and there was talk of getting him
into *Dynasty* as Joan Collins' long-lost husband. It was
all a far cry from the days of provincial rep and worthy
supporting roles.

A few minutes after eight the guests began to arrive.
Predictably, Tom and his wife June were the first; as
predictably, Hannah came in last. Eleanor was heard to
mutter something about prima donnas needing to make
an entrance. The guest list was about evenly divided
between Philip's friends and people he and Quennell
thought might be useful to his career. The least welcome of these were Owen and Fanny Trethowan, whom
Philip hadn't wanted to invite at all. It was Hannah who
had insisted; she pointed out that Owen was still one of
the biggest producers in London. Philip said that
Owen's tastes were too commercial and he had no wish
to be involved in a sex comedy or a ghastly whodunnit.
Hannah got annoyed and said that he was misrepresent-
ing Owen. His reputation was quite upmarket these
days; in the last year alone, he'd put on a Eugene
O'Neill and a Restoration. She reminded him that a

decision still had to be made on bringing *The Seagull* into the West End, and if there was recasting he'd be a certainty to get Trigorin—she could promise him that! In any case he ought to invite them to his party, as she had taken him along to theirs back in September. He did remember, didn't he? Yes, he said, he remembered.

Owen bounced in full of jocularity and bullshit. "Always knew you'd get there in the end," he said, slapping Philip's back. "What's it like to be a star? Got much on your plate at the moment?"

"Spinach quiche and Waldorf salad," answered Philip. "I think the green stuff's a kind of cucumber terrine. Please help yourself."

When everyone, including Hannah, had assembled, Tom de Vere clapped his hands for silence and gave a carefully rehearsed impromptu speech. While waiting for Hannah he'd passed the time with a bottle of Krug and quickly he became over-emotional. He sounded like a one-man Oscar ceremony and the audience reaction was suitably theatrical. Hannah in particular shrieked like a banshee. Philip thanked Tom for his kind words and reddened slightly as his guests drank to his past and future success. He was glad when the toast had been drunk and the party could begin in earnest. He had decided that he was going to get well and truly plastered tonight. He circulated bearing champagne amongst the little knots of party-goers.

Mark Gilbert and Tom de Vere stood in a corner complaining about working for the BBC. Tom thought there was an invidiously high proportion of morons in the upper echelons of management, and Mark despised the increasing signs of commercialism, the endless daft game shows, sub-intellectual current-affairs programmes and low-sud soap masquerading as drama. Quality, not truth, was the first casualty in the current war, the ratings war. Tom said what did you expect with all this crap about the licence fee? He was sick of smart-aleck politicians trying to make a scapegoat of the Beeb, especially as they were always using television as their vehicle.

Eleanor and a fat little casting director politely listened to June de Vere cataloguing the exploits of her son on the Rugby field. He was in his first year at Oxford and already tipped as a future blue. He'd scored two tries in his first match, against Oriel. He was reading English and had spent the afternoon writing a terribly clever essay about Wordsworth. She hadn't understood a word of it! Eleanor said the "Lines on Westminster Bridge" was one of her favourite poems. June said that when she was a girl she'd learned twenty-six verses of "The Bridge" for a school prize. She thought she could remember some. She began to recite it. Eleanor and the casting lady tried to edge away.

Peter Miles sat in a corner rolling a joint. Brendan O'Malley was drinking a Guinness from the bottle and complaining to an audience that included Paddy Elting and Fanny Trethowan about always being typecast as a drunken Irishman. Like Gondomar? Philip inquired. Philip noticed that Fanny was looking a bit miserable. She sat not saying very much and knocking back large whiskies. He said, giving her a refill, "Sorry but I don't have Trivial Pursuit in the house!" She perked up slightly. "You should have said, I'd have brought mine." Philip moved on hurriedly to replenish other glasses.

At the centre of the largest group Hannah held forth noisily. Women were conspicuously absent from her circle. This evening she was looking very vampish. She was wearing a lot of eye make-up and rouge and not much else. Her dress was so low-cut, it seemed to start below her navel. Through the outrageous slit in the side she occasionally flashed a black stocking top and a portion of creamy thigh. The men didn't know where to look, and stood with their heads bobbing up and down like Yo-Yo freaks. Philip paused to stare lingeringly down her cleavage as he resupplied her with champagne. As she laughed, her breasts danced mesmerically. He began to drool. He dragged himself away with difficulty.

Eleanor slipped her hand into his. She beamed at him and at John Quennell. "You must be very proud of him, John," she said. Quennell nodded vigorously. Eleanor continued, "You must have been so glad to get Philip on your books."

"Poor old Harry," said Quennell. "I knew he'd made a mistake."

"Did you?" Philip was abrupt. Quennell looked surprised. "Did you really?—Answer honestly!"

"Really, I did, Scout's honour! Harry Foster was a fool."

And so are you, thought Philip, if you expect me to believe that. If you thought I was so damned good, why'd it take you so long to pull your finger out? It was Eleanor got me this job, darling Eleanor, pushing, cajoling, sticking my name under Tom's fat nose at every opportunity. "Thank you, Eleanor," he whispered gently, leaning over to kiss her cheek. She seemed faintly bewildered, but gratified. She looked quite attractive tonight. She'd never been an eye-catcher, but she was kind and loyal and, Philip thought, unsuited to middle-aged spinsterhood. She'd make a wonderful wife and mother. She was one of those people who are incomplete alone. There was something slightly sad about her.

"What's this about H. Foster?" boomed Brendan O'Malley, doing an uncannily accurate impersonation of a drunken Irishman. "Any bets? Last orders, please; even money he was pushed."

"Don't be idiotic," grumbled Philip.

"Ah, wait till the missing diary comes to light, then we'll see who's idiotic!"

Philip moved on briskly to dispense more champagne. He didn't want to talk about Harry Foster, it was all in the past, done and forgotten. He'd had the odd heart-stopping moment over it, but not for months. His memory of it seemed rather vague; Harry's death was rather less relevant than Sir Walter Raleigh's. Mention of it irritated Philip. There were more important things to think about. Where was Hannah?

He saw her at that moment leaning back against the drinks table. Owen was holding her loosely round the waist and whispering intimately in her ear. Their attitude was playful, they'd both had a lot to drink, but Philip felt a pang of jealousy. The air in the room was stale and tobacco smoke stung his eyes. He escaped into the clean atmosphere of the hall and headed for the kitchen.

In the corner of the kitchen Peter Miles was pressing himself up against Annabel Two. She was making little moaning noises as he kneaded her breasts. He was grunting like a hog. Philip backed out into the hall and reached for the bathroom door just as it was opened suddenly from the inside. Fanny Trethowan stumbled out, clutching an empty glass and a scrunched-up ball of toilet paper. Her eyes were red and her make-up was smudged. She burped violently and staggered past him. He jumped into the bathroom and locked the door firmly.

He leaned against the basin staring at himself in the mirror. His eyes had a hard, cold look, his features were set rigidly. He was tense with frustration. His recent successes with assorted nymphets had awakened semi-dormant urges. It was as if, long dammed up, a torrent of sexual desire had inundated his senses. His old life-style seemed pedestrian and inadequate, pathetic even. His wants could no longer be satisfied by quiet after-noons leafing through a book while listening to Mozart. He hadn't read a book in weeks. Even beloved Wagner offered no self-contained satisfaction; Tristan's desire for Isolde magnified his own, and the highest artistic passion was only a flaccid imitation of the real thing, on which it acted as a violent catalyst, doubled in spades. To hell with it, burn all the books! smash the records! slash the exquisite prints of Botticelli nudes! All he wanted was to screw the arse off Hannah.

Always Hannah. Age had not withered her, he felt the power of her sexual attraction like the tide rising to the moon. Though he might forget about her for weeks, months, years, eventually she recurred. Eternally re-curred. Perennial desire. What was it Socrates said on turning seventy? Something like—thank God that I am free at last of the raging demon. And he was only forty-five. Could he endure another two and a half decades of it and keep his sanity? Even on his deathbed the thought of her would probably stir his impotent glands. She would haunt him as strongly at the end as at the beginning.

In my beginning is my end.

Was that *East Coker* or *Murder in the Cathedral*? Much of it was the same anyway. He'd played Fourth Tempter on the radio once, a marvellous part, wonder-ful language. He adored Eliot. Perhaps it was his dry-ness that appealed to him, the tone that suggested desiccated sexuality, an affinity of souls. Desire past and present was unified in his perception. Hannah would always follow him into the rose garden.

Time the destroyer is time the preserver.

That was definitely *Four Quartets.* It was definitely *The Dry Salvages.* Dry Salvages. The Dry Salvages of Moist Desire.

> Two and two, necessarye coniunction,
> Holding eche other by the hand or the arm
> Which betokeneth concorde.

East Coker? West Coker?

> North, south, east and west, know't, it will let
> in and out the enemy with bag and baggage . . .
> when the wind blows southerly I know a hawk
> from a handsaw!

Through the mirror he saw reflections of his mind, and his mind was inflamed. It felt as if his blood were burning. Fire was the element of desire, for a woman's face Ilium had been burnt. Not all the water of the Aegean could douse his passion. For years he'd been treating it with a garden sprinkler. If it fell it was only to rise again, a turning wheel, a gaudy glowing Ferris wheel.

> We shall not cease from exploration
> And the end of all our exploring
> Will be to arrive where we started
> And know the place for the first time . . .

"Philip, look at yourself."
"I'm looking."

"You've changed."

"I am in blood steep'd in so far that to return were as tedious as to go o'er."

"The king is dead. Long live the king. The old one was a weakly prince anyway. From the dowdy chrysalis a butterfly is born."

"A butterfly born from a moth, as a swan from a duckling. No more the moth. All my life I've flitted round the light and never dared to touch it. But I have cause and will and strength and means to do it. And I've had enough of infantile metaphors."

He swung open the door and strode out into the hall. He ignored the cheery greetings of Brendan and Paddy, who had been queueing for the bathroom. He heard Hannah's voice cutting through the general noise of the party. She was in the kitchen. He marched towards his siren.

Peter Miles was sitting on a chair with Annabel Two on his lap. Hannah was by the fridge emptying ice into a bowl. She laughed when she saw Philip.

"Why, darling, you've been ages. I thought you'd gone to take a bath!"

"The time for cold showers is over, Hannah."

He seized her by the wrist and all but pulled her off her feet. The ice cubes clattered like hailstones over the draining board. Before the last one had fallen he had dragged her out of the kitchen.

And pushed her into the bedroom. The wall shook as he slammed the door. As he turned the key in the lock she jumped back from him, her eyes wide with alarm.

"What do you want?"

"You."

He threw her down amongst the coats on the bed. She cried out but he stopped her mouth with his, forcing his tongue between her lips. Her hands pushed at his face but he brushed them away and pinioned her wrists under his left hand. With his right he clawed at her thighs. Knicker elastic snapped and the almost pointless scrap of lace fluttered into the air. She whimpered as he climbed on top of her.

Afterwards she lay crying softly into the pillow. He stood up and rearranged his clothes. Coats and jackets had been thrown all over the floor. He picked them up and dropped them back on the bed. A packet of cigarettes and a lighter fell out from one of the pockets. He pulled out a cigarette and lit it. He tasted nicotine for the first time in ten years. He sat on the bed and stroked Hannah's hair. She half-lifted her head. She was no longer crying. He offered her the cigarette. She took a deep drag and rolled over to lie on her back. She stared up at him.

"You realize that was technically rape?"

He shrugged. "I've committed worse crimes than that, you know."

He reached out a hand to touch her face. She turned her head to meet it and gently bit his finger. He bent down and brushed his nose against hers. They kissed. They heard voices outside in the hall. There was a knock on the door.

"Are you in there, Philip?" It was Tom's voice. "Time for us to be going, I'm afraid. Can we have our coats?"

"Tom."

"Yes, Philip?"

"Piss off, will you?"

THIRTEEN

February and March passed quickly. Initially Philip was glad of a break; the concentrated hard work of the previous months had exhausted him. But he had also grown accustomed to it and soon he itched for more. He marked time with a cameo role in a film for which he got special billing ("and with Philip Fletcher as Tony") and a lot of money. He turned down several similar parts. He was offered a commercial but decided to wait until after the release of the serial so that he could demand a bigger fee. Meanwhile he sat it out impatiently, waiting for the right script.

April came, breeding lilacs out of Philip's dead heart. Over Easter he took Hannah to Venice. They rode in a gondola, held hands on the Bridge of Sighs, made love in a four-posted bed. The bust of Canaletto

by the window trembled on its stand at the furious
creaking of the bed springs. Afterwards as they shared
Hannah's cigarette (Philip pretended that he'd given up
again), he asked if she remembered the time when he
had proposed to her. She looked at him coyly. They
stared into each other's eyes for a while, not blinking,
not moving, hardly even breathing. In the end what
made them break eye contact was the smell of the burning sheet—the cigarette had rolled off the ashtray and
was smouldering happily amongst the bedclothes. Nothing more was said on the subject for the while, but left
unsaid it had more force. The pauses between words,
the spaces in their lives tingled with electricity. Together, they oozed sensuality as a plant oozes oxygen.
He knew when he asked her again she would not laugh
at him, but the time did not seem quite ripe. Had the
cigarette not threatened dire combustion when it did,
who knew what might have happened; but the moment
had slipped through the net. It would recur, in good
time it would recur. Meantime they rode in gondolas
and held hands under a silver moon. And when they
went to bed they screwed like rabbits.

While they were away there was a screening of the
first episodes of *Sir Walter Raleigh* at the NFT as part of
a season of historical drama. Philip returned to plaudits
and a deluge of offers.

Mark Gilbert had been promised his first feature
and was going to film Conrad's *Victory* in the autumn.
He wanted Philip for Jones. When Philip heard that
Paddy Elting was writing the script, he accepted uncon-
ditionally. He reread the book avidly. Mark had already
flown out to Hollywood to cast about for a big box-
office fish to play Axel Heyst, but it was obvious to
Philip that Jones would be the showy role. Given a free
choice of parts, the sort of actor who leafs through a

script counting up the lines would plump unhesitatingly for Heyst, but Jones was the part with which to make an impression. It is a simple truth about acting—which the public all too often fails to realize—that it is far easier to portray evil than good. The greatest actors have stumbled at Othello; anyone with half an ear and an ounce of talent can do something eye-catching with Iago. And Jones was practically a Shakespearian study in evil: a vicious killer with the manners of an English gentleman, a "handsome but emaciated" misogynistic degenerate. On the printed page he exuded a deathly chill; on celluloid he would be Philip's guarantee of stardom.

Philip was already in demand. Not only professionally but socially. One morning Quennell phoned to say that the RSC had inquired after his availability. An hour later he rang back to say that a tabloid gossip columnist wanted to take him out to lunch. Grandly Philip consulted his diary and pronounced Wednesday free for a prandial interview.

He was slightly disappointed to discover that the appointed restaurant rated no more than mild approval in *Egon Ronay*. He was more than slightly irked to find that he had arrived first. He sat in a corner table by the window sipping a Perrier and consulting his watch at thirty-second intervals. When he ordered another Perrier, the journalist was already ten minutes late. Philip wondered how long he should give him. He decided on another ten minutes, but when twenty past came he did not quite have the courage to leave. He acknowledged ruefully to himself that as yet the hacks had all the cards stacked in their favour. He resolved that once he had achieved star status he would be chary about giving interviews and always meet on his own ground and terms.

At last the journalist arrived, puffy and red in the

face. He was a large-bellied, heavily built man of about
Philip's age, half-bald, contact-lensed and dressed in an
ill-fitting suit with ash on the sleeve and dandruff on the
collar. He squeezed Philip's hand between his pudgy
fingers, muttered an insincere apology and buried his
head in the menu, emerging for a moment to order a
large Scotch and light a cheap cigar. When the waiter
returned with his Scotch he ordered the most expensive
bottle of wine on the list, a dozen oysters and a lobster
thermidor. Philip's more modest order occasioned a
grunt.

"You lot usually stuff yourself when someone else is
paying," declared the journalist. His chuckle turned into
a cough as cigar smoke tickled his lungs.

Philip stared at him in frank disbelief. Fact is not
merely stranger than fiction, he thought, it's unreal. The
man opposite him would have been simply beyond the
brief of the most shameless caricaturist. Perhaps he
sensed what was in Philip's mind.

"Well, what did you expect?" he asked, pausing
briefly before slipping down his next oyster. "Nigel
Dempster?"

So far their conversation had been desultory. The
journalist took the end of the first course as his cue to
lower the tone.

"Supposed to make you randy!" he said, tapping an
empty oyster shell.

"Indeed," said Philip politely.

The journalist leaned in conspiratorially. "Don't
suppose you need much assistance in that department,
Phil. Birds must be chucking themselves at you . . ."

Philip's smile tightened into a horizontal slot. Fleet
Street's finest wheezed and lit another cigar.

"Are you married?" he asked.

Philip shook his head.

"That's my boy! Too much free crumpet about in your line, eh?"

Philip's horizontal slot curled downwards at the edges.

"You're not a poof, are you?"

"Certainly not!" said Philip, doing his best Edith Evans. "I am engaged to be married."

"Oh yeah?" The scribbler made a scribble in his notebook. "Who's the lucky lady, eh?"

"I think I'll keep that to myself for now," answered Philip primly.

The waiter appeared with the main course. For a few minutes the serious work of eating took precedence and the journalist stuffed his face enthusiastically with lobster. When he had scooped the shell clean of meat he snapped his fingers to order another bottle of wine and returned to the attack with a transparent display of reasonableness.

"You might as well tell me," he said. "I'll find out anyway. It'll make a good story, your getting hitched up."

Philip pushed away his half-finished meal. "Look, I thought I was here to discuss my work. Why don't you ask me about *Walter Raleigh*?"

"Ah, Phil!" The journalist extended his hands, palms outwards. "My readers don't want to hear about some berk in tights. It's the personal angle I'm after. Look, we're men of the world. A few words from me and you'll be a sex symbol. I can make you the next Dirty Den. Just tell me who you're screwing."

That had been it as far as Philip was concerned. He had declined a sweet and left before coffee could be ordered. He fumed in the back of the taxi all the way home. Hannah professed not to understand what he was making such a fuss about.

"What bloody business is it of his?" shouted Philip, stomping across the kitchen and thumping the fridge door for emphasis.

"Don't be such a prude, Philip," said Hannah drily, turning the page of her magazine.

"What do you mean, Hannah? What do you mean? Do you seriously think it's prudish not to want details of my sex life plastered all over some bloody tabloid rag? They'll be asking me to take my shirt off and pose with some topless tart next! Me! A serious artist! I'm not some second-rater from a ghastly soap opera, you know, I'm a classical Shakespearian actor!"

"Ballocks. Sit down before you have a hernia."

"Hannah!"

She carried on reading her magazine. He walked round purposefully to the other side of the table and leaned over it towards her, his weight on his clenched fists.

"Hannah, will you put down that magazine, please? I am talking to you."

"No, you're not, you're talking to yourself."

He snatched the magazine from her and threw it onto the floor.

"Look, Hannah, just because you've spent half your life trying to get into gossip columns, just because you'd prostitute your reputation for a line in the *Daily Mail* doesn't mean that I have to too!"

"You bloody hypocrite!" she screamed, rising to her feet. "You were over the bloody moon ten years ago, when I got you into William Hickey!"

"Yeah, and I was sick as a bloody parrot too when I read about all the bloody gigolos that followed me!"

"Philip, will you stop trying to tell me that just because I've slept around a bit I'm a whore!"

"A bit! When did you ever sleep around a bit? Lucrezia Borgia was a bloody nun compared to you!"

"Philip, I refuse to be baited." She walked towards the door. "You know perfectly well that I have given up casual sex in favour of serial monogamy, but—"

"What's that, one free screw with every packet of cornflakes?"

"Philip, I know you think you're very clever, but I'm not quite as stupid as you think. I am familiar with Freud, you know. It is perfectly obvious that your tantrums are the result of your fully justified concern about the length of your penis."

She turned smartly on her heels and slammed the kitchen door behind her. Despite himself, Philip had to admire her brilliant capacity for getting in the last word. After a moment's reflection he even permitted himself a smile. He went to fill the kettle.

At the sink he paused with his hand on the tap. He could hear faintly Hannah's voice through the door. Feeling curious, he put down the kettle and poked his head out into the hallway. Hannah was standing at the other end, her back to him, the phone stuck under her chin.

"I'll hold . . ." she drawled.

Philip stepped out into the hall. The sound of the kitchen door closing made Hannah turn. She glared at him malevolently.

"Yes?" she said into the phone, looking away. "Yes, it's Hannah Sheridan. I understand you wanted to know whom Philip Fletcher was screwing. Well, it's me."

Although he put tremendous effort into it, Philip was unable quite to manage the resounding crash Hannah's door slamming invariably achieved. Almost, it seemed, as if to taunt him, her exit through the front door a minute later made the house shake.

Later, in bed that night, they made it up to each other. Physical reconciliation with Hannah was always ecstatic, but already Philip was beginning to find their mutual remorse dulled by repetition. Kiss and make up was a facile formula; but it would be more sensible (he thought, while acknowledging his own share of responsibility) at least to make the attempt to take preventative rather than remedial action. Their constant bickering was tiring him out, and he always experienced a secret relief whenever Hannah went back to spend the night in Putney. They would have to do some serious talking about their relationship before long.

Thinking about the miraculous upturn in his career, Philip grew dreamy and philosophical. He began to plan his autobiography. Of course he would have to be rigorously selective in his choice of material, but that was standard; show-business biographies were almost always chiefly remarkable for what they excluded. But he considered that his own memoirs might serve a noble end—inspiration. Inspiration to others such as himself who had resigned themselves prematurely to failure, and inspiration to the young about to embark on the long, hard Thespian road . . . Researching through his old scrap-books one day, he alighted on the photograph of the Beaux' Strategem cast. Kit McCullers was standing in the middle of the second row looking very dashing in blue velvet coat and breeches. There was something curiously touching about the photograph, about all those bright, eager young faces. One or two of them he thought were doing very well. A lot of them had shown promise, including Kit McCullers. Philip had heard that the trial had been adjourned. Perhaps there'd be a good amateur dramatic society in Wormwood Scrubs. He tore out the photograph and threw it away.

Sir Walter Raleigh was due to begin screening at the

end of May. Tom de Vere wasn't happy about it, he wanted to wait and claim the prime autumn spot, but Philip was pleased. He wanted it to be shown as soon as possible, he wanted to be famous. He had decided to wait until his success was rubber-stamped before proposing to Hannah. Despite his first experience of Fleet Street he had a hankering to be married in the proverbial blaze of publicity. After all these years there was no need for a long engagement. They could marry in July to coincide with the end of the serial. The wedding photo was sure to make the front page of the papers.

He was informed that the transmission date for the first episode was May 25. At the beginning of the week he lay in an early morning bath running through his revised Desert Island discs. Hannah was crashing about in the kitchen. She'd made a token effort to curb her untidiness but not enough to soothe his nerves. They would definitely have to move into a big house as soon as they were married. Philip kept his voice down in the bath. He hadn't done much talking to himself of late, perhaps because there hadn't been the same old gaps in his life. All the same he still enjoyed occasionally being alone with his imagination. Now that Michael Parkinson had taken over, the Desert Island scenario would have to be reworked. The discs remained unchanged, but the conversation would be different. Mike would love him to steer their talk towards cricket. He swung the loofah over his head and eulogized Gordon Greenidge. Mike asked him about Hampshire's prospects for the season. Outside the phone was ringing.

"It's Quennell," said Hannah out in the hall.

Philip was annoyed at having his delightful conversation interrupted. "What's he want?" he asked irritably.

"The BBC want to know if you can appear on the *Terry Wogan Show* on Wednesday."

He leaped out of his bath like Archimedes. He thrust his dripping head out of the door.

"Well, do you?" drawled Hannah casually.

"Is the Pope religious?"

They had champagne for breakfast.

A little while later a researcher from the *Wogan Show* phoned to ask him out to lunch. He met her in town and she gave him a brief run-down of the sort of questions Terry would ask. It was all terribly amicable. She assured him that there was nothing to it, and his easygoing urbane style would be sure to go down well. He went home in high spirits and spent a pleasant afternoon listening to Radio 3.

He slept alone that night. Hannah had to go to a boring party in Richmond and Philip opted out. He was in a state of excitement and didn't turn out the light till after two. His mind had gone blank. He'd had countless conversations with Terry in the past, but now nothing at all came to him. Reality had shattered fantasy. He felt panic. What was he going to say? When at last he did get to sleep, it wasn't deep. He had a restless night.

He woke abruptly at seven o'clock. The sheets were soaked with sweat, his heart was beating furiously. He had had a nightmare.

"My first guest tonight," said Terry in the nightmare, "is an actor you may not have heard of but soon will. On Saturday night, when the first episode of the new historical drama *Sir Walter Raleigh* is screened, a star will be born. Ladies and gentlemen—Philip Fletcher!"

Applause. Bright lights. The camera lens zoomed in for a close-up.

"Now I have to tell you that I haven't been quite honest with you, Philip," said Terry, beaming. "We've got a little surprise or two for you tonight. A few friends of yours have dropped by and I know they're anxious to meet you. Ladies and gentlemen, would you give a warm hand to Mr. Gordon Wilde!"

Gordon came in to rapturous applause and sat down beside Terry.

Terry said, "You're looking a bit peaky tonight, Gordon."

Gordon wiped his blood-stained face with a sleeve. "Yes, make-up might at least have cleaned me up a bit!"

The audience howled with laughter.

"How are you, Philip?" asked Gordon.

"Never shake your gory locks at me!" shouted Philip.

"Hey, calm down!" said Terry. "I promise I won't put my hand on your knee again!"

The audience wet themselves.

"Thou canst not say I did it!" Philip screamed.

Gordon shrugged. "No, you've got me there, old chum. Afraid you've got clean away with that one."

"So there's no evidence that he murdered you?" asked Terry, who was now wearing a judge's wig.

"Not a sausage!" declared Gordon roundly, slapping Terry's knee.

"But wait a minute!" said Terry. "Here's our second mystery guest, just arrived from a quick circuit of Television Centre by the look of him!"

Harry Foster jogged through the audience wearing his grey track suit and carrying a volume of the *Encyclopaedia Britannica*. The upper half of his body was soaked.

"Been a change in the weather?" Terry asked.

Harry waved the laughing audience to silence. He sat down next to Gordon and looked at Philip. "Why didn't you say? I'd have brought my swimming trunks!"

"Silence in the court!" boomed Terry sternly, banging with his gavel on the podium that had appeared in front of him.

"I don't know what you're talking about!" cried Philip. "I've never seen these men before in my life!"

"You'll have to do better than that!" laughed Harry, opening up the *Encyclopaedia Britannica*. "It's written here in black and white. Shall I read you an extract?"

"It's inadmissible evidence!" Philip whimpered.

Harry ignored him. "Let's start here. October twenty-four. I was followed home again last night by an old man with an uncanny resemblance to Philip Fletcher's Firs, which of course I saw in Bristol twenty years ago. It's rather curious, today I could have sworn I saw Philip's Baron Tusenbach walking out of the newsagent in Dean Street."

"Let's put it to a vote," suggested Terry. "Audience, fingers on your buzzers!"

Philip faced the audience. They sat in an extension of the set from *Celebrity Squares* with a red and a white light in front of each of them. They were all wearing the hood of Sir Walter Raleigh's executioner.

"White for innocent, red for guilty!"

The red lights flashed in unison. From the front row appeared a line of ice-skating judges. They held up their placards showing a string of noughts.

Philip got up and ran to the back of the studio. The back wall disappeared and his feet slipped on an icy surface. The ice cracked and he was flailing in frozen water. He looked up and saw Superintendent Turnbull sitting on the edge of Whitestone Pond playing a grand piano. His smile turned to a frown as he struck a false note and a wire twanged.

"Over here!" came Harry Foster's voice, as he

tripped and fell. There was a mighty splash of water and Philip woke up.

Consciousness was a revelation of despair. He felt hemmed in, asphyxiated. His home imprisoned him, the four walls of the bedroom, the hot damp sheets imprisoned him. He threw off his duvet and dragged on his clothes. He ran out of the house, slamming the door shut after him. It was a bright, crisp morning. He stumbled down the street, gulping in fresh air like a drug. His mind was stale and befogged. His head ached.

He tramped aimlessly across Highbury Fields. A few early morning joggers were about; through the windows of the houses he saw people sitting down to breakfast. An old man in a donkey jacket was sweeping leaves from the pavement. Philip stopped and looked through the plate-glass windows of the swimming pool. A young girl flopped in at the deep end and a shower of water rose and fell. He turned away and walked on hurriedly.

At the tube station he stopped to buy a paper. He stood in the street racing through the pages. There was nothing about the trial. There was nothing abut Harry Foster's diary. No picture of Superintendent Turnbull holding up the evidence. Perhaps they were watching him now. Perhaps his phone was bugged. What if they broke in and searched the flat, would they find anything? Was there incriminating evidence at home?

He ran back to Highbury Grove. He was winded when he got there, he felt the effects of too many cigarettes in his lungs. All the same the first thing he did was to light a cigarette. He put the kettle on and sat down in the kitchen to think.

He took his coffee with him into the living room. He pulled his photograph album and scrap-books from the shelves and began to leaf through them. He tore out a picture of himself as Firs, and another as Tusenbach. He put a match to the photographs and watched them burn. He took his make-up box out of the cupboard and destroyed the old wigs and beards. The burning hair left a horrible smell. He sprayed an aerosol round the room and went into the kitchen to make more coffee. His clothes felt sweaty and uncomfortable. He ran a bath, washed, shaved and changed. He threw his old clothes into the laundry basket and took Firs' battered old pair of shoes and tatty costume out to the dustbin. He went back inside, opened all the windows and tidied up the house. He stripped the bed and put on fresh sheets. He Hoovered and dusted vigorously. Why, here's a spot! Fie! He swept and brushed and cleaned. Silver polish, brass polish, furniture polish, all was polished. The smell was not unpleasant. The perfume of Arabia.

At eleven o'clock he phoned Hannah. He was tired of household chores and had nothing to occupy his mind. He did not want to be alone.

"Come round," he said.

"I can't, darling. I'm going out to lunch."

"Please," he implored.

"I can't!"

"Come later."

"Is there something the matter?"

"I want to see you." He wanted to say that he'd like her to marry him. But not over the phone.

"I've got a busy day," she said. She was always claiming to have busy days. As far as Philip could make out, she spent a minimum of seventy-two hours a week in the hairdresser's.

"We'll go out to dinner."

"It's terribly awkward, darling. I've arranged something tonight."

"Well, cancel it!"

He realized he sounded desperate. He paused to try

and control himself. There was hesitation at the other end. At last she said, "I can't cancel it but I'll come round later. I can be with you by eleven."

"Then eleven it will have to be," he said grumpily and put down the phone.

He grabbed his coat and stormed out of the house. He couldn't think where to go, so he wandered back to the fields. He sat down on a bench and watched some children playing cricket. The batsman at the far end was an aggressive left-hander who kept hitting boundaries. The fielders ran with ever-decreasing enthusiasm to retrieve the ball.

"Today we're presenting a very special edition of Desert Island discs," he heard Michael Parkinson say. "We've been allowed into the maximum-security wing at the Scrubs to meet Philip Fletcher, well-known actor and murderer."

He couldn't be caught now, not now. He couldn't lose everything he'd fought so hard to gain. It was difficult to think clearly. He knew he was being paranoid, but he couldn't work out how much justification there was for his paranoia. There wasn't any evidence, was there? What about that damned diary; could there really be anything in it about him? And surely they'd have found it by now if they were going to? He remembered driving past Harry's house in a taxi a few weeks earlier. The "For Sale" sign had still been up, although there had been some legal wrangle over the estate. Owen Trethowan was the executor, he'd mentioned something or other about it at a dinner party. When the house was sold, perhaps the new owners would start knocking walls down (Hampstead residents usually did). They might discover the diary in a secret cavity. But surely the police had searched the place thoroughly—or had they only looked in the obvious places?

"This is all complete bloody nonsense," Philip muttered to himself. "They're not going to come up with anything now, not after six months. I bet it's just the police laying down a false scent to try and frighten me. Like in a detective story. Why me? They don't know I did it, no one knows . . ."

And yet
    . . . to be thus is nothing
But to be safely thus . . .

He stared vacantly across the fields. By now the lunch-time joggers were out, one was running through the cricket outfield towards him dressed in Harry Foster's shade of grey track suit.

"Wait a minute!"

Each night for two weekends he'd watched Harry's preparations for jogging. Each night he'd followed exactly the same routine. And each night Philip had been puzzled. He'd watched the windows light up all over the house as Harry went from room to room. First the landing light as Harry went upstairs. Then his bedroom where he changed and where he kept his equipment, the dumb-bells and exercise bicycle, on which he had a quick workout. Then he went upstairs for about five minutes to the small bedroom. Then he went into the bathroom and finally retraced his steps downstairs. The whole process took about twenty minutes.

What had he been doing in the small bedroom?

Surely not writing his diary . . . no, he'd go into this study for that. The police would have thought that. They'd have searched the whole house but they'd have concentrated on the study. But Philip had seen Harry's head through the window of the small bedroom. Invariably he had spent his five minutes there sitting down.

But why would he write his diary between his nightly limber and jog? Philip had observed his routine minutely; there had been no other regular time when he had sat down at a desk. And perhaps it wasn't such an illogical time to choose after all: he'd get warmed up, then give his pulse a few minutes to return to normal. He'd probably read that he should do that in the *Jogger's Manual.*

The more he thought about it, the more he became convinced that he was right. At the very least he knew that he would not be able to rest easy until he had checked it out. After two murders and a technical rape, housebreaking seemed a very minor crime to add to his list.

He looked at his watch. It was nearly one o'clock. He'd have to do it under the cover of darkness; it would have to be that night. Hannah had said that she wouldn't get to him until eleven, which meant half past at the earliest. If he broke in after eight, he'd have a couple of hours to look and still plenty of time to get back to Highbury. He walked home briskly.

He got out his make-up box and sat down at the bedroom table. A pity he'd burnt half his stock, but in any case it wouldn't be safe to adopt any of his regular disguises. He'd have to go as something new. He sorted through the grease-sticks and the tins of pancake. He came across relics from repertory productions of various thrillers. Perhaps he could go as Inspector Poirot, that would be ironical. No, he didn't have a suitable moustache. This was proving hard; he'd have to think of something entirely original . . .

His hand brushed over an unopened pancake tin. He read the label, "Negro No 1." He opened the tin and smeared a finger black. He studied his face in the mirror. His hair was dark enough, he'd conceal its Cauca-

sian texture under a hat. He'd have to be very clever
with the lips. Nothing he couldn't manage. His voice
rumbled in basso profundo:

"Farewell the tranquil mind; farewell content!
Farewell the plumèd troop and the big wars
That make ambition virtue! O, farewell . . ."

He watered the sponge and began to cover his face.
When the phone rang he only just remembered to
answer it as himself. It was the BBC. "We'll send a car
to pick you up at five o'clock tomorrow, Mr. Fletcher,"
said the girl. "Will that be all right, or would you like it
earlier?"
" 'Tis better as it is."
"Pardon?"
"Five o'clock's fine, thank you."
He'd almost forgotten about Terry. Perhaps that was
for the best; if he thought about it too much, he'd just
get nervous. Though normal stage fright rarely troubled
him, he had no idea how to appear as himself. He'd try
to put it from his mind and just react spontaneously
when it happened.
He returned to the table and applied the finishing
touches to his make-up.

FOURTEEN

Philip shambled with a rolling gait up the hill towards Harry's house. He wore an old green anorak with the nylon hood pulled up. In the darkness his features were invisible; the people he passed on the pavement probably didn't even notice the colour of his skin. He turned into Harry's street and stood between the telephone box and the tree watching the house. A man was walking his dog on the other side. Philip waited for him to pass.

He crossed the road quickly and opened the little gate into the front garden. A hinge creaked, but not loudly. He closed the gate after him and darted towards the side of the house. A little alley ran between Harry's and the next house. He manoeuvred his way past a dustbin and crept onto the patio at the back. He'd noticed a light on in the front of the next house, but at the back it was dark. He sidled along the rear wall feeling the windows. By the kitchen door he found a window to suit his purpose, small but just large enough to squeeze through, and consisting of a single pane of glass. He took out a little torch and checked the inside catches. There were two, one simple, the other a tough-looking burglar-proof lock. He had been expecting that.

He stood back and listened carefully for a full minute. He heard nothing. He pulled a half-brick out of his pocket and held it six inches from the window. He jabbed the brick into the middle of the glass.

Shards of glass crashed noisily at this feet. The noise of breaking was loud and sharp. But before the effect of the first blow was complete he struck again, knocking back the jagged pieces that remained. It was not an elegant break-in, but at least it had been quick. Only a few sharp edges remained. He poked them out with his Swiss army penknife. The way was clear.

Again he waited in silence. Again he heard nothing. It had all been so sudden that his hope was that if someone had heard, they'd think themselves mistaken. He waited to see if any neighbouring lights went on. None did. And no voices rose to challenge him out of the darkness. He climbed through the window.

He came through onto a table covered with glass. His gloves and clothes were thick, there was no danger of cutting himself, though he felt his anorak snag in several places as he pushed his torso through. It was a tight squeeze, but at last he found himself standing on the inside. He took out his torch and walked through the kitchen.

He stopped to glance out of the hall window. Another dog-walker was about, ambling carelessly down his side of the road. He was glad to see him pass so close by; if he had not heard the break-in, then it was unlikely anyone else had.

On tiptoes Philip made his way upstairs. He did not pause on the first floor—it didn't even seem worth checking the study—but pushed on at once to the second. He edged himself into the small bedroom and closed the door.

The room was sparsely furnished. There were a small bed, a table, a desk and a chair, with one bookshelf above. There was a closet containing one plastic coat hanger. Philip went to the desk and slid into Harry's chair. There were no drawers. The desk was bare except for a standard lamp and a china mug decorated with a portrait of the Princess of Wales, which contained a felt-tip pen, a Biro, a packet of paper clips and an elastic band. Philip ran his fingers along the wall above the desk, looking for secret cavities. Finding none, he bent down and felt the floorboards. They were all secure. He went to the closet and pushed about behind the coat hanger. Nothing. He returned to the desk.

He looked up at the row of books. There was one odd volume of *Spotlight* (Actresses A–K 1972–1973), two novels by Jeffrey Archer, a dictionary, the *Oxford Book of Quotations, Hollywood Wives,* the 1984 edition of *Contacts,* a gardening manual and a very large Bible bound in white leather. They all looked well thumbed, apart from the gardening manual. He removed the books one by one to feel the wall behind. Still no secret cavities.

The Bible was so heavy he needed two hands to lift it. After he had replaced it he sat staring blankly for a while, searching in vain for inspiration. He glanced out of the window and saw the telephone box on the other side of the street. He rummaged in his memory for clues. He came up with nothing new. Every night he had witnessed the same procedure: come in, turn on the light, sit at the desk for five minutes. That was it. He had not carried anything to the desk. If he had been writing in his diary, then it must lie within his reach at the chair. It must be . . . here. What else could he have been doing? Reading? What? Obviously not the gardening manual. Surely not a dictionary or an old volume of *Spotlight*. The Bible? Was it possible that he was a secret religious fanatic given over to regular sessions of holy meditation? If so, it was the best-kept secret in London. And yet, it had a well-used look. It didn't tie in with Harry at all. Intrigued, he took it down again.

He opened it and scanned the flyleaf with his torch. It was a sumptuous edition, illustrated with Rembrandt's religious paintings. At the bottom of the title page he saw printed in block capitals: THIS IS THE FAMILY BIBLE OF and underneath in faded violet ink: HENRY GEORGE FOSTER with spaces beneath for the names of his spouse and children. Of course the spaces were blank. Philip had a vision of Harry's mother lovingly inscribing it. Perhaps it had been a confirmation gift. There was no date. It struck Philip as rather pathetic. Little had poor Harry's mother known what an unholy brat her son would turn out to be!

Philip remembered seeing a rather fine Rembrandt in Amsterdam years ago. Was it the *Annunciation*? That rang a bell. Idly he flicked through the leaves till he got to the New Testament.

And there it was.

The Apocrypha, the Gospels and the Acts had all been neatly excised. Only the edges of the pages remained, enclosing a hollowed-out oblong, in which sat a black volume embossed with a single word in gold letters: DIARY

His hands trembled so violently he could hardly lift

it out. In his excitement he tore several pages of St. Matthew. He opened it and read:

My diary by H. Foster, aged 38.

19 August 1979: I feel absurdly self-conscious starting this diary, despoiling these crisp virgin sheets. That reminds me. Picked up a very tasty little number in the National foyer last night. Programme seller. Drama student. Went dewy-eyed when I told her I was an agent. Not *quite* a virgin, I admit, but deliciously gauche in bed. Had her in the all-fours position. She looked completely bemused. Big turn-on. Did it three times. Felt knackered this morning. Not good. I think she was called Sarah or Sandy or something. **

Philip flipped over a few pages. They were filled with Harry's neat, small handwriting. And they were filled exclusively with sex:

. . . December 12. Fantastic blow-job from Nikki! **** . . .
. . . February 24. Could only get it up once. Janet tight as a coin slot. Disappointing. * . . .
. . . March 17. Did it five times with Sharon. *5 times!* Felt great today. Exercise paying off. *****

And so on. Page after page of recorded gratification, compiled with the meticulous humourlessness of a Masters and Johnson report. Hundreds of women, steady relationships and one-night stands, rigorously catalogued and marked. At first Philip found it luridly compelling. By the time he got to 1981, he was disgusted. By

1982 he was bored. Briefly he checked July 1984, the
month when Harry had given him the boot, just to check
if he had been mentioned. There was nothing. As far as
Philip could tell, not a single man appeared in the book.
Philip read the last entry:

. . . September 18. Getting older! Must step up
fitness routine. No sex for three nights and still
feel shattered after Jenny! Worried about sore
patch on cock. Better go to Paddington and get it
checked. Second dose this year would be disastrous.
September 19.

He'd written that in, the next day's date, September
19, but he'd not lived to make the entry. Philip felt an
urge to make it for him:

September 19. Pushed into Whitestone Pond by
P. Fletcher. Drowned. No sex today.

So that was it.
There was nothing more to it. And all that fuss, all
that excruciation had been for nothing. For the self-
obsessed ramblings of Harry's adolescent brain. No
wonder Harry had been paranoid about anyone finding
it! What a shame it had eluded the police! Or perhaps it
hadn't . . . Philip sat back in the chair, rested his
elbows on the arms and pressed his fingers together. He
felt a frown settling on his forehead. This is absurd, he
thought. What am I doing pretending to be an amateur
cat burglar? If he, the amateur, had found the diary,
what about the police? Surely experts wouldn't have
been fooled by Harry's book-in-a-book technique? That
one was as old as the hills. He vividly remembered it

from a creaky old forties' thriller. Of course the police had found it. If they'd been looking. Was there any reason to suppose that they had been looking? Quite probably not . . . Many-tongued Rumour had driven him to this extreme; idle gossip, dressing-room chat. If the police had searched the house, it would only have been as part of a routine inquiry. There had never been a murder investigation. That had been in his head. In his dreams. A pity, in a way. Under the glare of a murder inquest a leak of the diary would have been inevitable.

A centre page pull-out special in the *News of the World* would have annihilated Harry's reputation once and for all. Philip wondered why he was still so keen on annihilating Harry's reputation. Was he so obsessed with revenge? Harry deserved annihilation. What on earth did women see in men like that? Some women's tastes were so odd. Harry was particularly repugnant. The diary proved it.

Of course it would have to be spiced up for serialization with some snappy headlines—the overwhelming impression Philip gleaned from the collected entries was of Harry's monumental colourlessness. It was almost incredible that so much concentrated sexual ecstasy could sound so dull. All those twee little stars and flat descriptive comments. It was about as exciting as reading a guidebook. Philip supposed that it wasn't really a book for reading but for dipping into. The deluxe edition should come with screw-in bedside table legs. And a foreword by some media celebrity.

Philip replaced the diary in the Bible and closed the heavy volume. A brass clip at the side secured the loose pages, double protection from idle prying eyes. He heaved it back onto the shelf. He could rest easy now. He would suffer no more qualms about Harry. He checked the time. It was a quarter past nine. He ought to be getting a move on. It would take a while to get all the make-up off, and you never knew, Hannah might be on time for once. Now all he had to do was have a quick rummage downstairs and leave the impression of a burglary. He'd just lift a few trinkets on the way out and dump them somewhere going home. It shouldn't take more than a few minutes.

He glanced out of the window. A big saloon car was just pulling up outside the house. The engine and lights were turned off and a fat little man got out. He walked round to the passenger door. I'll have to wait a minute till he goes, thought Philip. The driver opened the passenger door and glanced up towards the house. The light of a streetlamp caught briefly his upturned chin.

It was Owen Trethowan.

For precious seconds Philip stood frozen to the spot. His brain had seized. What in God's name was Owen doing here? A pair of woman's legs swung out of the passenger seat. He wasn't showing round a prospective purchaser, was he? He was executor, after all.

"Christ!"

Philip ran. He was half-way down the top flight of stairs when he remembered that he'd left his torch sitting on the desk. He tore back up frantically and stuffed it into his pocket. He ran down again, losing his balance at the first turn and bashing his hip against the banister. He leaped the last four steps and crashed onto the first-floor landing. He steadied himself against the wall and pushed off down the last flight of stairs.

A key turned in the front-door lock.

Philip stood transfixed between the third and the fourth stair. The door swung open and a pair of shoes scraped on the doormat.

"I'll just switch on the hall light if I can find it," said Owen.

The light came on and flooded up the stairs. For a moment only it touched on Philip's heels. He crouched out of sight on the landing. It all depended on what happened now . . .

Footsteps creaked on the stairs, Owen's heavy tread and a lighter one behind.

"I've brought some whisky. Got any cigarettes?" Owen asked.

"Uh-huh," came the reply.

Philip backed away down the landing. Two doors were behind him, both closed. He hesitated. Between the doors was a cupboard. He pulled it open frantically and tried to get in. It was dark, he couldn't see inside the tiny space, but he felt a boiler pipe and had to bite his lip as he banged his shin against something solid. He fell in, wedging his buttocks up against some kind of metal box and pulled the door shut as the landing light came on. He sat crunched like a sardine, his head in his shoulders, his feet bent back under his body while he clung for support to a metal pipe. He hardly dared breathe as footsteps came towards him. He could hardly breathe anyway.

He heard the door to his right open, and a moment later close again. The footsteps were behind him now. Lights were switched on and curtains drawn. He heard low murmurings and a woman's giggle. So that's it, he thought—you dirty bastard!

As quickly as he dared, Philip pushed open the cupboard door and uncoiled himself. He squeezed himself onto the landing like toothpaste out of a tube. He stood blinking in the light, gasping for breath. He glanced behind him and wondered how on earth he could have fitted in amongst the tangle of pipes, meters and switches. He pushed the cupboard door to. He took a step down the landing.

A door handle rattled. He spun around. The door through which Owen had gone was opening slowly. He heard Owen's voice.

"Yes, it's freezing, I'll switch the gas on so we can light the fire."

To Philip's right was the other closed door. He grabbed the knob, flung it open and jumped through on tiptoe, pressing it shut at once and flattening himself against it. He stood like a statue, amazed that he could hear Owen's heavy breathing above the furious beating of his heart.

Philip inched his body down the back of the door and put his weight on his knees. He sniffed disinfectant. He was in the bathroom. He reached out and felt the cold enamel of the bath, grasping it firmly for support. He twisted his neck and put his eye to the keyhole.

He saw the shiny bald patch of Owen's head at eye-level. For a horrible moment he thought Owen must be trying to peer through the same keyhole, then he realized that he was staring into the cupboard which Philip had just vacated. Philip's heart pounded a furious reprise. Owen was muttering to himself, an almost inaudible running commentary.

"Bloody stiff, this cock. Ugh! Bugger! Went to all that trouble to get the bloody thing reconnected. Ah—that's it! . . ." Owen stood up. Philip saw him dusting down his knees. "Done it, darling!" Owen shouted. "You can turn the fire on now. Back in a sec, just going to wash my hands . . ."

Philip saw a pale blur flash across his keyhole and then the doorknob turned above his head—

Philip scrambled to one side as the door opened. Owen flicked on the light switch and backhandedly pushed the door to as he waddled down to the other end of the bathroom. He flipped up the toilet seat, unzipped himself and began to pee. He hummed tune-lessly to himself.

Philip crouched beside the door, as helpless as a grouse beaten from cover. The door was not quite shut; if he'd only left it open Philip would have been hidden, but he had only to turn back and—

Owen snatched a piece of toilet paper and blew his nose like a trumpeting elephant. It was a startling sound. Galvanized, Philip seized the moment.

He sprang to his feet, pulled open the door and dragged it back behind him as he darted out onto the landing, all in one swift movement. The echoing roar of Owen's nose-blow covered his exit.

"Darling, what are you doing in there?"

The voice floated out onto the landing from the other room. Not even a nasal encore from Owen could muffle it; it sliced through Philip like a knife and laid a dead hand on his heart.

"Coming, Hannah. Got the fire going?"

"Uh-huh."

Philip heard Owen turning a tap and water running into the sink. He stood like a dummy on the landing, numbness creeping through him.

Through the open door on his left he saw a mirror on the wall, and in the mirror Harry Foster's bed, and Hannah lying on the bed.

"Finished!" shouted Owen.

Philip heard him drying his hands. He looked around in panic. He threw himself back into the cupboard.

His position the second time was even more uncomfortable than the first. Something sharp stuck up his backside and brought tears to his eyes. He gritted his teeth as Owen stepped past his ludicrous hiding place and went into the bedroom.

Philip pressed his ear to the wall. He could just hear the conversation in the bedroom.

And Hannah's laugh, tingling with a sexual charge, echoing round his stuffy little cupboard.

The numbness was gone. Philip burned with bitterness and anger. It was a nightmare. What in God's name was she doing? He wanted to murder her. He wanted to leap on Harry Foster's double bed and smother her face in the pillows. He moaned in dreadful anguish.

"Put out the light, and then put out the light!"

He heard bedsprings creaking through the wall, and Hannah's heated groanings, more potent than her laugh.

"Christ!"

His voice was like a bark in the tiny sound-box. He was gripping the pipes with manic frenzy. Suddenly one gave in his hands, he heard a shearing grind as metal peeled off from the wall and he fell with a painful jolt down the side of the boiler.

"What the bloody hell was that?"

Philip held his breath. He didn't even know if he could move, he was wedged in tight. The amorous background noises had stopped. There was a silence in the bedroom.

"I don't know," he heard Owen saying through the wall. "I'd better have a look."

Footsteps and the sound of the door again. Owen was on the landing. He had a look round the bathroom.

"Don't know what it was," he said, standing directly outside the gas cupboard.

"Sounded like someone was in pain," said Hannah, her voice faint but anxious. "It was horrible. It set my teeth on edge."

"Nothing to worry about, I'm sure."

"Have another look, darling, perhaps it was up-stairs."

Owen moaned softly to himself. He grunted something and began to climb the stairs. Philip heard his heavy footsteps through the ceiling.

"Got to get out of here . . ." Philip muttered painfully to himself. He screwed up his nose. There was a funny smell. He sniffed two or three times and almost gagged. It was gas.

"My God, I'm being poisoned!"

In a frenzy he squirmed out of the cupboard and crumpled on all fours, panting.

"Owen?"

He glanced behind him. The bedroom was open. He caught a glimpse of Hannah in the mirror, and Hannah caught a glimpse of him.

The bathroom door was to his left. He rolled through it and under the sink as Hannah screamed.

Owen came running down the stairs.

"What is it? What's the matter?"

Philip heard Hannah pattering onto the landing. Her voice was breathless.

"I saw something out there!"

"What?" Owen sounded impatient.

"It was a black man, Owen. There's a black man on the landing!"

Owen roared with laughter. "Oh, Hannah, you really are the limit!"

"I tell you I saw something! Black as the ace of spades!"

Owen sighed. "I think you're letting your imagination run away with you—"

"Don't patronize me, you stupid bastard!"

She slapped his face. Philip, under the sink six feet

away, couldn't resist a snicker. Despite himself, he was beginning to enjoy this.

The bedroom door was slammed. Philip heard the sounds of muffled argument. He got up warily. He leaned against the sink and saw his face in the mirror. The only light was from the landing, spilling through the half-open door, but he could see a black and glistening outline and could appreciate that he must have given Hannah quite a shock. Daft bitch, he thought. He almost felt sorry for her. They were still arguing in the bedroom.

He stepped out carefully onto the landing. He paused to listen, but the raised voices were indistinct. He shook his head wearily.

He toyed briefly with the idea of ambushing them when they came out and stabbing them to death with his Swiss army penknife. A few minutes ago, if he'd known it was she, he could have done it, a crime of passion, but not now, coldly. He wasn't that sort of killer. Harry Foster was one thing; and as for Owen, well, he'd been wanting to murder him for ages, but Hannah . . . no, he had never murdered someone he had loved.

"Well, that's in the past now," he muttered rather sadly to himself.

It was sad, he thought, as he turned away and walked down the landing. What an idiot he'd been, to think that the leopard could have changed her spots! Better, he supposed, to find out now rather than after the wedding. After the wedding! That was choice! He wondered if she'd still be along later on. He hoped not, it would be tiresome to have to kick her out in the middle of the night. He'd feel much happier about it in the morning. At least he wouldn't have to put up with her strewing her tights and knickers all over the floor anymore. It would have been bound to end in divorce anyway . . .

A floorboard creaked.

"What was that?"

He stopped in his tracks. He was half-way to the stairs.

"Owen! I said what was that?"

Her voice through the door was shrill. Owen grumbled something.

Philip held his breath. It had been a fairly innocuous creak. He didn't think that Owen was going to move again, which was just as well, because this time he really was out in the open. He gave a little sigh of relief.

Then suddenly the bedroom door was flung open, and Hannah was standing there stark-naked, staring him full in the face.

She slammed the door shut and screamed.

Philip bolted down the stairs. He tore like a thing demented through the hallway and into the kitchen and flung himself through the broken window, falling heavily onto the concrete outside. He pulled himself to his feet and raced round the side of the house.

He stopped at the end of the alley-way. He could hear their voices floating through the upstairs window, Hannah's loud and manic.

"How dare you speak to me like that! I'm getting out of here, Owen, give me my dress!"

"Hannah, are you mad?" Owen's voice was a plaintive whine. "I've heard of seeing fairies or pixies, but black men!? What is the matter with you?"

Philip ran on the balls of his feet through the front garden, suppressing a desire to giggle. He crossed the road and darted behind the phone-box. He peeked his head round to take another look.

Owen flipped back the bedroom curtains. Even at a

distance Philip could see that his face was puffed with
anger. Hannah drifted into shot, waving her arms about
wildly. She jabbed a cigarette into her mouth and lit it.
She hit Owen, for the second time. Philip rubbed his
hands with glee. Hannah turned her back on Owen and
the window. He saw her walk towards the bedroom door
waving her cigarette. She disappeared from view.

An almighty explosion thundered in Philip's ears.

The shock threw him to the ground, he rolled upon
the pavement, stunned and half-blinded. Gaping stupidly, he clambered to his feet and stared at the remains
of the house opposite.

There was a great hole where the roof had been.
The windows had all been blown out, glass was flying
everywhere. A great tongue of flame licked out of the
bedroom window.

Philip staggered away as lights came on all down the
street. Doors were flung open and people stumbled out,
shouting crazily. He heard children screaming.

"Bloody hell," he said, looking at the mayhem.

A man with a dog brushed past him and dived into
the phone-box. The dog yelped as the door closed on
him. Philip heard the owner barking into the receiver.

"Fire, quick, it's an emergency, there's been a gas
explosion!"

Philip ran away down the street, hearing already in
his head the fearful wail of sirens. He stopped briefly at
the top of the road and glanced back.

The whole house was an incendiary mass. Great
clouds of black smoke rolled across the garden. It
looked like something out of the apocalypse.

Philip pulled up his hood. He sloped down the hill
towards the station. A man was running up towards him.
He stopped when he drew level and tapped Philip on
the shoulder.

"What's going on up there?" he asked, dumb-founded.

Philip shrugged. "Dunno, man." The man in question looked hesitant. Philip made a "search me" gesture.

"Life is full of surprises!"

FIFTEEN

Philip sat in his armchair listening to Elgar's cello concerto. He loved its melancholy power. It was the middle of the night, the room was in darkness. Through a gap in the curtains he saw the tiny glow of a streetlamp. When the music stopped he sat in silence staring at the light.

He lit a cigarette and held the match to his watch. It was four o'clock. He felt exhausted but couldn't sleep. At least he ought to try to eat something; he hadn't had anything since lunch-time.

He walked into the kitchen, shielding his eyes from the fluorescent glare of the strip-light. He rooted around in the fridge and found a lump of cheese and half of a grapefruit that he'd left for Hannah's breakfast two days ago. He wedged the cheese between two slices of bread and nibbled unenthusiastically. He noticed a trace of make-up on the back of his hand.

He went into the bathroom to wipe it off. The bath was still smudged with black stains. He scrubbed them away. He looked at his face in the mirror. His skin was an unhealthy, colourless shade and his eyes were red and black-rimmed.

He went to lie down on his bed. It was cold; he got up again to put on his dressing gown and noticed Hannah's photograph on the sideboard. He carried it over to the bedside table. It was quite an old photograph; her agent had been telling her for some time to update it. Hannah had resisted, as she had always resisted any implication that she might not be so young as she once was.

"Poor Hannah, dead and gone, not with a whimper but with a bang."

In a way she might have approved. He couldn't imagine her getting old. He thought that he had improved with age, and would probably go on improving for a few years yet. But Hannah had been building sandwalls against the tide for years now. Her life had become geared more and more to the process of graceless decline, a plethora of diets and fads, a merry-go-round of visits to beauticians and cosmetic surgeons. If she found a grey hair it meant a sleepless night. Her life was in thrall to the bathroom scales.

"I could have strangled you, Hannah, with my own bare hands, when I realized it was you in there with that ghastly, loathsome heap of blubber. You're not exactly ideal casting for Desdemona, but it would have had a certain symmetry. Why Owen, darling? What appalling taste! What an insult! The nasty sty. Making the twobacked beast with Jumbo. Not a pretty sight. If you had to do it with anybody, why not someone more attractive

at least? More attractive? I can't think of anyone more
revolting. I suppose I did murder you really. The gas.
There's a kind of symmetry in that too. At least Owen
got his just desserts.

"I can't see that it would have worked anyway, being
realistic. It's not a good idea to keep secrets in a marriage, and my secrets are a little unusual, to say the
least. There were you thinking of me as plain old Philip,
never guessing for a moment that I was one of the most
successful murderers in England. It's a difficult secret to
have to keep; I might even have told you in an un-
guarded moment, and I don't think that would have
worked, either. It may well have turned out for the best.
Well, perhaps not from your point of view, but you had
secrets too, remember! I wonder, did you recognize me
when you saw me on the landing? I doubt it, but you
might have done. Just as well there are no witnesses to
my break-in. The police might have asked some nasty
questions!

"Nonetheless, it's all been a bit of a shock. If it really
had happened accidentally, if I hadn't known, if I hadn't
been there and a policeman had turned up on my door
to break the news that you were dead, I'm afraid I
would have gone to pieces. I'd have wept buckets for
you, Hannah. Perhaps I'd have seen it as God's judgement on my misdeeds. Of course I don't believe in God,
but that doesn't rule out the possibility of him believing
in me. I wonder if you're up there now, being fitted with
your wings. I can't imagine you in white somehow. If I
find you not there, I shall seek for you in the other
place. I wonder if I should arrange a memorial service.
It would be rather impressive, theatrical. Rather moving
too. I'm afraid I might break down. Yes, I think I
would."

Philip got up and went to his chest of drawers. He

took out a clean handkerchief and blew his nose. He returned to the photograph.

"I suppose it's a bit old-fashioned of me to resent your infidelity in this day and age. Jealousy is the worm in the bud, I'm afraid; I can't help it. I suppose it would be hypocritical of me to mourn, seeing as I considered killing you myself, albeit only for a moment. But all men kill the thing they love. The coward does it with a kiss, the brave man courtesy of North Thames Gas. I'm sorry, that was tasteless. You were a good sort really. And I was in love with you."

He picked up the photograph and examined it carefully, as if memorizing the details. Then he tucked it under his arm and walked back to the living room. He took the Elgar off the turntable and put on Berlioz' Requiem. He placed the photograph on the mantelpiece and stood in the middle of the room listening to the violins and the violas. The horns and woodwinds added their say before the choir swelled. Not for nothing was it called the *Grande Messe*. It always made him think of Napoleon's tomb in the Invalides.

It was light when the music finished. Philip didn't draw the curtains. He had still not slept, he was lightheaded with exhaustion. He went to lie down, but sleep did not come easily. When at last he had dozed off, he was woken almost at once by the doorbell.

Furious at being disturbed, he slouched off into the living room to see who it was. Lifting the curtain with his finger, he could just see into the porch. He dropped the curtain back into place at once. There was a policeman standing on the doorstep. The bell rang again. Philip stood motionless. After a minute he heard the heavy tread of the policeman's boots walking away. He breathed a sigh of relief and went back to bed. He really didn't want to face the police now. He climbed under the duvet and turned out the light. Quite soon, he was asleep and dreaming.

He was sitting at his table sipping champagne and endeavouring not to appear nervous. He was stiffly upright in his dinner jacket, trying to concentrate on what the peculiar woman on his right was saying. It was such an effort. He wanted to be looking round the whole time, to crane his neck and see who else he could spot in the crowd. They were all there! Jack Nicholson was at the next table in his sunglasses, next to Meryl Streep. And there was Jane Fonda chatting to Jack Lemmon. It was so exciting! What was the peculiar woman going on about? Why wouldn't she shut up so he could eavesdrop on Barbra Streisand and Walter Matthau? These people were getting quite hysterical. It was very important, Philip thought, to maintain decorum. Maintain his Englishness, that was the correct thing. It was vital to be correct. Whatever happened, he mustn't let the side down. It wouldn't be cricket.

"Excuse me," he said to the peculiar woman, "but are you familiar with the rules of cricket?"

The peculiar woman ceased her chatter and stared at him blankly.

"Evidently not," he continued smugly. "Then it shall be my pleasure to enlighten you." He explained to her that it was a game for two sides of eleven players and that one was in while the other was out. This was not the same as getting out when you were in, because when you were out when you were out, it meant only that you were in the outfield, whereas if you were out when you were in, it meant that you had to go back in and await your turn to be out, unless, that is, you had already been out, in which case you could put your feet up and relax. There were a great many more ways of getting out than was commonly realized, but even being clean-bowled involved an infinite variety of possible deliveries. One could fall victim to the bouncer, the yorker, the grass cutter, the leg spin, the wrist spin, the one that swung, the one that kept straight, the googly, the fast, the medium-fast, the fast-medium or the downright slow, and combinations of the above too numerous to list. The most difficult thing of all for a novice to grasp was probably the law of l.b.w. Would she like to hear an explanation of the law of l.b.w.?

The peculiar woman's eyes glazed over. She made a strangled noise and fell off her chair. A stretcher party came and took her away. He noticed that in profile she bore a curious resemblance to Tallulah Bankhead. Philip folded his napkin and adjusted his tie.

"So excitable, these Americans," he said knowingly to Michael Caine.

Of course Mike wasn't the only Englishman there, although not a lot of people knew that. There was Sir John Gielgud, walking up to the podium, large envelope in hand, acknowledging the crescendo of applause. Sir John opened the envelope and took out a slip of paper.

"And the winner of tonight's raffle is . . . oh no, wrong envelope."

Sir John took out another envelope and opened that.

"Seeing as the choice of the Academy this year is so glaringly obvious, I shall dispense with the usual list of nominations and read out only the name of the winner of this year's Oscar for Best Actor, who is, of course, Philip Fletcher for *Victory*. And here to present the Man of the Match Award is the chairman of Cornhill Insurance."

This dream was getting confusing. What was Ian Botham doing at the microphone? And why was the telephone on his table ringing? Why was there a telephone anyway? He got up and staggered towards it.

"Hello?"

"Hi! Steve Spielberg here. How'd you like to make a movie with me?"

"Hello? Mr. Fletcher?"

"Huh?"

He stood in the living room rubbing sleep from his eyes and trying to work out which way round the receiver should go.

"Good God! How did I get here?"

"Mr. Fletcher, are you there?"

"Is that Mr. Spielberg's secretary?"

"Pardon? This is the BBC, Mr. Fletcher." The girl sounded anxious. "The driver we sent round to collect you said there was no answer when he rang. Thank God you're in. We're cutting it very fine."

"What?"

"Mr. Fletcher, you're due to appear on the *Terry Wogan Show* in just over an hour!"

"My God—what's today?"

"Tuesday."

She said that another car was on the way. He should just make it to Shepherd's Bush in time. He'd have to go almost straight on.

He ran into the bathroom to wash. He tried not to catch his eye in the mirror; he knew that he looked awful. He put on a jacket and tie.

The car came almost immediately. Philip sat in the back trying to compose himself. He felt too disoriented to be nervous. The black cab ploughed doggedly through the rush-hour traffic. They didn't hit the Marylebone Road till after six. It took another half-hour to reach Shepherd's Bush.

Most of the audience was already in. Of course no

one recognized Philip. For the time being. The exposure was just beginning. He was going to be on the front cover of the next *Radio Times,* whose readers would have the chance to win a Philip Fletcher Golf Convertible.

A blonde PA met him at the stage door. She was the girl who had spoken to him on the phone, she was a no-nonsense hockey-sticks type of girl with BBC written all over her. Probably called Cristabel, thought Philip. He heard sounds of laughter from the auditorium where the warm-up man was doing his routine. The girl showed him to a dressing room. "Terry's most disappointed not to have had a chance to speak to you," she said. "He likes to have a word beforehand, but he's been well briefed. I'll come and get you in five minutes; perhaps there'll still be time for a quick chat."

Philip sat down in a chair facing the mirror. The bright lights around the glass accentuated the paleness of his face. A make-up girl came in. She smiled at his reflection and began combing his hair.

"Should I just let it flop forward?" she asked, uncovering the thinning patch at the front. He nodded. She flipped the comb and the hair fell naturally into place. "I think it's very distinguished," she said, fingering his receding temples. She chatted breezily as she powdered his face. "Better get a bit of colour into you or you'll disappear under the lights. You look a bit nervous. Relax. Terry's smashing, really easygoing. You're the star of that new serial, aren't you? I love that historical stuff. Really romantic! Been interviewed before?"

"Not on the telly," said Philip. He was beginning to feel excited.

"I expect they'll all be after you soon," said the girl. "Must be a big night for you."

"I can't begin to tell you."

She stood back from him, studying his face in the mirror. She seemed pleased. "That's better. This really means a lot to you, eh?"

"Of course," said Philip, smiling benignly. "It's what every actor dreams of—recognition, popularity, success. You don't get asked onto the *Terry Wogan Show* unless you are somebody. I've waited twenty-five years for this. I've watched countless chat shows and interviews, wondering if my turn would ever come. And as the years went by I became more and more convinced that it wouldn't. I went through my twenties without a whiff of anything. That's all right, I thought, there are some actors for whom nothing happens until they're thirty. Look at Michael Caine. I was never a juvenile, I thought that my time would come when I was a bit more experienced, more mature. But my thirties were as blank as my twenties. When I turned forty I thought, that's it! you don't become a star this late in life; if it hasn't happened by now, I'm not going to. I wasn't a failure; I was a working actor, respected, known in the business. But I was not Prince Hamlet, just another attendant lord, third or fourth billing, usually. The leading man's friend, not the leading man. I used to lie awake at night, wondering what it was that was lacking in my chemistry. Why were people who I knew were no better than myself playing starring parts, when I was not? I was envious all right. Not so much of the good people. You can't begrudge someone getting recognition when they deserve it. But there were others who didn't deserve it and their success frustrated me. I took it personally. If only I'd been less ambitious! But if I had been, I'd have probably given up years ago. A teacher at drama school told me that stamina was the most important quality an actor could have. More important than talent. You know what Kean used to ask would-be actors? 'Can you starve?' You've just got to stick it out, you never know when a lucky break will come. I can still hardly believe it's happened to me. Almost overnight my life's changed. People are going to recognize me in the street. They're going to know my name, whisper it as I pass. I've seen that happen. Producers are phoning up to offer me jobs; I don't have to chase after them. For more than twenty years I've wondered what it would be like. And now I'm going to find out. In a few minutes Terry Wogan will introduce me to the nation, and a studio audience who know nothing about me will applaud enthusiastically. Up and down the country millions of viewers will be glued to their sets, listening to me talking about myself. Millions I say. Can you conceive of it? All those ants, to have power over all those ants. People will actually want to hear me talking about myself. Me. I'll get fan letters, requests for photographs and locks of hair, offers of marriage from lonely spinsters in Weston super-Mare. All my dreams will be realized. All my dreams. Not many of us can hope for that. Not many of us can say that we've achieved what we set out to do, reached our full potential. Joined the Olympians. Perhaps you think I'm exaggerating, a case of believing my own publicity, falling in with the media hype. Well, why not? Tonight means more than the icing on the cake to me. It's a public seal of approval. Of course I'm no different now from how I was last year. I'm the same person and I'm the same actor. That part of me, my talent, my technical equipment, hasn't magically been transformed. I haven't become anything new. What we can be is in all of us. What's changed is other people's perceptions of me. I'm still the same me, but producers who once flicked idly past my photograph in *Spotlight* will pause at it now and accord that little monochrome portrait respect. For what I have become in their eyes. Suddenly I am a name. It's a snowball effect. If one wants me, then another will. You're never so much in demand as when you're in demand. And I'm in demand. Terry Wogan awaits me. The nation awaits me. Not for a fantasy or trick of fame. Tonight I'm to be the bride. Yes, my dear, you could say that this really means a lot to me."

There was a knock on the door.

"My call, I take it," said Philip. "Come in."

The door was opened hesitantly. Eleanor Thompson walked in. "Philip," she said, her lips quivering. Her eyes under her glasses were red, her cheeks pale. She stood uncertainly in the doorway. Philip got up, taking out his handkerchief. He said to the make-up girl, "Would you mind leaving us alone for a moment?" She picked up her things and went out with a curious look at Eleanor. She closed the door.

"Sit down," said Philip gently.

She took off her glasses and dabbed at her eyes with her handkerchief. Tears were pouring down her face. She could hardly speak. "Oh, Philip, I'm so sorry . . . I can't begin to . . . it's so awful!"

He went over and put his arms round her. How strange, he thought, that she should cry so. She'd never even liked Hannah. He stroked her hair. "How did you hear?" he asked softly.

"It's in the *Standard*. I came straight over. My poor, poor darling, you must feel terrible . . ."

He sat down beside her and took her hands in his. "Have you got a copy of the paper?" he asked.

"Oh, Philip, how can you be so calm? You're so brave!"

"Life must go on, darling. Don't think I'm callous. But I'd like to know what it said in the paper."

"It said . . . oh God! It was horrible. They said there was a gas leak, an explosion, and Hannah died instantly. Her photo's all over the front page. I'm afraid they've gone to town on it."

"Mm. Thought so . . ." muttered Philip. "Well, you can't blame the papers, I'm afraid. It's not every day they get such a bizarre story. 'Famous Actress and Producer Blown to Smithereens in Freak Accident'!"

She was looking at him in blank disbelief. He realized that he must have sounded utterly callous. He mustn't shock her, not Eleanor, his staunchest ally. He threw his head suddenly into his hands and moaned plaintively.

"The bastards!" he added for good measure.

Eleanor patted him on the back and made a valiant effort to stifle her own renewed tears.

"At least there's a hope that Owen may pull through," she said.

"What?"

His furious exclamation startled her. She jumped.

"So—sorry!" he stammered. "I'm just overwrought."

There was a knock on the door. The blonde PA stuck her head in. "Terry would love a quick word with you, Mr. Fletcher. Shall I say you're coming round?"

Philip nodded. She closed the door. He got up and went to the basin. He ran his hands under the cold tap and cupped them to take a sip of water. He dried his hands on the towel. He said, "I thought Owen was dead."

"No. He's badly injured. In hospital. But they pulled him out of the wreckage."

Philip stood uncertainly in the middle of the room.

He patted his pockets for his cigarettes but found he'd left them at home.

"You don't have a copy of the paper, do you?"

His sudden shifts of tone were clearly alarming her. Her eyes were wide open with anxiety.

"No, Philip." She shook her head. "You'd better sit down. I don't think you're well enough to go on tonight, I'll—"

"Nonsense!" barked Philip, springing to the door. "Wait here a minute."

He had remembered that when he came in, the doorman had been reading the paper. He closed the dressing-room door after him and headed off down the corridor towards the exit. His pulse was racing. Horrible suspicions crowded his mind: What if Hannah had recognized him? What if she'd told Owen? Already questioned by the police about two deaths, his involvement with a third would surely seem more than coincidence.

A door opened behind him and he heard voices. One of the voices stopped him dead in his tracks. He turned round slowly.

A girl was walking down the corridor away from him, chatting to a man at her side.

". . . yes, Mr. Fletcher's just down here . . ."

"I think he'll be quite surprised to see me," said Superintendent Turnbull of Scotland Yard.

They stopped and the girl knocked on his dressing-room door.

Philip backed away on tiptoe. They hadn't seen him.

"Come in." He heard Eleanor's muffled voice.

A door opened at Philip's shoulder and a woman stepped out. Philip darted in past her, just registering her look of bewilderment, and slammed the door behind him.

Two women were standing chatting by a row of wash-basins. They stopped and stared at Philip, who began to turn bright red. He glanced furtively to left and right and saw a cubicle door standing open.

"Terribly sorry!" he blurted out. "Emergency!"

He plunged into the cubicle and locked it. He pushed down the toilet seat and climbed on, crouching against the wall.

"Well, I never!" declared one of the women indignantly.

Philip heard their footsteps across the tiled floor. They went out smartly. Philip squirmed.

He looked at his watch. He was due on in a few minutes. This was appalling. The police couldn't drag him off now, not now, when he stood on the threshold of fame. They couldn't deny him his moment of glory . . . Hannah must have talked to Owen. And Owen must have talked to the police. She'd known it was he all along. They'd know he'd been in the house. They were going to pin her death on him! It was a travesty of justice! He hadn't even meant to kill her. They couldn't do him for the one crime he hadn't actually committed!

He was shaking. He was a complete nervous wreck. He loosed his tie. He couldn't breathe. He groaned.

The door to the toilets opened and footsteps came towards him. They stopped outside his cubicle.

"Mr. Fletcher?"

It was the blonde PA in her best head-girl voice.

"Mr. Fletcher, I know you're in there. Come out at once, please."

"I'm sorry. I'm not feeling very well."

"Mr. Fletcher, you really shouldn't be in the Ladies', you know. Your presence is causing some distress to female members of staff. If you're really sick, please come out and I'll call you a doctor."

"In a minute."

"We don't have a minute, Mr. Fletcher. If you're too ill to go on, we will have to rearrange the schedule and we will have to do so at once." She tapped a foot impatiently.

Reluctantly Philip flipped up the lock and opened the door a few inches. He smiled with what he thought was becoming charm.

"Are you alone?" he asked in a whisper.

"Pardon?" she said stiffly.

He poked his head out and glanced towards the door. He beckoned her a little nearer. She did not move. He cleared his throat.

"I know my behaviour must seem a little odd," he said, "but I've got this, er, curious allergy towards certain individuals. Is Superintendent Turnbull waiting outside, please?"

"Why should he be?" she blurted out in exasperation. "The Gents' is just opposite. Why on earth should you be allergic to Superintendent Turnbull?"

"I'm afraid he's in love with me," said Philip confidentially.

The PA blinked.

"I see," she said after a pause.

"Would you mind just checking for me?" Philip asked.

She walked slowly to the door. She opened it, stuck out her head and looked to left and right. She turned back to Philip and shook her head deliberately. Philip gave her a thumbs-up sign. He joined her at the door and confirmed for himself the amorous policeman's absence.

"Okay," he said, giving her a nudge.

She walked off down the corridor. He followed a few paces behind, keeping one eye over his shoulder.

"Are you feeling better now?" she asked.

"Oh yes, thanks."

They stopped outside the studio door. They heard the sound of laughter from within. The PA conferred with another girl and put her finger to her lips for Philip's benefit.

"It's started," she said. "You're on next. Follow me."

They went round the back of the set. A man wearing earphones came over and gave Philip whispered instructions. He didn't hear half of what he said but understood where he was to make his entrance. He was shown a cue-light. He could hear muffled conversation on stage. He wondered whom Terry was talking to. He'd meant to ask, but it was too late now, the man in earphones was waving to him. Philip coughed and adjusted his tie. He hoped he looked all right. He'd snatched clothes out of the cupboard almost at random. He should have combed his hair. He should have had a shave. He should have brushed his teeth. He must remember to buy a new flannel, the old one was—

Terry's voice like music floated to his ears. He heard his name. He walked forward as in a dream.

The cue-light went green. Philip strode into the applause.

SIXTEEN

Philip stood woodenly in the white bright corridor holding a bunch of flowers. An orderly went by, a cleaner pushing a Hoover, a man in dressing gown on crutches. The door opposite him opened and a matronly matron stepped out.

"If you could wait just a moment longer," she said. "His wife's in there now, I think it's best to leave them alone."

"How is he?" Philip asked.

"Very weak, but improving. It's a miracle he survived at all. He was blown clean out of the window, he's got a lot of broken bones. But at least he wasn't badly burnt."

Philip nodded sympathetically. He looked at his watch. There was only a quarter of an hour of visiting time left. It would be no use to him at all if Fanny was still there when he was eventually allowed in. Well, he'd just have to come back tomorrow. He sniffed the flowers. The smell was pleasantly refreshing, anaesthetizing the pervasive hospital odours. He looked at his watch again and saw the seconds ticking by. He also saw that the matron was staring at him. He met her eye and she looked embarrassed.

"Excuse me," she said with a cough, "you must think I'm very rude. But didn't I see you on television last night?"

"Er, yes," he muttered quickly. "Not terribly impressive, I'm afraid . . ."

Not terribly impressive. That was the understatement of the year. It had been a catastrophe.

The applause had been tremendous. He had felt it, like a wave, hitting him as he went on. Absolutely amazing, he'd thought, all those people clapping and not one of them even knew who he was. Not a single one of them, except for the man who rose beaming from the sofa to extend a hand.

"We've met already," said Superintendent Turnbull to Terry.

Philip felt his knees buckle. He collapsed into a sitting position, almost missing the sofa. The audience laughed at him. Philip stared gormlessly into the rows of half-lit faces, sensing his nerves disintegrate.

My God, he thought, they're going to arrest me on the air. Live. A first for British television.

Terry had asked him a question. It was like in the nightmare. Oh, his prophetic soul! They were all looking at him, Terry on his left, the policeman on his right, the audience ahead and, through the cameras, countless millions of people, all witnessing his downfall. It was too much. He held out his wrists meekly to the Superintendent.

"I'll come quietly," he said.

This comment went down rather well. Philip found the laughter bewildering. What were they doing to him? Surely they didn't expect a public confession?

He heard Terry asking another question, something about Sir Walter Raleigh. Who? he thought. "Yes," he said in answer to the question, sure of at least a fifty-percent chance of success. There was a silence, clearly he'd said the wrong thing. "I mean no," he added quickly. That was obviously no better. Could he ask for the question to be repeated? he wondered, or would they deduct marks from his final score? He could see Terry, hardened by years of experience, mastering the situation. He asked another question.

"Pass," said Philip.

Which was almost exactly what he had done. Passed out. Fainted into the arms of Superintendent Turnbull under the eyes of millions. It certainly had been a first for British television.

"Are you feeling better now?" asked the matronly matron.

Philip jumped, surprised in his reverie. "Er . . . yes, thanks, it was just strain."

That had been what Eleanor had said; it had been the first thing he'd heard on coming round. He was lying on a couch and a doctor was taking his pulse. Eleanor was in earnest conversation with the blonde PA.

"I should never have let him go on," Eleanor was saying, "he's had such a shock, poor dear."

"I realized he wasn't all there," said the blonde PA, "but I'd no idea he was going to flip."

Philip was indignant. He spluttered a protest and Eleanor soothed him. But later, when the others had gone, she left no doubt in his mind that she shared the general view of his instability. She repeated what the doctor had told him: he ought to seek psychiatric help.

Later, thinking about it on his own, it struck him that perhaps they were right after all; perhaps he really was going mad. The thought of being subjected to psychiatric investigation chilled him, not least because of what revelations his subconscious might make under hypnosis. He felt his paranoia coming on again. That was his problem, paranoia. He'd never understood what it meant before; now he realized that, in his case at least, it was a kind of mental tunnel vision: one just couldn't see the wood for the trees, the most innocent of happenings oozed with a sinister subtext. Take Superintendent Turnbull, for instance.

Superintendent Turnbull, successful detective retiring from the force, widely publicized author of his memoirs, being groomed for the post of media pundit and cutting his teeth in interview with Terry Wogan . . .

Of course it had been an extraordinary coincidence, quite startling, in fact, but what on earth had given Philip the ludicrous idea that he was about to be publicly arrested? The Superintendent had been quite concerned about Philip, he'd come to see him later. Gazing up from his couch into the broad avuncular face, Philip had seen only compassion, not the least hint of suspicion. The suspicion had all been Philip's own invention. They'd never had anything on him. He'd never been more than the subject of routine inquiries. He had made up his own case against himself. It was hideous really. A chain of alternative causation uncoiled irresistibly in his mind: they weren't after him, Harry's diary was a red herring, he needn't have gone to the house at all, and—

"What on earth is going on in there?" asked the matron. She went and put her ear to the door. It was an unnecessary move. Even from where he stood Philip could hear quite plainly a pronounced thumping noise and a series of strangled groans. Suddenly there was added a piercing shriek.

The matron flung open the door and strode in. Feeling highly curious, Philip followed.

Owen Trethowan, bandaged from head to toe, both legs raised in splints, was lying helplessly in bed while Fanny screamed in his ears and pummelled his chest.

"You two-faced bastard! Don't think I don't know what you were up to in there with that slut!"

Owen yelped as she hurled herself across the bed. The matron, who had shoulders like a stevedore, pulled her off and flung her back against the wall. Fanny, though winded, attempted to renew her assault on her husband, but the matron slapped her hard across the face.

"Pull yourself together, you stupid woman!"

Fanny burst into tears. The racket in the tiny room was fearful. Fanny was sobbing, the matron was shouting at her crossly, Owen was moaning and groaning. At least Philip assumed it was Owen. It was difficult to tell under the bandages. But the lower part of the face was uncovered, and the fat cheeks, blubbery lips and double-chin looked familiar. There seemed to be a flicker in the eyes too. A new, rather hysterical note entered Owen's whimperings.

"How are you feeling, Owen?" Philip called out above the din. "You're not really looking yourself."

Matron dragged Fanny, kicking and screaming, to the door. She wrested herself free briefly and turned back to loose a Parthian dart:

"I know all about your dirty goings-on, Owen. I'll kill you if you get out of here alive!"

You'll have to join the queue, thought Philip. "Good afternoon, Fanny," he said pleasantly.

She didn't answer. She and the matron, like an improbable pair of lady wrestlers, disappeared through the door.

Philip went and stood his flowers in the sink. He turned back to Owen and couldn't help smiling.

"Forgive me for saying so, old chap, but you look just like the curse of the mummy's tomb."

Owen tried to grin. It ended up as more of a grimace. "Philip, old thing . . ." he said in a confidential tone. His voice was a little faint, but otherwise normal. Philip responded by taking the chair next to the bed and inclining his head towards him. "Philip, I—I don't want you to get the wrong idea. What Fanny said just now, she's just—"

"What idea would that be?" asked Philip innocently.

Again Owen tried his tortured grin. Philip continued to look blank.

"About me and Hannah," said Owen. "It's all just idle gossip. I was showing Hannah round the house, that's all. It was a tragic accident. I'm terribly sorry."

"Why were you showing Hannah round the house, Owen?"

"Um, I think she wanted to buy it. You know. For you to live in."

"Yes, she did have some funny ideas, didn't she?"

The door opened and the matron came back in. She went straight to Owen and fiddled with his dressings.

"Are you all right?" she asked. "She didn't do you any damage, did she?"

"Never felt better!" said Owen with a weak laugh.

"Good," said the matron. She turned to Philip. "I'll have to kick you out soon, I'm afraid. Now, Mr. Trethowan, if you need anything, just call." She indicated the emergency button on the bedside table. Philip noted where the cord went into the wall. The matron went out again.

"I bought you a present," said Philip. He took a brown paper bag out of his pocket and held it up for Owen to inspect the contents. "Chockies," said Philip. "Coffee creams, to be exact."

Owen's piggy eyes lit up. "My favourite!" he declared.

"Hush now!" whispered Philip. "Don't tell Nurse! Strictly against the rules, you know!"

Owen nodded impatiently. It was amazing, thought Philip, how the most transparent lies became opaque where self-interest was concerned. He popped one of the chocolates into Owen's mouth. He masticated noisily.

"Like another?" asked Philip.

Owen gave a vigorous nod. Philip stuffed them in, one after another. It was like feeding geese.

Cluck! Cluck! Philip thought to himself. "All right?" he asked.

"Mm!" said Owen, who seemed to have regressed into a state of Billy Bunterhood. "De-licious!"

"I'm surprised they taste that good," said Philip ruminatively. "I couldn't bring them in a box, I'm afraid. Couldn't conceal them, you see. It was important I conceal them. That's probably why they're a bit sticky. There. All gone. Shucks." Philip screwed up the empty bag and put it back in his pocket. "They can't be feeding you properly here."

"Actually the food's rather good," said Owen. "I just never could resist coffee creams!"

Philip laughed along with Owen. It was fun encouraging him to laugh, it obviously afforded him so little pleasure.

"Look, Philip, about what I was saying—"

"Oh, forget it, Owen. Idle tongues, as you say. Ssh! Here comes matron. Not a word about the tuck now!"

Owen pressed his finger to his lips, indicating mute complicity.

"Five more minutes," said matron, sticking her head round the door.

"Hannah's funeral is going to be on Friday," said Philip after she'd gone. "I don't suppose you'll be able to make it."

Owen paused for a moment, gathering his thoughts, then he launched into a kind of clumsy oration. He listed Hannah's innumerable good qualities, mostly fictitious, and lamented the passing of one of the finest actresses of her generation, which was overdoing it, to put it mildly. He then railed against the vicissitudes of fate and gave a lengthy and false description of events the other night in Harry's house, culminating in the fatal explosion. Philip found his mendacity comforting. The more he lied, the more Philip was able to justify his loathing. The more he complained, the more he seemed deserving of his fate. Such qualms as Philip might have had soon vanished.

The matron came to announce the end of visiting time. Philip shuffled off to the door.

"Be seeing you, Owen," he said. "Get better soon."

"Thanks, Philip. Thanks for everything!"

Philip followed the matron down the corridor.

"Damn!" he said. "I've forgotten my scarf. Excuse me a moment."

The matron waited for him while he retraced his steps. He walked swiftly back into Owen's room and went to the chair where he had left his scarf. "Forgot this," he explained to Owen. He stooped down smartly and pulled the emergency-call socket out of the wall. He straightened up and had a good look at Owen. He appeared to be rather uncomfortable. His arm gave a little nervous twitch.

"Goodbye again, Owen. I mean it this time."

Philip rejoined the matron in the corridor. "He's asleep," he told her. "Better not disturb him."

She nodded. "Sleep's the best thing for him now."

"Is he going to be all right?"

"He should be."

"But you never know?"

"I'm afraid not."

They stood at the end of the corridor chatting for the next ten minutes. Philip found that she required little prompting. He got her going on the NHS and listened with feigned interest to her stream-of-consciousness monologue. "Really?" he interjected occasionally, or "You don't say?" Eventually a nurse came to seek her out with a request for help. Philip waved a cheery goodbye and made for the exit.

On the way out he dropped the empty chocolate bag into a bin. He stopped to look at his watch. Twenty minutes since Owen finished the chocolates. He obviously hadn't suspected anything. Philip acknowledged to himself that it had been a pretty accomplished job, but then he was, after all, a pretty accomplished murderer. He'd taken enormous pains. First he'd had to dissolve the strychnine (harder than it sounds!), next he'd had to mix it carefully with the coffee, creaming and cooling the liquid into a fondue. Then fill the neatly bisected chocolates, seal them up and hey presto!—poisoned coffee cream. It was a curious thing that strychnine, which has a very bitter flavour, should be rendered tasteless in coffee. Amazing what you learned doing the rounds of the reps in creaky old thrillers. Philip checked his watch again. That should be about it, he thought. If they hadn't pumped his stomach out by now, he'd be a goner. And good riddance too.

It was certainly going to be his last murder. Although there were still a great many loathsome people at large in the theatre, he thought that he'd done his bit, it was time to bring the curtain down on a distinguished career. One actor, one agent and one producer. It would have been nice to have included a director to make up the quartet, but he was so spoiled for choice he really wouldn't have known where to begin. No, the longest-running shows had to close eventually. Better not to gild the lily.

He bounced happily down the steps outside. He made a mental note to get rid of the rat poison at home. He thought he'd covered his tracks pretty well. At worst they could only suspect, and he could live with suspicion. He wasn't going to fall into the paranoid routine again! No, if anybody got it in the neck, it would probably be Fanny. He sang to himself as he walked up to the main road.

> "Hey diddle-de-dee
> An actor's life for me!"

There was a cab rank round the corner. He could take cabs all the time now. How pleasant it was to have money, heigh-ho!

He got into the first cab and settled back to enjoy the ride. He sang under his breath:

> "There's No Bus'ness Like Show Bus'ness
> Like no bus'ness I know . . ."

Suddenly he began to giggle. There certainly wasn't! he thought. The cabby glanced at him in the mirror. At the next traffic lights he glanced again and his frown became more marked.

"Didn't I see you on the telly last night?" he asked.

Philip groaned. "It was pretty nerve-racking, I'm afraid," he said, leaning forward. He smiled ruefully. "I'll tell you something for nothing. That old saying, it's true. Showbiz is, well, it's just murder!"

The black cab sped through Camden Town with Philip's laugh echoing round the back.

ABOUT THE AUTHOR

SIMON SHAW was educated at Cambridge and, after a stint at the Old Vic Theatre School, became a professional actor in 1979. He is the author of three novels of suspense: *Murder Out of Tune*, *Killer Cinderella*, and *Bloody Instructions*. He lives in London.

Don't miss

KILLER CINDERELLA

by Simon Shaw
Coming soon from Bantam Crime Line

Mark and Maddie Harvey hardly had a fairy tale marriage. Maddie's shrewish temperament and blatant infidelities were enough to drive any man to the edge—but still, Mark had never intended her any harm. Still again, no one could have foreseen the violence waiting to happen . . .

"Look," he said, trying to sound calm and reasonable. "We may have had our differences, but let's at least try to live in a civilised fashion. You could have put enough in the kettle for me, you know, I did ask you. The coffee's finished. Is there any more?"

She shook her head, once. He shrugged and made an exasperated noise.

"Well, you could have bought some more. It's not much to ask."

He went back out to the kitchen and found an Earl Grey tea bag, which he dunked unenthusiastically in a cup of hot water. He added Long Life milk and a spoonful of castor sugar. It tasted like sweet milky water.

He returned to the living room. Maddie had turned off the main light, leaving only her table lamp to read by. That was thoughtless of her. Or had it been deliberate? The knot of irritation tightened in his stomach. He turned the main light back on again.

"Do you mind?"

The first words she had spoken to him in days evoked no response. He was staring at the sideboard.

"Why have you moved my things?"

His voice was a hoarse whisper. She tutted and muttered under her breath before returning to her magazine. He advanced on the sideboard in an agitated state and angrily pushed to one side the vase of flowers which she must have just replaced there. The bowl was behind it, and he saw that she had put the model on a chair.

"What have you done with my cup?"

She didn't answer. She turned the page.

"What the. . . ."

He had seen it now, or at least the bottom of it, the baize base of the black plinth. The cup was upside down in the waste-paper basket. His prize-winning cup.

"What did you. . . . ?"

He could hardly speak. The cup had become detached from the plinth, to which it had been firmly glued. She must have thrown it into the basket with considerable force to have done that. One of the handles bore a slight scratch. He put the plinth back down on the sideboard and the cup on top of it. It would be all right. He could fix it, but—

"How dare you!"

It was a scream of rage. At least he had found his voice. She couldn't ignore it.

"I could say the same!" she shouted back, throwing the magazine down and rising.

"How dare you damage my things!"

"How dare you destroy my life!"

"You stupid bitch!"

"Don't talk to me like that!"

"I'll talk to you how I want! It's my home, isn't it?"

"We'll see what my solicitor's got to say about that!"

"Stop going on about your bloody solicitor!"

"Don't swear at me!"

"Fuck off!"

"Fuck off yourself! I know damn well what you've been up to, you and your sick friends! Lizzie saw the look Martin gave you after they'd beaten up poor Roddy. You were all in it together, you're all in a conspiracy against me, against us, against the only man I've ever loved, who's worth more than the lot of you put together and all your stupid little cups and bowls and toy soldiers, you vindictive, spiteful, vicious man!"

"They're not toy soldiers."

"Don't interrupt me! I haven't finished!"

"Well I have! I've had enough of listening to this crap!"

"You're a disgusting coward! You can't even face up to Roddy man to man, you've got to get your friends to do your dirty work for you!"

"Face up to Roddy! It would be like throwing a cripple in the river!"

"How dare you talk like that about the man I love!"

"He's a wimp, Maddie! A pathetic, fat dumb no-hoper with MORON stamped all over his forehead in indelible ink!"

"I hate you!"

"You deserve each other! Good bloody riddance and the best of luck to him. If you need anyone to give you away at the marriage, give me a call, I'd be delighted, although none of us can pretend you're the bargain of the century!"

"You Nazi!"

"Oh, that stung! I thought you'd never get around to that one. Excuse me a moment, I've just got to pop out and annexe Poland."

"Don't be cheap! Thank God I'm going to have Roddy to protect me in future!"

"I'd rather have a brown shirt than a brown tongue."

"Don't be disgusting. I'm glad our child won't be raised in this atmosphere."

"Oh not that again! You're about as pregnant as this carpet, darling!"

She hit him. She was a big woman, there was a lot behind her slap. He staggered backwards, slipped and fell, clutching his jaw. He tasted blood. She was standing over him, shaking with indignation.

"I'm going to speak to my solicitor first thing Monday morning. I'm going to get a court order on you, get you out of my home and away from me as soon as possible."

"Your home!"

"Yes, I'm the one who slaves and cleans and makes it a home. You can get out, and take all your stupid things with you!"

"Maddie, no!—"

It was a piercing scream, enough to shatter glass.

"No!"

A crystal shower glittered in the air. Fragments caught the light, like tiny shooting stars that fell and gleamed as moondust on the carpet. The noise of breaking glass was loud and sharp. The wall behind him hummed; the plaster was dented where the crystal bowl had disintegrated against it.

She was speaking. He didn't hear it. She had turned, she was walking away, past the fire, towards the door. She had knocked over the cup in passing; it was rolling gently on the carpet from side to side.

He was screaming at her. He didn't know what he was saying. She stopped, she was shouting back. They were in front of the fire. She was red in the face, she was shaking her fist. His hands were round her throat. He shook her.

What was she saying? He couldn't understand it. There was a roar in his head, like the tide going out, the shooshing of sea over the pebbles. She was kicking him, his shins ached. He couldn't hear her now, although he could see her mouth opening and shutting. Her face was even redder. The thick veins stood out on her forehead. Her eyes bulged, like ping-pong balls. Her hands were vices on his wrists. She fell back. He had to let her go.

"You stupid bitch!"

She didn't answer. She had sunk back into the armchair. She was clutching at her throat, making a curious rattling noise. She looked almost comical. He would have laughed but he was still too angry.

"It's not even my bowl! I've only got it on loan for the year!"

His cheeks were hot. He brushed them with the back of his hand and found them wet with tears. He slumped on to the sofa and covered his face with his palms. Maddie gasped weakly.

"And the cup! You'd better not have damaged the model!"

He jumped up and ran back to the sideboard. He picked the diorama off the chair and examined it anxiously. It seemed to be all right. Maddie groaned.

"Oh shut up! Don't expect any sympathy from me!"

He put down the diorama and picked up the cup and loose base. It was definitely scratched.

"There's no need to behave like this, you know, there's no need. I didn't have anything to do with hurting Roddy, really I didn't, and I've never meant to hurt you either. We've had our differences, that's all, and you're always overreacting, you're always damaging things. Like that time you threw the teapot at me. That was my mother's teapot, I was very attached to that. You never think about the hurt you cause, do you? I've got feelings too, you know, you and your precious Roddy don't have a monopoly. How do you think I feel in all this? Pretty miserable, I'll tell you. Pretty miserable and lonely. I haven't got loads of friends to turn to like you have. If you kick me out of my own home where am I to go? I'm not trying to deny you your share, but you seem pretty keen on depriving me of mine. It's the injustice, Maddie, I resent. Let's at least behave decently towards each other and not break each other's things up. You've got less to be bitter about than I have, you know. At least you've got someone to look after you. . . ."

Suddenly it became unbearable. He sobbed. A tidal wave of self-pity swept over him.

"Excuse me. . . ."

He ran out of the room. In the hallway he almost knocked over Roger, who had just come downstairs.

"Is things all right, Mark, I've been hearing the most terrible racket. . . ."

He didn't reply. He didn't even hear the end of the sentence. He had run into the bathroom and locked the door behind him. He closed the toilet seat, sat down on it and burst into tears. There was a pain in his chest. There were aching twinges in other parts of his body, especially his fingers. He cried his eyes out, ripping great chunks of toilet paper off the holder on the wall. Eventually his sobs became dry. He washed his face and bathed his eyes with Optrex. He blew his nose one last time, thoroughly, and unlocked the bathroom.

"I'm sorry Rog, I'm a bit. . . ."

He didn't know what to say. He stood in the kitchen doorway, staring at the floor. Roger was making a cup of tea. He seemed to have found a fresh pack of tea bags from somewhere.

"S'all right Mark. No business of mine. Fancy a cuppa?"

He sounded quite bright and friendly. At least, he sounded considerably less gloomy than usual. In anyone else his tone would have probably passed for indifference.

"I've had a good thought, you know," he said, tapping his nose meaningfully.

"Oh yes?" said Mark, sounding interested, which he wasn't, knowing perfectly well what species this "thought" must belong to.

"New technique I've worked out," Roger explained, fractionally lowering his voice. "Quick and painless. One hundred per cent success rate. No mess. Do you think Maddie would like a cup of tea?"

"I'll ask her."

He knew that she wouldn't, but he needed an excuse to get out of the kitchen. Anything was preferable to a conversation with Roger about suicide. Even Maddie.

He went back into the living room. She was still sitting on the armchair. The magazine she had been reading was on the floor, where she had thrown it earlier. He picked it up and turned to the back, where he found the Problem Page, his favourite.

"Roger says do you fancy a cup of tea?"

She didn't answer. He pursed his lips and carried on reading.

"I thought you wouldn't. I only asked. She doesn't want one, Roger!"

He read in silence for half a minute. He laughed softly to himself. A woman had written in to ask if her husband was a pervert because he kept wanting to do it in different places all round the house and not in the bed. She was worried about the postman peeking through the window and she didn't like it because it was uncomfortable on the floor. She wanted to know what she should do. It seemed obvious to Mark. Get a bean bag. He could sell her one cheap, secondhand.

"Amazing things they write in these magazines," he said, only half aloud. He didn't expect a response from Maddie. She had obviously decided to return to her old taciturn ways and wasn't gong to talk to him again. No doubt he'd be having to write to her wretched solicitor for an update on the tea-bag situation.

"Shall I bring it in, Mark?" Roger called from the kitchen.

"Thanks Rog, that's good of you!"

He put down the magazine.

"Maddie, don't stare at me like—"

His hands fell limply to his sides. The blood drained from his head. He gaped at her with wide-open lifeless eyes. Eyes as lifeless as her own.

"Put it here Mark, okay?"

He didn't answer. He didn't even nod. He couldn't have done. There was no motion in his body, save the shallowest of breathing. Roger didn't seem to notice. He put the tea mug down on the small table.

"Night, Mark. Night, Maddie."

He didn't look at either of them. His eyes were on the floor, as usual. He sloped out of the room. Thoughtfully, he closed the door after him.

Mark heard him go up the stairs. He heard the scraping of his feet on the ladder to the attic. He could hear all the tiny sounds of the house, the faint creakings and groanings, and outside the wind.

He knew what had happened. He had known it at once, in the same split second he had set eyes on her. It hadn't even occurred to him that it might be a trick of light, a vision, a dream. And yet those would have been quite natural responses, if only for that fraction of a second. No, he knew what had happened.

He got up from the sofa. Strength came to him from somewhere, he did not feel it within him. There was nothing within him but a soggy pulp. He moved ethereally, but at the same time clumsily, as if finding himself in possession of an alien body and operating it by remote control. During an eternity he stepped across the carpet. He stood in front of the armchair.

He touched her face. It was warm, but a cold shock ran through him. He realised that the whole of that side of her body was warm, but it was the fire. There was no warmth in her blood. No life in her veins. Her ping-pong eyes seemed to be staring across the room, at the place where he had been sitting, but they saw nothing. They had not even seen him when he had sat there, a minute ago, reading her magazine. The soggy pulp inside him ran nauseous. He tried to keep the thought down, the thought which was trying to rise like bad oysters, the thought which ran:

I sat here and read the magazine and laughed in my head at her, while she sat opposite, dead.

Available now from Doubleday Perfect Crime

BLOODY
INSTRUCTIONS

by Simon Shaw

Philip Fletcher, the murderous actor who starred in
MURDER OUT OF TUNE, returns. Now, he may be a
successful murderer in his own right, but Philip does
object to being wrongly accused when a body turns up.
In desperation he turns amateur detective, a role for
which his life of crime has amply prepared him . . .

Philip Fletcher, the well-known actor and murderer, was sitting in a restaurant waiting for a woman.

And not for the first time, he thought to himself resignedly, breaking open another bread roll. At least the bread rolls, and the restaurants, were getting better. So too were the women, although in the present case, most unusually, sex was not an issue. Martha Kielmansegge was above and beyond that sort of thing these days, and she had never been interested in men anyway. This had been quite a relief to the men.

Martha Kielmansegge. It was a name to conjure with, and he had conjured with it, shamelessly. It was a restaurant popular with media people, and Philip had been gratified to notice on his entrance, a quarter of an hour earlier, three well-known actors and one internationally famous actress sitting within earshot of the reception desk, along with the usual assortment of photographers, TV producers and quotidian riff-raff to whom Philip had paid no attention. His delivery, precisely pitched and modulated in best rolling Windsor rep style, had been aimed exclusively at his peers and rivals:

"Martha Kielmansegge's table, please."

One actor had spluttered into his soup; another had turned as red as the rare beef on his plate; the third had exited immediately to the lavatory, probably to throw up. Only the actress retained her sang-froid, a trick acquired over decades of conflict with the world's paparazzi. She almost raised an eyebrow at him as he passed. Philip was impressed.

"Good God!" said the third actor, returning from the lavatory a minute later. "It's Philip Fletcher, isn't it?"

Philip tried his General de Gaulle look, the female llama surprised while bathing.

"Oh yes," he said after a moment's blankness, "Jeremy Woodward, isn't it?"

"Wyngarde."

"Yes. My dear old thing, how are you?"

"Fine. Yourself?"

"Mustn't grumble."

"Working?"

"Oh, one or two things in the pipeline, you know . . ."

"Things in the pipeline," in actors' parlance, means "out of work," like the *passé* "resting." Somewhere in the sands of the imaginary desert there must be an awful lot of actors lying in the sun waiting for the pipeline to burst.

"Lunching alone?" asked Jeremy Wyngarde.

Philip depressed the corners of his mouth in amused condescension. Jeremy Wyngarde noticed something hanging on his wrist. It was his watch.

"Good heavens, is that the time? Must get a move on, I've got a voice-over at two. Lovely to run into you, Phil."

He returned to his table, none the wiser. Philip returned to his bread roll.

The restaurant was filling up. The waiters were brisk; the diners had an air of clinicism: they weren't so much having lunch, they were doing lunch. The four thespians each had a single companion and their appearances were interchangeable: they were either agents or managers, lawyers or accountants; men in suits. The suits were expensive. They had to be. One glance at the prices was enough to tell Philip that.

He scanned the menu for the umpteenth time. That was the problem with sitting alone in restaurants, waiting for women. He should have brought a book to pass the time, but the days when he had always travelled with a dog-eared paperback thrust into his side pocket were past. Nowadays his own suits were too expensive to bear the disfigurement. He wanted something to occupy him. He ordered another drink, then took his diary from his inside pocket and turned to the page at the back marked "Notes." It contained two vertical rows of neat block-capitalled headings. The first list read:

MY LIFE AS AN ACTOR

AN ACTOR'S LIFE

THE ROAR OF THE GREASEPAINT

TREADING THE BOARDS

MY LIFE, BY PHILIP FLETCHER

The titles had been written down some time before, in pencil, and they were already faded. He had written them in another restaurant, while waiting for another woman. That too had been an occasion on which he had failed to bring a book to read. In the event he had been kept waiting for so long that it had occurred to him he might as well try and write one.

And why not? Philip wondered to himself afresh, surveying the—frankly uninspiring—list of potential titles: Think of all the complete morons and utter nonentities who flood the market with their styleless drivel year after year . . . Philip thought about them. Some of them were even in this room. He wondered what sort of an advance Jeremy Wyngarde had received for his recently published outpouring *Follow That Act!*, a book which by all accounts ought to have been subtitled *Memoirs of a Talentless Bore*.

That was the chief problem with showbiz autobiographies, of course—they were excruciatingly dull. The average reader only wants to know two things about an actor's life: how much is he making and who is he screwing? The former is never vouchsafed; the latter a catalogue of omissions. What one actually gets is a mechanistic list of events and jobs, like an extended theatre programme note, accompanied by a selection of dreary snapshots. There were exceptions, but they were precisely that, and why should it be otherwise? After all, the more successful the actor, the more time he spends working; the less time, therefore, he has in which to do anything very interesting.

Philip had. He really was one of the exceptions. He cast his eye over the second list of titles:

MURDER MOST FOUL

KILLER THESPIAN

ACT OF DEATH

MURDER IN THE STALLS

MURDER OUT OF TUNE

He liked the last one. It had a ring to it.

With a sigh he closed his diary. Three murders he had committed: death by blunt instrument, death by water, death by poison; each in itself might have furnished an arresting title. He had also caused inadvertently the fatal explosion which had killed his fiancée, Hannah, the only one of the deaths he regretted. It was a remarkable story, but, alas, it would have to remain untold. He had considered writing it in secret and depositing the manuscript with his solicitor, "to be opened only in the event of my death," but what if it should fall into the wrong hands? The consequences didn't bear thinking about. It was the dully discreet *My Life, by Philip Fletcher* or nothing.

And he was loathe to embark on that. Without the odd murder to spice it up his life would read no better than Jeremy Wyngarde's. After all, what had he done? What had he ever done? An unremarkable childhood, a standard adolescence, two anecdote-free years at drama school then two decades plus of obscurity, scratching around, trying to root out a living like a truffle pig with an intermittent sense of smell. Only in the last two years had there been anything to crow about: his *Sir Walter Raleigh* for the BBC, his *Uncle Vanya* at Chichester followed by a successful West End transfer and an Evening Standard "Best Actor" nomination (he should have got it, a fact of which everyone in London seemed to be aware except for the judging panel), a quick stint at the National (rave reviews all round) and a three-parter for ITV in which he had played the romantic lead—with unmitigated success, to judge from his postbag. He had made a film too, a low-budget version of Joseph Conrad's *Victory* in which he had played the psychopathic misogynist Jones, a performance which, in all fairness to himself, he could only describe as quite brilliant. Frustratingly, though, the producers had failed to find a distributor, despite nice noises at Cannes. It was depressing to think that probably his greatest performance (apart from one or two cameos employed in pursuit of the occasional homicide) was destined to lie unreleased for years, no doubt ending up in some late-night midweek slot on Channel 4 after a fortnight at the Curzon, Mayfair. He had been counting on that performance to cement his still tenuous reputation as a leading man, to open the door into the lucrative movie world. What he had been doing was all very well, but it had made him merely comfortable, not rich. And he wanted to be rich. He needed the money.

Money was a big problem. Although he had more than he had ever had before it wasn't enough. He had an expensive mortgage now, and had indulged himself in the acquisition of expensive tastes. These were, unfortunately, irreversible. Furthermore, and most alarmingly, he was in hock to the government. Seemingly every last penny in his bank account was earmarked for the Inland Revenue. He seemed to spend his entire spare time filling in VAT returns. Success—that which he had sought so fervently and which had eluded him for so long—was not the uncluttered rose-bed of his dreams. Though it did have its compensations: Jennifer, Jeanette, Helen, Laura—first-class compensations, all. Philip smiled to himself. He thought of some more compensations: Alison, Sue, Gail, Amanda. His smile became a grin.

"Philip Fletcher, I presume."

Philip started guiltily, like a schoolboy caught poring over dirty pictures, which was more or less what he had been doing.

"I'm Martha Kielmansegge."

He rose awkwardly to his feet and took the proferred hand. It was long, thin, and bony; like her. It was also encased in a black silk glove. But the iron grip almost made him yelp. She affected not to notice.

"I'm sorry to have kept you," she said, sitting down and snapping her finger at the waiter. "A meeting dragged on, I'm sure you understand. Large dry martini, please"—this to the waiter; to Philip: "You look different without your beard."

Philip had never grown a beard in his life. She meant either Walter Raleigh's beard or Uncle Vanya's, the two performances which she'd told his agent she'd seen. Philip smiled to himself. He took the remark as a compliment; he liked people to think he looked different from how they remembered him: the vanity of the character actor. She, on the other hand, looked exactly as he had expected:

The yellowish, slightly slanted eyes he met across the table were the same that had stared at him from countless photographs; the hair steel-gray and short-cropped; the Audenesque folds of her face loosely drawn over the still impressive cheekbones. But it was the eyes which were most distinctive: sharp and quick; she had the look of a ruthless mandarin on the make.

She wore tweed, and she wore trousers. And she called them trousers too, not pants, and certainly not slacks; they were made in Savile Row. Her lips were pale, thin and colourless; she wore just a little eye make-up. There were no rings on the black-gloved fingers with which she was fitting a mentholated cigarette into a holder.

"Smoke?" she enquired, pushing the packet over.

"From time to time, but never those."

She laughed, a rasping noise. Her voice was the stuff of health warnings.

"At least you can in this town. I've just come in from L.A. Smoke over there these days you're about as welcome as an Iraqi with herpes. Have you ordered?"

"I was waiting for you."

"Don't. Ever. I exist solely on a diet of alcohol and nicotine. You're on your own, Phil."

She snapped her fingers and the waiter reappeared. Philip ordered a Dover sole and a half bottle of Chardonnay. She ordered another martini.

"Place is full of actors, huh?"

"How can you tell?"

"You're all the same, Phil. The lean and hungry look."

"They can't all have been waiting for you, Martie."

"Don't call me Martie. Ever."

"Willingly, but on one condition—that you don't call me Phil. It's Philip. Not Pip, not Phil, not anything else. Just Philip."

Her thin lips extended into a smile.

"I think we're going to get along just fine, Philip. Please call me Martha. Everyone always has, except Noel Coward. And I'm not telling you what he called me."

Philip smiled politely. He knew perfectly well what Noel Coward had called her, everyone did, it was in the diaries. But perhaps, just like everyone else, she needed the occasional self-deceiving fiction to sustain her, in this case that a confidence breached should be unacknowledged. Philip considered it only good manners to oblige.

She reminisced fondly about Noel while Philip waited for his food, and when it came she continued talking, about Dolly and Bob, and Jerome and Irving, and half a hundred others whose names were caviare to the general but common to the currency all theatre folk spend like water. In such a conversation surnames are redundant; the equivalent, indeed, of the red badge of ignorance. Yet such was the scale of her anecdotal catalogue that in anyone else it must have seemed pretentious, or at least forced. But it flowed, and it was genuine. When she talked about who had said what to whom and did what (or who) where, it was impossible to disbelieve her. At least Philip found it so, and he was not the first: for forty years now Martha Kielmansegge had been there, at the heart of things, the hub: she had flown her flag on Broadway, in the West End and all over the world—it was all her stage. For nearly half a century she had been producing theatrical hits, and most of what she touched had turned to gold. That touch was a little tarnished now, but only in the inevitable way of things, under the trivial vagaries of fashion. She was still a mighty force in threatreland, as Philip had known that everyone in the restaurant would know. Jeremy Wyngarde's face was a picture.

"I expect you're wondering why I asked you here," she said at length.